A Home Subscription! It's the easiest and most convenient way to get every one of the exciting Coventry Romance Novels! ...And you get 4 of them FREE!

You pay nothing extra for this convenience; there are no additional charges...you don't even pay for postage! Fill out and send us the handy coupon now, and we'll send you 4 exciting Coventry Romance novels absolutely FREE!

SEND NO MONEY, GET THESE
FOUR BOOKS
FREE!

━━ ━━ ━━ ━━ ━━ ━━ ━━ ━━ ━━ ━━ ━━ ━━ ━━

C0181

MAIL THIS COUPON TODAY TO:
COVENTRY HOME
SUBSCRIPTION SERVICE
6 COMMERCIAL STREET
HICKSVILLE, NEW YORK 11801

YES, please start a Coventry Romance Home Subscription in my name, and send me FREE and without obligation to buy, my 4 Coventry Romances. If you do not hear from me after I have examined my 4 FREE books, please send me the 6 new Coventry Romances each month as soon as they come off the presses. I understand that I will be billed only $10.50 for all 6 books. There are no shipping and handling nor any other hidden charges. There is no minimum number of monthly purchases that I have to make. In fact, I can cancel my subscription at any time. The first 4 FREE books are mine to keep as a gift, even if I do not buy any additional books.

For added convenience, your monthly subscription may be charged automatically to your credit card.

☐ Master Charge ☐ Visa

Credit Card #_____

Expiration Date_____

Name_____
(Please Print)

Address_____

City_____ State_____ Zip _____

Signature_____

☐ Bill Me Direct Each Month

This offer expires March 31, 1981. Prices subject to change without notice. Publisher reserves the right to substitute alternate FREE books. Sales tax collected where required by law. Offer valid for new members only.

MAID–AT–ARMS

Enid Cushing

FAWCETT COVENTRY • NEW YORK

MAID-AT-ARMS

Published by Fawcett Coventry Books, a unit of CBS Publications, the Consumer Publishing Division of CBS Inc.

Copyright © 1980 by Enid Cushing

ISBN: 0-449-50156-6

Printed in the United States of America

First Fawcett Coventry printing: January 1981

10 9 8 7 6 5 4 3 2 1

Chapter One

As the black stallion reared, the stable-boy went off backwards.

Lady Jennifer Welland sighed impatiently, and seized the leading reins from a perspiring groom, who was trying unsuccessfully to cope with the excited black.

"Here, give me those!" she commanded, her husky voice scornful. "Jake, stop your sniveling, boy. Get up and try again. It's ridiculous that you can't stay on Selim. There's nothing wrong with the horse."

"Beg pardon, m'lady, but Mr. Willy, he used to say that horse had the devil in him," the groom muttered, with a watchful eye on his mistress. Lady Jennifer was known to be somewhat free of temper.

"Mr. Willy has nothing to do with this," Lady Jennifer snapped, so dismissing mention of her guardian's late and unsatisfying nephew. "Jake, mount up!"

If the black was to be feared, so was Lady Jennifer. Reluctantly, young Jake chose the lesser of two evils. He put one foot reluctantly into the stirrup. The horse swung away from him, snorting, rolling eyes in warning.

Lady Jennifer kept a firm grip on the bridle and talked soothingly to the horse before she again ordered the boy into a second try.

"Are you putting the lad to prove anything in particular, Jenny?"

Unnoticed by the girl, though not by the attending groom, who touched his hat hastily, a horse and rider had come up behind them in the yard. Both the man and his mount now regarded the scene with interest.

Lady Jennifer did not even look around. "Selim has to have some exercise, Rufus," she said firmly. "He can't stay stable-bound forever."

"It would seem to me to be a reasonably simple and less temper-exhausting matter to turn him loose in the meadow," Lord Rufus Randall suggested.

"We tried that," Lady Jennifer retorted. "Then it took six of the stable-hands to catch him. Come on now, Jake. Try again."

However, supported by what he felt was a powerful reinforcement, this time young Jake remained where he was. "That horse don't want to be rode, m'lady," he said stolidly.

"Nonsense, Jake, he won't do anything to you. Come along, get up!"

"Do you propose to spend the entire morning expostulating with a horse?" Lord Randall queried. "I believed *we* were to go riding."

"Of course I'm going riding," the girl returned crossly. "All right, put Selim back in the stable, Jake. We'll try again this afternoon."

"Yes, m'lady," muttered the unenthusiastic stable-boy, accepting gingerly the reins his mistress thrust in his direction.

The groom was leading out a bay mare. Another stable-boy came running to give the rider a foot up into the saddle, and she swung aloft with practiced ease. "Don't let Selim loose," she cautioned before she whistled to the large mastiff lying by the stable door. "Come along, George."

"Do you have to have that hound along?" Lord Randall asked.

"Certainly. He needs exercise, too. Don't be stuffy, Rufus."

She was already turning out of the yard. Lord Randall fell in beside her while the big dog coursed ahead of them.

Once clear of the gates, Lady Jennifer touched her mare lightly with her quirt. Obediently, the bay fell into a smooth canter.

"I don't know why the boys are so frightened of Selim," the girl said abruptly with a frown which pulled her brows near into an impatient line across a brow too sunbrowned to be fashionable for any female. "There's nothing wrong with him. He's an excellent goer."

"It's possible they feel that, as your guardian's one and only heir The Honorable Willy was killed in a fall from your wonderful Selim, they might well be the next victims," Rufus replied with that reasonable note in his voice which could always give a twitch to her temper.

"That's ridiculous!" Jennifer threw up her head indignantly. "Willy had the worst seat I've ever seen, and he was cow-handed to boot. You know it as well as half the county!"

"Willy would have hardly agreed to that," Lord Randall murmured.

"Willy had an exaggerated opinion of himself as a horseman, as well as in other fields. Why, he even took the whip to Selim once. That was the act of a hare-brained fool, and you know it, Rufus."

"I might be mistaken, but the thought at this moment occurs to me that you are perhaps better acquainted with Selim than you would have your guardian know," her companion said, a slightly different note in his usually lazy voice.

Jennifer was silent for a moment, but her color rose slightly. "Well then—yes," she said defiantly.

"In fact, I might even venture strong odds you have ridden him yourself upon some occasion—some rather private occasion?" His probing continued.

"Yes, I have," she answered with her usual candor when faced with some new proof of what was supposed to be more of her lack of proper behavior. Then she added quickly, "But I ask that you don't tell anyone, Rufus."

7

"And, might I enquire just when you have indulged in these pleasant rides?" He returned, with that quirk of lip she had long ago learned to watch for to measure his current mood.

She chuckled unexpectedly. "At night—when nobody else is awake. Really, Rufus, it's wonderful galloping across the countryside. Selim loves a good gallop and so do I."

"Er—sidesaddle, I suppose, m'lady?"

Now her smile was close to a guilty grin. "Well, not exactly. And mind you don't say anything about this at all, Rufus. Remember. Guardie would have a fit of apoplexy if he knew."

"I see," Lord Randall murmured. Now his lips were openly curving upward. "I assume I am to take it that you do *not* ride sidesaddle."

"Goodness, I couldn't control Selim if I had all that weight of skirt hanging about," she said defensively. "Besides, it's much better at night not to."

"Yes, I think I can agree with you on that," Lord Rufus nodded. "Up to your old tricks, are you, Jenny?"

"Well, *you* can't possibly guess how deadly dull it is to be a female." Lady Jennifer was still unaccountably on the defensive. "You're not told always anything that's fun or exciting is just 'not proper.'" Her voice took on a mincing note and her lips pursed in a grimace of affected horror. "You're not supposed to just sit around and sew and knit and read and wait for some good match to come calling. It's awful, Rufus."

"A sad prospect indeed. I feel for you, Jenny." Lord Randall agreed with a heartiness which made her glance at him in suspicion. "Tell me, how is Jonathan faring these days?"

"Oh, Jonnie's off in town having a good time, writing poetry, and playing the fool. Guardie's forever talking about when he was young, and how he didn't have time to scribble verse, listen to music, and generally make an ass of himself."

"No doubt," Lord Randall nodded. "I can't imagine the Duke finding much pleasure in the weighty task of rhyming. I take it you do not still yearn to exchange garb with Jonathan, to place yourself in his stead during his present occupations? Or are those far too dull for your taste, along with sewing and knitting and the rest you listed?"

"No chance," Jennifer said scornfully. "Jonathan can have his versifying and the rest, if he wants it."

"Tell me, Jenny, did your guardian ever become aware of the numerous occasions on which you er, diddled him. I believe such was the term you used—in the past?" Lord Randall enquired, again with that quirk of lip.

Jennifer giggled. "I don't think he ever did," she said. "He still can't understand why Jonathan doesn't ride more now than he does, when he was so enthusiastic about horses a few years ago. He really never did know the difference, Rufus. No more than he can understand why I can't play the pianoforte for him now—I used to be so good at it, he tells me. We had fun then, Rufus, changing about. I wish..." her voice was suddenly wistful, but she did not continue.

"You were two unregenerate wretches," his lordship observed calmly. "When I remember how you rode out with the hounds at that county meet while a skirted and beruffled Jonathan toyed with tea and cakes and exchanged titters with delicately nurtured maidens at the Manor, I am in two minds whether to beat you, even now."

"Jonathan had a wonderful time that day," Jennifer laughed wholeheartedly. "Mr. Wimple had just made plain his intentions to Mary Quayle, and she was telling the girls all about it—Jonathan regaled me with the details later."

"You both ought to have been soundly beaten, and set on bread and water for a fortnight at least," said his lordship pensively.

"Rufus, do you remember the time Sir Peter Davies over at the Lodge had that party three years ago? They played all those forfeit for a kiss games—or maybe you don't remember, because you stayed off in the trophy room with Sir Peter—anyway, Jonathan was the belle of the party and was always being caught on purpose. You must have heard about it."

"I also recollect that the Jonathan of the evening also made quite a name for himself as well," Lord Rufus said dryly. "A fine pair up to no good—that was the two of you."

"We used to have fun," Jennifer nodded at her memories

of mischief successfully carried through. "Nobody could ever tell the difference."

"The only noticeable difference was that the fair Jonathan displayed a fine sense of more maidenly conduct than his sister appears interested in showing," Lord Rufus pointed out.

"I should have been the boy," Jennifer sighed, not for the first time. "Truly, Rufus, it's horribly boring being a girl— I don't see how Jonathan enjoys those soirées he's forever attending. And Guardie can't understand it, either. I should be married and Jonathan should be in the army, then we'd be perfectly normal so far as Guardie's concerned. Why, do you know what he's being busied about lately?" her voice rose.

"I can't imagine," his lordship replied.

"You know that scruffy Mr. Wallace over at Barnowl Lodge—the one with the long neck and pimples? He's offered for me, no less, and Guardie's written me earnestly, imploring that I consider his suit most seriously. Can you imagine! Mr. Wallace!"

"I take it you don't regard this ardent suitor up to your standard?"

Lady Jennifer sniffed. "There's one thing I'll say for you, Rufus," her tone was forthright, "you have never made a fool of yourself by offering for every female you meet."

"You may rest assured that I shall never offer for you, Jenny," he said solemnly.

"That's what I mean," she declared. "I don't have to put on any airs for you. It's a big relief."

"Thank you," he said meekly.

"Oh, Rufus, you know what I mean. Don't be so silly. Besides, it's all very well for you, you're a man, and you can go where you want....Anyway, you don't stay in any one place long enough to get bored. When are you going north?"

"I believe I'll leave this afternoon," he answered. "I've sent Masters on ahead to have the house opened."

"Are you driving yourself?" she asked.

"I'm taking the coach," he said. "Much too fatiguing to drive all that distance."

She snorted. "You mean you're too lazy," she said flatly.

"Catch me not taking the reins when I could be driving my own horses!"

"But you see, my dear, I don't share your energy," he said pleasantly. "I prefer to do things the easy way. It is far less fatiguing and trying to the nerves to be driven than to drive. Just think—one can nap away most of what might otherwise be a dullish trip."

"You've got just as much energy as I have if you want to use it," she said sagely. "Don't try to be so stuffy with me, Rufus, it won't go over. Look, how about going around by the Old Spinney? George flushed a hare there the other day, and it kept him amused for hours."

"By all means, let us give pleasure to George," he agreed, and swung right, beside her.

It was a clear, mildly crisp spring day, the ground was firm. The horses lengthened their pace into a run, as their riders gave them their heads, and cleared the ground at a smooth gallop, slowing only slightly as they approached the various walls and hedges and gathered to jump. The pace was too rapid for conversation, and Jennifer even forgot her companion in the pleasure of the run. She sat her horse well, and her hands were gentle and capable on the reins. The wind tossed her red curls into a tangle, and her face was alight and smiling.

Lord Randall was riding a handsome chestnut, which easily kept up with the bay. Not for the first time, Rufus followed where Jennifer led. She knew all the bypaths in the neighborhood. He smiled dryly as he thought that once upon a time he had been the first to show them to her.

A sudden picture flashed into his mind of the first time he had seen her; a child of eight, far from home, and obviously lost. He had been riding then, too, and he stopped beside her, and had said in the condescending tone which an eighteen-year-old will use to a mere child—and a girl at that—"Hello, little girl. What's your name?"

"I'm Lady Jennifer Welland, and I'm eight years old, and I've come to live with my guardian, the Duke of Burghley, at Six Chimneys, because my Daddy and my Mummy died last month. And what's your name and where do you live and how old are you?" She had answered boldly back without obviously pausing for a full breath.

"I'm Rufus Randall, and I live over there at The Cedars, and this is my own horse. And what are you doing here?"

"How old are you?" she had evaded his question.

"I'm eighteen," he said with dignity.

Clearly she was not impressed. She sniffed. "I have a brother who is eight," she informed him. "We're the same age. We're twins. He's a lord—Viscount Welland."

"I suppose I'll have to see you home if you're lost," he said with the scorn that only a young man of those years could summon.

She drew herself up haughtily. "I'm *not* lost. I just don't know how to find the way back."

That had been twelve years ago. He had left The Cedars shortly after, and in the intervening years he had spent only the odd month or so at home. But each time that he had been there, he had, for some reason he never quite understood, made a point of riding over to see how the little redhead and her brother were getting on. They not only looked incredibly alike but also sounded remarkably so, for Jennifer had a deep, husky voice for a girl, while Jonathan's was light and slightly shrill for a boy. Tales of their escapades were rife in the neighborhood. Jennifer had developed into a tomboy of—as the proper might term it—near scandalous proportions. From the day that she had first clambered aboard Rufus's own horse and hung on behind him to be taken back to her guardian's house, she had gone on climbing on one horse after another, until her riding exploits were talked about in every pub in the county. Always with a chuckle, though. The Lady Jennifer was popular. She was a "rare good 'un," the locals agreed, and were not so astounded as some of the county gentry were when "Lord Jonnie" won point-to-point races. The locals had their own opinion of who had been doing the riding, and wagered a tidy sum every time on "the young Lord."

They had arrived at the Old Spinney now, and Jennifer drew rein and turned a flushed face to him, brushing futilely at some strands of flying hair.

"Look, Rufus, isn't it wonderful how far you can see down

the Great North Road from here? You should see it in the moonlight. It winds like a river."

"I suppose you're an authority on that?" he said dryly.

She laughed. "Oh, this is one of my favorite spots," she declared. "George! What's George doing? What's he got after now? George!"

There was crashing in the underbrush, and she spurred towards it.

"Let him alone," Rufus suggested. "He sounds like an elephant. Probably started a hare."

"Come back, George!" She whistled. The dog barked before more sounds of wild activity in the thicket followed.

He came at length, but with obvious displeasure, for he kept running back and forth and barking furiously.

"He must have started a whole family of hares this time, to judge from the noise he's making," Rufus observed tartly. "Why do you keep such a rough, noisy beast, Jenny?"

"Because I like him—and don't keep calling me 'Jenny,'" she flashed. Why did Rufus so often make her feel like she was a village brat with a dirt-smeared face and a hole in her apron? They could be good company, and then all at once she sensed he was bored with her—or found her a nuisance.

"If you could manage to make your hound come along with us, I think we'd better start back," he suggested. "I dislike mentioning it, but I do have things to see to before leaving."

She sniffed. "As if your time wasn't all your own, I suppose, and the coach would take off without you. Really, Rufus, I can't understand you at all."

"Don't try, my dear," he said mildly. "I can't think of any reason why you should."

"And don't you try that la-di-da tone with me," she said darkly. "Maybe it's successful with those ladies of the town you know, and maybe that's the way they all talk in London, but I know you better than that, Rufus Randall, and don't you forget it."

"I'm not likely to when you keep reminding me, my dear," he murmured.

"And don't 'my dear' me, either," she said fiercely. "I'm not your dear."

"No, my love," he said meekly.

She glared at him, but his expression was so studiedly meek that she laughed instead. "You fool, Rufus! Really, I don't know why you come down to The Cedars at all now. There isn't anything there to interest you. The hunting season is over. And you never take much interest in your land. No reason at all."

"No, I don't think there is, very much," he agreed thoughtfully.

"There, you see," she said triumphantly. But strangely enough, she was sorry he had been so quick to agree this time. It was an odd way to feel, and she shook herself mentally, and said as briskly as before: "Are you sending your horses back to Walfram?"

"Not immediately," he said. "I'm not sure when I'll be going back to Walfram, so they might as well be exercised here."

"Really, I don't understand why you keep such a good stable," she said roundly. "You don't even seem the slightest bit interested in what mounts you have here."

"You might observe that I'm riding one now," he pointed out.

"We could always mount you," she said.

"On Selim?" he said. "Thank you, my sweet, but I think I'd prefer to be astride one of my own nags."

"There's nothing wrong with Selim," she began hotly, until he raised one hand arrestingly.

"Please, Jenny," he begged. "Not again."

"Don't keep calling me 'Jenny,'" she said again automatically. "No, but Rufus, really there isn't..."

"Jenny," he murmured gently, "no."

"Very well, but I think you're very stupid," she said firmly, and touched the whip to her horse lightly. "Come along, Regina, His Lordship is in a hurry."

They returned home by yet another path, Jennifer led the way unerringly, taking a five-bar gate in her stride. Rufus's eyes opened wide as he saw the gate looming ahead, but the girl's mare went over it with the utmost nonchalance, and his own horse followed. He came up beside her as they slowed for a turn, and called across to her:

"Do I take it that you're accustomed to this path, too, at night?"

She flashed him a smile. "Certainly. Selim's an excellent jumper. So's Regina." She patted the mare's arching neck.

"Indeed," he murmured, and kept up with her easily as her bay swung into a smooth gallop again. She was an expert horsewoman all right. No one would ever accuse her of having a poor seat, or of being cow-handed.

This path brought them by his estates first, and she drew rein at the entrance to The Cedars. "Don't bother coming on with me, Rufus. I know you're in a hurry. Make sure that that fool groom of yours rubs Copper down thoroughly. I'm not too sure he's been doing his job properly." She slackened her reins again, and the horse moved ahead obediently. "Good-bye," she called, raising her hand in salute. "Thanks for your company."

She touched heels to the horse and swept off down the roadway. Lord Randall watched her disappearing with the big dog running after her before he turned his mount into his own driveway. It occurred to him he was almost sorry that he was leaving. A curious afternoon, and for once he had not found anything boring in company or in occupation.

Chapter Two

The moon rose full that evening, flooding the countryside with a brilliance which reached through windows, beckoned one out into the shadow-checkered night. More restless than usual, Jennifer paced from one window in the long drawing room to the next, returned at length down the room.

· Seated in a tall wingchair, drawn cosily close to the fire, and sheltered as much as possible from any prevailing drafts, Mrs. Medley, a faded, much-widowed dependent of the Duke's, worked with peering dissatisfaction at some needlework. From time to time she regarded the restless Lady Jennifer fretfully. Her position as companion was not ever, she thought privately, an easy one.

"Jennifer, will you please stop pacing back and forth in that fashion which makes one nerve-ridden to watch! Sit down, my dear, and compose yourself as a young lady should," she said at length, in a mournful, near whisper of a voice. "You are quite distressing me."

"Sorry," Jennifer spoke casually, and certainly not apologetically. She had long since dismissed most of what Mrs. Medley said as being of small importance to her own affairs. She paused momentarily by the front window. "Cousin Leticia, didn't you ever feel you'd like to walk in the moonlight?"

Mrs. Medley was scandalized. She was easily thrown into that state, as most of what Jennifer said brought about her instant disapproving reaction. "Most certainly not," she said firmly. "Such an outlandish thought never entered my mind. I hope you are not entertaining odd whims, Jennifer. Let me assure you, it would never do. Young ladies do not walk alone in the moonlight. Nor do they roam about at night." She gave a stout pull to her thread, and uttered then a small sound of irritation as it caught and snapped.

Jennifer sighed rebelliously. "Young ladies don't do anything," she muttered.

Mrs. Medley dealt firmly with the thread. Having triumphed over that, she proceeded to deal as sternly with her charge's lack of conformity.

"My dear, truly you must not speak in such a fashion." Shocked disapproval was a standard weapon of Mrs. Medley's. As always, she sought secondary support from her ever present bottle of smelling salts. "It always distresses me to have to chide you so, my dear, but I feel that it is my duty. You *must* indeed be more circumspect, Jennifer. I heard comments that you were out riding with Lord Randall this morning, unaccompanied."

"Not entirely unaccompanied," Jennifer protested. "George was with us."

"My dear—a dog! You should have had Simpson with you. Does he not know his duties?"

"Besides Guardie lets me go without any groom hanging behind. He always has," Jennifer replied defensively.

Mrs. Medley opened her mouth, and closed it in wordless protest. She felt her position as dependent cousin on His Grace, the Duke of Burghley's favor keenly, and was given to little fluttering motions whenever that gentleman was present. Actions which, if she only knew, irritated her patron no end. The Duke had been a soldier, and fluttery, fading women were not to his taste at all.

"Don't be silly, Cousin Leticia. I've known Rufus all my life. He's almost like my own brother."

"He is, none the less, an Eligible Young Man," Mrs. Medley said firmly, her tone lending 'Eligible Young Man' capital letters. "What must he think of you for riding about alone with him?"

Jennifer snorted. "He'd think that I had picked up some very stupid notions if I were to play coy with him, now," she said flatly. "Truly, Cousin Leticia, you don't need to feel upset over Rufus. He thinks of me as nothing more than his sister, and I doubt that he considers me much more than eight years old, even now."

With that supposition, quite unknowingly, she did Lord Randall an injustice.

Mrs. Medley pursed her lips. She was not convinced, but although a stupid woman she recognized the inevitable occasionally, and bowed to it with as much grace as she could muster. With an injured air of resignation she finished the last stitch, bringing to life a sickly pink silk rose, carefully folded up her work, put her needle away in the needle book, and the needle book away in the sewing cabinet that stood beside her chair; gathered up scraps of silk from about her skirt, and got to her feet with rustling dignity. In a voice close to that of a prophetess pronouncing some coming doom, she announced she did not intend to await the arrival of the nightly tea tray but intended to go to bed, and it would be well for Jennifer to do likewise.

Jennifer swung from the window. "By all means," she agreed cordially. "Have a good rest, do, Cousin Leticia. I'm sure you'll feel better in the morning."

Mrs. Medley answered remotely that she certainly hoped so, in a tone that implied she believed quite the contrary would be the truth, and trotted out of the room. She was not, however, too weakened to call to Collins, the butler, as she went through the hall, and request that he bring to her room a tray with a little light refreshment, since she was not awaiting tea in the parlor.

Jennifer threw herself into the chair, recently so neatly occupied by Mrs. Medley, and ran her fingers through her curly red hair, shaking it loose from the ribboned restraints proper dressing had put upon her very unruly lengths. Her face, in the reflected glow from the fire, was handsome—not pretty. Her cheekbones showed strongly, and her chin was steady and firm. She was a tall girl with broad shoulders, and despite her petticoats she lounged in the carelessly graceful attitude of a young boy. There was nothing meekly feminine about her, neither about the straight lines of her mouth, nor in her clear hazel eyes, which could turn hard as green agate with anger. She was twenty; she could ride a horse like a man; and shoot straighter than most, and, although this was an accomplishment unknown to many, could outswear a stable-hand. Yet, curiously enough, she was not really lacking in the attractions of her own sex. She merely disregarded such.

She sprawled there, until the hands of the ormolu clock on the mantelpiece traveled almost a complete round from the time of Mrs. Medley's retirement. Then, aware of the silence in the house, Jennifer swiftly crossed the room and ran noiselessly up the stairs to her room.

Once there behind a locked door, she struggled out of her gown, flinging it back on the bed. Kicking off her shoes she jerked open the heavy door of a massive wardrobe and dove into the back of that to drag out a tight bundle. A few vigorous shakes freed a pair of black breeches and a matching jacket. She pulled on an old dark shirt, tugged on riding boots. Her red hair was hastily tucked out of sight beneath a battered hat. A black kerchief about her neck and black gloves on her hands and her beloved disguise was complete, save for the last item she pulled from her bureau drawer. Jennifer inspected that small pistol carefully before shoving it deep into her pocket. She hadn't told Rufus, of course, but she had discovered once or twice a pistol was a handy thing for these midnight rides.

Blowing out her bedside candle, Jennifer opened the door and peered cautiously into the corridor. The house's silence held complete. A moment later she shut her chamber door softly and ran on tiptoe down the hall, using the servants' backstairs and a door whose latch was very familiar to her fingers even in the dark. The night air was like wine, she thought, as she sped into the stableyard.

There was a party at the village schoolhouse that evening, and most of the staff had permission to attend. There was only old Peter left hereabouts, and he was no source of worry, for he had been her accomplice on many a midnight flitting—if not actively, at least ready to keep her secrets.

Selim's saddle waited over a wooden horse outside in the tack-room, his bit and bridle hung on a nail nearby. Jennifer gathered the tack up swiftly and let herself into Selim's box-stall. The big black nickered and moved restlessly until she spoke. After a snort in her direction, he allowed the girl to saddle and bridle him, standing with a patience far different from the skittishness he had displayed that afternoon.

Jennifer let him out confidently and he stood while she closed the box-stall again. As docile as a meek-mannered mare, he followed along to the way which led to the back pastures.

Jennifer swung into the saddle. As her weight settled, Selim pawed the ground a little. Her steady hands and the firm grip of her knees quieted him, and he paced sedately out into the network of shadows and moonlight.

Once clear of the encircling fences, Jennifer gave the powerful stallion his head. He broke into a smooth gallop, covering ground until Jennifer felt as if they both were free of the earth—flying. At one moment, as Selim crossed a stretch of smooth turf, she half thought she heard hoofbeats behind her, and she turned to look behind.

Making up their headstart as rapidly as he could, George pounded in their wake, seeming to move with very little effort at all.

Jennifer reined in Selim to allow the mastiff to catch up with her. The big dog leaped, forepaws in the air, voicing his pleasure with a single sharp bark.

"George, be quiet!" she ordered, then added: "However did you get out? Well—so be it—you'll find you're going to have quite a run tonight."

George might not understand her warning, but he recognized the implied welcome in his mistress's voice. His tail whipped back and forth as the stallion once more went into action. Selim lengthened his stride and the fields flashed by.

Without conscious intent, Jennifer followed much the

same path that she and Rufus had ridden earlier. She finally pulled the blowing Selim to a canter, urged the mount to a slow walk as she reached the higher ground overlooking the Old Spinney.

A growl from the panting George alerted her. The mastiff's big head was turned somewhat; his tail was stiff. He faced the Old Spinney squarely.

"Quiet, George," Jennifer's voice was not far above a whisper. "Steady, boy!"

Far down the Great North Road, looking oddly like a top-heavy beetle with waving antennae stretched before it, a traveling coach and four was galloping towards them.

At that hour—Jennifer might not have a watch to hand but she was countrywise enough to know her time by the clocks a poacher or other nightfarer used—a coach here was something to wonder about.

Only the oncoming coach had not riveted George's attention. The dog was watching the Old Spinney itself—not the road beyond. Unconsciously, Jennifer stiffened. Selim pawed the ground restlessly as the girl's hand tightened on the reins.

At one place not very far below her, the growth of the Spinney spread to the verge of the Great North Road. Its trees and brush almost overhung the way to the other side. Not too long ago this had been a favorite spot for Gentlemen of the Road. It was said that the infamous Black Tom had had his headquarters nearby. Those times were past, Jennifer told herself firmly. Or at least they were supposed to be.

Unfortunately, she must be wrong. For, just as the traveling coach drew alongside the wood, there echoed the sound of a shot on the clear air. Audible to Jennifer's ears, came the traditional gruff command: "Stand and deliver!"

Suddenly a heady recklessness took command of Jennifer, fed by both the desire for adventure and her usual ever present curiosity. Giving a quick glance about, she dug her heels into Selim's flank to charge down the hillside. As her mount plunged forward, she suddenly thought to pull the black kerchief up over her face, giving herself barely time to tug out the pistol before the stallion scrambled for footing at the road edge.

Moonlight imparted a sharp clarity to the scene. A helpful

glint of that light on the pistol which the highwayman held was all that Jennifer needed.

Taking quick aim, she fired. The weapon whirled out of the man's hand. With an oath he wheeled about, to stare astounded at the new player in his old game.

"Put your hands in the air, and stand back there." Even in her excitement, Jennifer remembered to keep her voice gruff.

The man, clutching a numbed hand, obeyed slowly, moving with greater haste as Jennifer flourished her own weapon.

"I mean quickly," she ordered. "You," nodding at the coachman, who was having his hands full with his four excited horses, "get going!"

The coachman would gladly have obeyed, but unfortunately in the excitement the traces had snarled. The footman up beside him was, not surprisingly, unnerved, and his fingers fumbled as he attempted to give aid.

"Hurry up!" Jennifer prodded.

The coach door was shoved open. A portly gentleman made an ungainly descent to the road, puffing, settling his hat with an impatient bang of one hand.

"It's an outrage," he was fuming, "an abominable outrage, on His Majesty's highway—in broad moonlight! Never heard of such a thing nowadays. My dear sir we are most grateful to you, most grateful indeed."

Jennifer struggled to keep her voice low. "Get back in the coach if you will, sir," she said brusquely. "Just leave this scoundrel to me."

The elderly gentleman had been followed by a much younger man; a handsome youth, in dark green regimentals. He stared wide-eyed at Jennifer. Even in the moonlight, surprise and then apprehension crossed his mobile face.

The footman, dismounting from his precarious seat, had at last untangled the traces and came back to the coach.

"Sir," Jennifer fought hard to maintain her own composure, "there is no need for you to linger. Leave this bungling fellow to me."

The young officer now displayed an amazing burst of energy; adding his entreaties swiftly to hers, he urged the portly and still fuming gentleman back into the carriage. "For indeed, sir, we must be on our way. Everything seems to be well in hand here."

The old gentlemen was loath to go.

"This ruffian must be handed over to the authorities," he declared.

"I'm sure this gentleman will attend to everything," the officer said hastily. "Indeed, we must get on. The hour is very late, and you know, sir, how the night air is injurious to you."

"Look sharp there now," Jennifer said again, and waved the pistol once more in the direction of the bewildered highwayman. "Not a move from you, mind. That'll do. Sir, this man will be no trouble now, I assure you."

The young officer having succeeded in getting his outraged companion into the carriage, the footman slammed the door after them.

As the coach swept past Jennifer, the officer's face visible at the window was now only a white blob in the half moonlight. Jennifer averted her head and held Selim on tight curb while the coach rattled out of sight. Although her gaze was on the quaking highwayman in front of her, her mind was off with the rapidly disappearing carriage. She came back with a start when the highwayman said pleadingly: "Look, gov'nor, can't I put me hands down now? I'm stretchin' 'em clean outta their sockets."

"What the devil did you think you were doing?" the girl exploded. "How long have you been on this lay—that's what you call it, isn't it? No, keep your hands up for a while."

"Well...honest gov'nor, all I wanted was something to buy me a loaf of bread or som'thin' to eat. I ain't a regular bad un, honest I ain't."

"Where are you from?" Jennifer demanded. The man's accent was strange to her.

He named a town in the Midlands. "I used to have a good job there, gov'nor," he said and there was bitterness in his voice. "Then they started to build them new mills. Now they don't care about us what used to do the weavin'. Turn us out they do—without nothin'."

"That's no reason to play highwayman," Jennifer said sharply.

"When you is hungry, gov'nor, you is like to do anything as will put somethin' in your belly," the man answered sullenly. He started violently at a crashing in the bushes behind him. The massive George leaped onto the road. "Lor', gov'nor, what's that?" he gasped.

"It's only my dog," Jennifer snapped. "You can put your hands down, now that he's here. You wouldn't be able to get away with anything. He'd have your throat out if you tried it."

He lowered his arms and began massaging his hands almost unconsciously. But he now kept a very wary eye on George who sat, his tongue hanging half out between teeth which looked far too sharp and ready for action.

"What are you going to do with me, gov'nor?" he said.

That was a question bothering Jennifer. She found it somewhat difficult to answer. Of course, she couldn't dare take the man to the nearest Officer of the Peace and turn him in without swearing out a warrant for his arrest. Such action would mean giving her name, which she could not do. Unfortunately, this man had seen fit to hold up the carriage of no less a person than the Duke of Burghley, who was a personage in these parts.

At length she answered truthfully, abruptly. "I don't know. If this is the first time you've tried this..."

"Lor' gov'nor, I'd swear it so on whatever you'd want me to," the man said harshly. "It happens to be the God's truth, but I don't expect you to believe that."

"I haven't any money," Jennifer said curtly. It was true, she hadn't. "But if you will give me your word that you will not attempt to rob again, I'll do what I can for you."

The moonlight showed the astounded expression on her captive's face. "What, gov'nor?" he gasped.

Jennifer was thinking fast. "Go, tomorrow morning to the big house beyond the village—The Cedars. Ask to see the stable-man. Tell him His Lordship sent you. That you want a job. If he has one, you'll get it; if there isn't anything for you to do, you won't. Are you willing to take the chance?"

"This ain't no turn up—with the law waitin' there?" The man was skeptical.

"You'd have to take a chance on me," Jennifer said crisply.

"I tell you it's straight, if you want to believe. Will you try it? It's that or the constable."

"Sure, sure, I'll try it," the man said hastily.

"Just one thing more," Jennifer said, "forget that you saw me tonight. Do you understand that?"

"Forget that I saw you tonight," the man repeated, obediently. "Yes, gov'nor. I'll be glad enough to make sure of that, for one thing." His assent was given with emphasis.

"And give me your pistol," Jennifer finished. She was alert for trouble, but the man stooped at her bidding, picked up the pistol and gave it to her, butt-end first. She dropped it in her pocket, then paused a moment longer. "Good luck," she said as she dug her heels into Selim's flanks.

With a bound, the big horse broke into a gallop, leaving the man gazing after her with a look of wildest disbelief.

Disbelief and something else. A look of dawning hope.

"God, what a gov'nor!" he breathed almost reverently. Then he began slowly and wearily to trudge up the Great North Road towards the village.

Chapter Three

By cutting across country, recklessly urging Selim to his best speed, Jennifer reached the house before the traveling coach. She whistled her private signal to old Peter as she swung off Selim's back behind the stable.

As she led the stallion into the stable, the groom hurried from the tack-room to take the reins she handed over.

"Get him unsaddled and rub him down as quickly as you can, Pete," she said urgently. "Guardie's on his way. I met the coach down the Great North Road, by the Old Spinney. Just remember, Selim hasn't been out tonight at all. And, oh, Pete, one other thing. Tomorrow morning, as soon as you can get up go to The Cedars and see Joseph. Don't tell him I spoke to you, but make an excuse to say that if anyone applies for work, you could do with an extra hand if they haven't any call for him. I can't tell you any more than that now, Pete. Look after it for me, will you?"

Old Peter beamed toothlessly, and nodded several times.

"Aye, m'lady, that I'll do. Tomorrow morning, bright as the sun is up. Never you have a care."

Jennifer tossed a brief, "Thanks, Pete," over her shoulder, before slipping out into the shadows. With George beside her, she ran noiselessly across the yard to the big house, and plunged up the dark stairs and along the corridor to her room.

As she ran she peeled off her gloves and tugged the hat from her head. Now she struggled out of the tight jacket, pulled the shirt over her tumble of hair, caught the heels of her boots in turn in the standing bootjack and jerked out of them with all possible haste, at the same time pushing her trousers down over her hips and stepping out of them. Bundling the discarded clothes up, she hurled them into the depths of the wardrobe, every sense alert for the first sound of the approaching coach.

She heard it now, crunching the gravel of the driveway with its heavy wheels. She seized her voluminous nightgown, pulling it on, to fasten the ruffled high collar. Then she grabbed up a peignoir, tying its sash firmly about her slender waist before she seized a comb to reduce her tangled hair to some semblance of order. Stepping into slippers, she opened her bedroom door.

Commotion in the downstairs hall announced the arrival of His Grace. Jennifer closed the bedroom behind her and ran lightly down the great front staircase.

"Guardie, whatever are you doing, arriving at this hour of the night?" she called out. "And Jonathan," she caught sight of her brother behind him, "what are you doing here? Why...Jonnie..." on a rising breath, for the moonlight at that road meeting had not allowed her any mistake. Her brother *was* in all the glory of dark green regimentals. Jonnie—a soldier! She quite forgot their earlier clandestine meeting in the full surprise of that moment.

Jennifer flung herself into his arms, and hugged him tightly. "Jonnie, whatever are you doing in those clothes?" she cried.

But before he could answer she whirled from him to her guardian. "Guardie, it's so good to see you. Come on into the drawing room. There was a fire there. If I'd known you were coming, I wouldn't have gone to bed so early. Collins, bring some port for His Grace. I'm sure you could do with something to warm you after such a journey. Have you come all the way from London?"

She propelled him, still chattering, into the drawing room, where the embers of the fire were being prodded to life by a hastily summoned underfootman.

"Cousin Leticia retired hours ago, and although she vows and declares she doesn't sleep a wink all night, I'm sure she won't have heard you arrive. Come along, Guardie, and tell me what brings you here so unexpectedly."

His Grace allowed himself to be steered towards the wing chair, which Mrs. Medley usurped whenever possible, and subsided into it with a grunt of satisfaction. His red face was well equipped with fierce mustaches which he fingered possessively from time to time, and sharp brown eyes. He'd been a soldier fighting through the Peninsular Campaign from 1809 with Sir John Moore, to 1814 with Lord Wellington, as an officer in the old 95th Rifles of the Light Division. Jennifer's father had been one of his junior subordinates, and among her earliest memories Jennifer stored the sight and sound of gatherings of comrades-in-arms as they drank and exchanged tall tales far into the night—not that she was supposed to have been present on such occasions of course, but there were ways of sneaking down from the nursery. After her father had died as the result of a hunting accident, and her gentle, pretty mother had followed her husband to an early grave, Jennifer and her brother had come here as the wards of His Grace, the Duke of Burghley. Then evenings of wonderful stories grew ever more frequent and, as Jennifer grew older, there was never anything better that she liked to do than to sit and listen to retired warriors rehashing old times. Just now, this old war-horse was breathing fire and brimstone once more.

"Damned outrage!" he snorted. "Wouldn't believe it, Jennifer. Wouldn't have believed it if it had happened to someone else. If any person had told me about this, I tell you I wouldn't have believed it. Damned outrage! On His Majesty's highway! In this day and age, mind you. Those fellows need discipline. They need a touch of the lash. Who expects to face a rascal's pistol near in sight and sound of his own home! Preposterous!"

"Guardie, whatever are you talking about?" Jennifer demanded. "What happened?"

"My coach was held up! Damned truth, it was! Down by the Old Spinney. Most outrageous thing that ever happened to me." His Grace's face was near a dangerous fiery shade now, and his snorting rage was at the bursting point.

"A highwayman, Guardie, truly? What did you do?" Jennifer counterfeited, as well as she could, a mixture of wide-eyed astonishment and horror.

"Damned fellow shot off a pistol, scared the wits out of that ass of a coachman, set the horses rearing. I tell you such a thing would never have happened if I'd been younger. Never expected such a thing. Before I could do anything, that damned wretch had the carriage door open, and was ordering us to hand over our belongings. Outrageous! Positively outrageous!"

"Guardie, how dreadful! Did he take very much?"

"No, he didn't get a chance," His Grace said reluctantly. "A stranger came along and shot the pistol out of his hand. Damn fine shooting, that. Couldn't have had much of a sight on it either. Not very good light. Gad, I'd liked to shake the hand of the man that did that. Damn fine shooting! Damn fine pistol, too. Fairly long range. *Damn* fine shooting!"

"Yes, but what happened then?" Jennifer pressed impatiently. She wasn't interested in hearing the details of the shooting; she knew them too well. But she did want to hear what else His Grace might have observed. Guardie was anything but stupid. If he had the least suspicion....

"This fellow sat his horse there as easy as you please. Ordered the coachman to pull the horses together, and when I attempted to thank him, he ordered me back in the carriage. Not a very friendly person. He said he'd attend to the rascal. I wanted to stay, but Jonathan here thought we should get on. It didn't seem right to leave that one man to look after that gallows-bait. Outrageous! Positively outrageous! In broad moonlight, on His Majesty's highway! Never heard of such a thing in the past twenty years!"

"Did you get a good look at this stranger?" Jennifer asked. "Do you know who he was?"

"Wouldn't be calling him a stranger if I knew who he was,

would I?" her guardian demanded with some reason. "No, his face was in shadow. Dressed in black—rode a great, huge black horse, too. Never saw it around before." Jennifer felt her lips twitch. "The fellow was wearing a broad-brimmed hat. Had something up over his face, too. Probably up to no good himself; still, that wasn't my affair. Wonderful horseman. Sat his horse there, and it was a big horse; restless, too. Held him steady. Shot straight as a die. Gad, what damn fine shooting!"

"Did you get a good look at the highwayman?" Jennifer asked.

"No, couldn't see him, either. His face was in shadow. Kept it that way, too. Careful like. Damned outrage!"

"Well, it's all over now, Guardie," Jennifer said soothingly. "Have some port. And tell me, what brought you down here so suddenly?"

His Grace accepted the glass, and said in a more moderate tone: "Thought we'd better come down here to see you. Jonathan will be leaving soon. Wanted to say good-bye."

"Jonathan ... leaving? Going where?"

Her brother spoke for the first time. "Halifax," he said gloomily.

"Halifax? Where's Halifax?" she repeated blankly. "What on earth are you going to do there?"

He made a sweeping, oddly feminine gesture. "Place's in Canada—I'm for garrison duty."

"Garrison duty? But Jonnie, you don't like the army."

His Grace fired up again. "About time he had some discipline. Gad, do you know where I found this brother of yours, my dear? At Lady Ashbury's salon, no less, listening to a fop reading poetry. Poetry! And he was all ready to spout off verses, too. Imagine that for your brother! I tell you, at that point I had had enough. I told him to come home with me. Not going to have my ward behaving like a pampered pimp, reeling round in ladies' salons and boudoirs, listening to poetry. 'As long as you're in my charge, young man,' I said to him, 'you're going to have some discipline.'"

"But ... but ... the army," Jennifer protested.

"It's the Rifles, ain't it?" her guardian snapped. "Damned lucky I was, too. I went up to the War Office to see if any commissions were for sale. Found there was a captaincy in the Rifle Brigade, so I bought it for your brother. Damned lucky! Didn't think I'd be able to get one in the Rifle Brigade. Pretty hard to buy into that regiment, you know. Wanted something on duty now. Not one of your home regiments; no good at all. This one's stationed at Halifax, Canada—a good ways from that London hothouse. Be the best thing in the world for your brother. Teach him a little discipline."

"But Guardie, I thought you didn't approve of the purchase of commissions," Jennifer expostulated.

"All right at a time like this," her guardian said firmly. "Not on active service, of course; in war-time doesn't do at all. An officer has to learn in the field. Nothing higher than an ensign, then. Of course, I wanted a lieutenantcy, but there were none available, so I took this captaincy. Pretty expensive, too."

"Well, I'm sure it's very kind of you to take so much interest in Jonathan," Jennifer said hastily, "but the army... Halifax.... How long will he be away, Guardie?"

"A year. Two years. Three years, if he wants to stay on. Certainly a year, until he's twenty-one," her guardian said flatly.

"A year! Oh, Jonnie!" His sister cast such a horrified glance at her brother that he felt forced to speak up.

"A year ain't so long, Jenny," he said quickly.

"But Canada is so far away, Guardie." Suddenly she stopped. A light gleamed in her eye. She leaned forward. "Guardie, can I go, too? Can I go to Halifax? I could take Katie with me, and I could stay at one of the hotels there while Jonathan was in garrison. You've often told me of how the women traveled with the army in the old days. Why can't I do it now? That...that would be wonderful, Guardie. It would be such fun then, seeing Halifax. Why...that's so far away in Canada—a whole new world! It would be simply wonderful. Guardie, couldn't I do that?"

"Well, now...you certainly can't," her guardian was firm. "What would you do over there?"

"But, Guardie, you told me so often yourself, how Lady Smith married Sir Harry after the siege of Bajadoz in 1812, and campaigned on the field with him for the next two years. Why can't I go to Halifax with Jonathan?"

"That was different," her guardian said stoutly. "She married him."

"Yes, but *this* is different, too. This is peace-time. Why can't I go over with my brother? Guardie, it would be wonderful. Can't I go, please?"

"No, of course you can't," her guardian was firm. "Never do at all."

"But, Guardie, you know so many people over there. Why, didn't you say that Lord Bradbury was the Lieutenant-Governor in Nova Scotia? Why, Guardie, if he was over there, you could transfer your guardianship to him. He wouldn't mind, would he? You've always said he was a good sort and a good soldier."

"No," her guardian said firmly. "It won't do, Jennifer. I tell you it won't do."

"Why not, Guardie? It would be wonderful."

"No," said her guardian, and to forestall further coaxings, he got to his feet. "I'm going to retire. I tell you *NO*, Jennifer. You can't go. Preposterous—wouldn't do at all. Good night." He made what near amounted to a hasty retreat.

Left alone by the fire, brother and sister looked at each other. Jennifer spoke first as usual.

"Well, Jonnie, apparently you went too far this time."

"How was I to know the old gentleman would come into Lady Ashbury's salon? It's the last place in London that I would have expected to see him," her brother said sullenly. He leaned against the high mantel and ran his fingers fretfully through his hair which was the same color as his sister's. "Jenny, what *am* I going to do?"

His sister got up and faced him across the breadth of the mantel. "I think you're going to Halifax, Jonathan," she said frankly. "When did all this take place? Why didn't you write me? I *do* think you could have let me know, and not land down here like this, all ready to sail. When *are* you sailing?"

"Jenny, there wasn't any time for anything. I give you my word it was a rush from start to finish. I don't know whether I've got everything, even now. It's been terrible."

"Yes, I know," his sister agreed, "but what happened, Jonnie?"

"Guardie came to Lady Ashbury's salon as he said, and he took me off home with him as he told you. Then, the very next morning he went up to the War Office. He bought this commission. He came back and told me, and ordered me off to the outfitters."

"But when was Lady Ashbury's salon?" Jennifer demanded.

"Two weeks ago—Tuesday."

"Well, I warned you Guardie was furious about you going to those places," Jennifer said darkly. "I must say I think you've asked for it. You know he doesn't approve of them. I can't see what you like in them, either, but I suppose it's all right. Anyway, if you'd only gambled, or gone about in the Society circle, or flirted with the girls, Guardie wouldn't have minded it at all. I told you he didn't like all this poetry thing, Jonnie. It's your own fault."

"It wasn't any of his business," Jonathan protested, but without conviction.

"He certainly considers it his business, Jonnie, and don't you forget that," Jennifer returned. "You know perfectly well he's responsible for us until we're twenty-one, and I do think you might have been more considerate of his wishes. It wouldn't have hurt you for another year."

"Jenny, don't you pick on me, too. I've had all I can take." He threw himself into the big wing chair. "Jenny, I can't stand the army."

"No, I don't suppose you think you can," his sister agreed. "But you're going to have to learn to."

"Everything will be so rough; so coarse," he shuddered. "Jenny, I won't do it. I'll run away."

"You'll do nothing of the sort, my boy," his sister retorted furiously. "Don't be a coward, Jonathan. You're going to go to Halifax, and you're going to make the best damned officer..."

"Jennifer!" her brother was honestly shocked.

"Oh, stop Jennifer-ing me," his sister snapped. "When are you sailing, Jonnie?"

"Next week," her brother said forlornly. "The *Cambria*.

She's supposed to be a fast one—several weeks they say." He shuddered visibly.

"Only several weeks!" Jennifer's eyes were alight. "That's wonderful, Jonathan. Oh, if I can only get Guardie to let me go with you. Then it wouldn't be so bad. I could have a wonderful time there, in Halifax; I know I could."

"The old man won't let you go," her brother said glumly. "You know he won't. Besides, what could you do over there? Probably be worse there, and you're always saying how bored you are here."

"I'm sure it would be different in Canada. Why, they probably let the females ride astride over there."

"Talking about riding," Jonathan sat up with a jerk, "Jenny, I give you my word, I was never so surprised... Whatever were you doing out tonight? What were you on? Was that Selim? Why..."

His sister grinned. "Oh, yes. Nice horse, too."

"Jenny, if His Nibs had ever recognized that horse, I give you my word... I didn't know what to do. Why, if he'd caught one look at you... Why, Jenny, I was so shocked! Whatever were you thinking of? Whatever made you get yourself up in that rig and go out at midnight, alone?"

"It wasn't midnight, Jonathan," Jennifer said briefly. "I left at ten o'clock. It was only eleven then. Besides, nobody else can ride Selim. Somebody has to. Jake fell off him twice this morning."

"But you know Guardie told you never to ride Selim. I think he's going to sell him or something."

"No, he can't sell Selim," his sister said decidedly. "He mustn't do that."

"How are you going to stop him?" Her brother was sidetracked.

"I'll send him up to The Cedars. Rufus is away; he won't mind."

"If Rufus is away, how do you know it will be all right?"

"Joseph will take him in. I know that. He'll look after him for me," his sister tossed that problem aside with ease. She began to pace the hearthrug. "So you're leaving in a week, Jonnie? That would give me loads of time to get my things ready. I've got all the clothes I need. All I have to do is pack

34

them, and I'm sure I can get passage on the same boat. I'll take George with me, of course, and we should be able to get horses over there, shouldn't we, Jonnie?"

"Never mind all that, what did you do with that fellow?" Her brother refused now to be sidetracked.

"What fellow? Oh, you mean the man on the road? Let him go, of course. What else could I do with him under the circumstances?"

"You let him go? Why, the man was dangerous!"

"Not so much. He was just hungry—and a lot scared—I think."

"How do you know?"

"I asked him. He comes from the Midlands. No work. No money."

"They all tell you the same tale. Jennifer, you're an out-and-out softhearted fool at times!"

"Well, I didn't notice you acting too heroically," his sister retorted. "In fact, the way you chivvied Guardie back into the coach was masterly."

"What else could I do?" her brother was stung to retort. "I didn't dare let him take a chance on recognizing you."

"I could have managed Guardie. Anyway, you got him into the coach and off you went, and that was that." She began pacing again. "Jonathan, I think this all is going to work out all right, if you'll just keep your head and let me do the thinking and handle Guardie right."

Eight days later, on the twenty-first of May, a group of three persons and a large dog stood together on the deck of the *Cambria*, bound from Liverpool to Halifax, Captain Walker commanding. It was a clear May day, and England was at her best. Many of the passengers lining the rail and fluttering handkerchiefs at the waving relatives on shore, were crying unashamedly: even one of the group of three was sniffing loudly.

The ship stood out from the quay, a strong and willing wind obligingly filling the run-up sails. She moved majestically down the Channel; her next destination, Halifax.

"Jonnie, isn't this wonderful?" Jennifer, her hazel eyes dancing and her red curls ruffled by the wind, turned to her brother in elation. "I can hardly believe it! Oh, Katie, do stop sniffling. You know you've always wanted to travel. I told you I'd handle Guardie and make it, too."

An extra loud sniff was her reply. "'Tis doubtful, Miss Jenny, if we'll ever get there," Katie mumbled. "I'll be down in the cabin unpacking." She turned and left them, making her way uncertainly along the rolling deck.

Jennifer laughed. "Poor Katie. "I think she'll already be glad when she's on land again. Oh, Jonathan, aren't you looking forward to it?"

"Yes, I think I am," her brother agreed fervently. His face was turning a peculiar color, his hands gripped the rail tightly.

"Jonathan, don't tell me you feel seasick *already?*" There was a hint of amused scorn in her voice and her brother turned angrily.

"It's fine for you, you've always had a good stomach. I don't see why you wanted to come on this trip in the first place, and now that you are here at least do me the favor of not being amused because I feel seasick."

"Poor Jonnie," her voice was solicitous, if her lips were twitching. "Maybe you'd better go below."

"Another thing," an old grievance surged to her brother's mind, "I don't see why you insisted on bringing along this fellow, what's his name—Bates? as my groom. I don't want a groom. I'm not going to set up a stable."

"But I expect to," Jennifer said airily, "and Bates was well recommended."

"By whom? It's all very queer to me."

"He came from Rufus's place," Jennifer said patiently. "I've told you all this before, Jonathan. Joseph, the head man there, said he was a wonderful hand with horses. He was a new man so they could spare him if we wanted to take him to Canada with us, and Bates wanted to come, and it was too good an opportunity to miss, because you know Guardie could never have spared us a groom."

"Well, where is the fellow now?"

"Probably down below making himself useful—he said he'd act as your valet until we got our horses."

"You know Guardie said I'd have a batman," Jonathan

began, then bit his lips hard. Sweat stood out on his face. "Jennifer, I—I—" he began in an altered tone. Then, "Oh, God!"

Jennifer, helping her brother down the steep companion-way a few minutes later, was not displeased that the conversation had terminated when it had. Because it was completely possible that Jonathan could have asked some very uncomfortable questions, and she had no intention of telling him that the "wonderful hand with horses," their new groom, was none other than the highwayman whom she had thwarted. It was, she reflected with amusement, quite an interesting arrangement!

Chapter Four

Two days out from England, the *Cambria* ran into heavy squalls, then into storms, mountainous seas and high winds, which blew her off her course and battered her from the height of one wave to another. She creaked and groaned and plowed her way ahead, lying first on one side, then rolling to the other.

The passengers held vastly differing opinions on the voyage. Some of them regarded it merely as a means of passage from one country to another; something to be endured if not enjoyed; an unpleasant interval which would pass, given a requisite amount of time, and they set themselves to withstand discomfort as best they might. These stolid ones played interminable games of cards in the great saloon and stayed up half the night sampling the liquid stabilizers carried in fair quantity (and quality) by the *Cambria* for the gratification of her passengers. If some of these passengers rolled on their way to their berths, all the unsteadiness of their gait could not be entirely accounted for by the motion of the boat.

But most travelers spent much of the trip in their respective cabins, wherefrom unearthly moans and groans could be heard, interspersed by more unpleasant sounds, as the suffering inmates first feared the end of all earthly travails was at hand, then prayed this should be and regretted that it was not.

It had not required the buffeting of any storm to send Jonathan to his bunk, and Katie was a close second. By the time night fell on the first day out, Jonathan's complexion was the color of an anemic pea, and so far as he was concerned, life was no longer worth the living. He had collapsed on Jennifer's bunk that first afternoon, and had been so miserable that Jennifer had left him there, retiring to Jonathan's single cabin across the way.

Nothing daunted Jennifer. She accommodated her gait to the bucking jolts of the *Cambria*, and tucking her curls under a close-tugged shawl went up on deck. There were still a goodly number of other passengers afoot for the second day, and she passed the time pleasantly enough.

But the third day was another matter. Wrapped in her shawl, she had mounted a steeply pitched companionway to the deck, only to be met at the top by a gust of wind so fierce that she stopped to catch her breath before she ventured further. A swarthy ships officer, whom she later learned was Mr. Jones, hurried across to the open door and, touching his cap courteously, warned her that it would be best not for her to attempt any visit to the deck; such daring was certainly not for females.

"But I'll be perfectly all right," she protested. "Mr. Williams is up there, I saw him go only a few minutes ago."

"It's all right for the gentlemen, ma'am," Mr. Jones said earnestly, "but there ain't no female what can stand up to this pitching, m'lady, begging your pardon. You see, m'lady, it's all them skirts, begging your pardon I'm sure. The wind, it fills 'em and you just can't tell when it'd blow you. Please, m'lady, much the best you stay below."

Having battled even a fraction of the wind Jennifer was forced to see reason in Mr. Jones's earnest warnings. She sighed and returned to the ladies' saloon, where the atmosphere was so thick that she fled in distaste to the large cabin which she had intended to share with Katie. She had looked in on the sufferers earlier in the day, and they had appeared to be resting comfortably—in fact Katie had been moving about the cabin setting it to rights—so she had left them with a good conscience. But now—she drew back on the threshold and swallowed hastily. For both Jonathan and Katie had been vilely ill and were stretched out on their bunks, their faces wet and white, moaning fretfully. She shut the cabin door behind her and grabbed the nearest basin, thrusting it at Jonathan almost angrily.

"Jonnie, why didn't you call the stewardess?" she asked sharply.

"Oh, God, Jenny, go away," her brother moaned. "Of course we called the stewardess. Why doesn't this damned boat stop for just one minute. Oh, God!" He moved convulsively, and Jennifer got the basin to him just in time.

"Katie, how are you?" she demanded, stupidly enough. It was obvious how Katie was.

"M'lady, I don't know why I came with you," Katie groaned. "Oh, Lady Jennifer!" She attempted to sit up, and her mistress again was just in time.

"Better lie still," she said. "I'll see if I can't find the stewardess."

"It won't do no good, m'lady," Katie told her mournfully. "She's only got one pair of hands and it seems like most all the ladies aboard is calling her. She told me I'd best look after my mistress myself, she couldn't do nothing. She thought Master Jonathan was you, m'lady."

"All the more reason why she should have come," Jennifer said sharply. "I'll find her at once."

She left, but Katie had been right. The stewardess was so busy flying from one cabin to another that Jennifer realized it would be useless to try to attract the woman's much divided attention. She returned alone, and set about doing what she could to set the cabin to rights.

"M'lady, you shouldn't be doing this," Katie tried again to get up, but sank back with a moan. "Oh, my head!"

"Be quiet, Katie, try to sleep," Jennifer advised. "Jonathan, shouldn't you make an effort to get up on deck? I'm sure fresh air would be good for you, and…" However, even as she spoke, she realized her brother was in no condition to stand the gales above.

"Just let me alone, Jenny," he pleaded. "Go away and leave me alone. Oh-h-h!"

She did what she could for them, lurching across the cabin at each roll of the *Cambria*, and stowing away loose objects which had been flung this way and that. Down here in the cabin, the rolling was intensified, the air heavy with the foul odor of sickness. She longed for the upper deck, and savagely cursed those skirts which kept her below.

In the midst of gathering up Jonathan's coat and trousers which had fallen off the hook where Katie had first hung them, she paused suddenly and eyed the clothes speculatively. She glanced at her brother, lying inert on her bunk, rolled in one of her dressing gowns. After all, what could be the harm? No one would know the difference. Jonathan was not likely to be above decks for some time, and by then she could reclaim her skirts. Besides, in this weather, skirts were definitely a nuisance. With every passing moment she could appreciate even more Mr. Jones's apologetic comments.

"I'll take your uniform to the other cabin, Jonathan," she said. "There's more room to stow it there."

"I don't care what you do with it," her brother groaned. "Throw it overboard, if you want to. Damn Guardie! Oh-h-h!"

She picked up his dark green jacket and the matching trousers, and opened the cabin door cautiously. Nobody was about. She was able to slip quickly along the passageway to her brother's cabin, where George greeted her enthusiastically with a loving attempt to knock her down and lick her face.

"Quiet! Get down, George. I'll take you up on deck soon," she promised recklessly.

It was only a matter of minutes before she was free of her encumbering dress and under-petticoats, and had pulled on Jonathan's trousers, which fitted her quite as well as his garments always had in the past. It was fortunate, she considered, that padded fronts to an officer's uniform had become

41

a recent military style. That addition concealed admirably, she was sure, the variation between her figure and Jonathan's. There was little difference in the length of their hair. Fashion for gentlemen decreed flowing locks and sideburns if possible (although Jonathan, much to his continued chagrin, had not yet been able to attain this height of elegance, being still far too downy-cheeked, he believed)—while ladies attached curls to their coiffure to supply the necessary upstanding crown of elegance, their own hair short and puffed over the ears.

Too much wind tó risk Jonathan's shako, but she could well use his cloak. Though she had no mirror to judge by, Jennifer was sure it would take a most astute person to pierce the masquerade.

She snapped a leash onto George's collar, and led the eager dog out to the open deck without incident. Once up there, she hastily sought possible shelter. For the wind had sharpened enough to almost whirl her off her feet. She wrapped Jonathan's cloak more closely about her, and tightened her grasp on George's lead, while the big dog pressed against her and whined.

A rope lifeline had been rigged so that the hardy souls venturing on deck could cling tō that as they made their way along open spaces. Jennifer clutched that anchorage firmly. With George close beside her, she fought her way against the wind along the length of the deck to a relatively-sheltered spot near the bow of the ship, where she halted gratefully until her breath returned to her. Even if this was a battle, it was better than staying below in the ill-smelling cabin.

A large crate carried as cargo had been lashed to the deck. Jennifer scrambled on top of that and leaned back with satisfaction against the bulkhead. George crouched at her feet and shifted uncomfortably as the *Cambria* lurched and rolled, while the wind blew with a sullen ferocity and the shortened canvas whipped and strained overhead.

Jennifer felt keenly alive. Her hair blew in wet frenzy, some locks plastered against her cheek as she laughed and did not avert her face from the spray. This was really living! No staying below deck for her, when she could get up here!

An oilskinned figure fought his way along toward the captain's quarters and the bridge. Sighting Jennifer he crossed the open deck with difficulty.

"Beg pardon, sir," he yelled against the wind. "Captain's request, sir, would you care to come aloft?"

"Aloft?" Her eyes traveled up the rigging.

"To the bridge, sir. The captain saw you come above decks. He thinks you'll be better off aloft."

"That's very good of the captain. I shall be pleased to come," Jennifer returned promptly. Such a notion was rather more than she had bargained for, but to refuse such an invitation might bring her even more attention.

She swung off the crate, gathered George's lead and Jonathan's cloak to her, and struggled over to the companionway down which the sailor had come. The wind caught her full-face and nearly hurled her against the following sailor.

"Best give me the dog, sir," the sailor shouted. "I'll attend to him."

She handed over the lead thankfully, now able to use both her hands to clutch the guard rail. The cloak billowed out and she felt as if she were going to sail through the air in another moment. The helpful sailor grabbed at that encumbrance quickly.

"Go ahead, sir," he yelled, and Jennifer did, gaining the sanctuary of the pilot's cabin, drenched, windblown and breathless, but smiling gamely.

"Thank you, very—much—Captain," she got out, between gasps. "The—the wind—it—it took—my breath—away."

"Aye, it's a bit strong," Captain Walker agreed, motioning her to a locker seat. "Sit ye doon until ye catch your breath. Man, you're a glutton for punishment, Captain. When I spotted ye making your way for'rad, I said to myself, 'There's a mon who'll not rest long above deck.' Then there you was, stretched out as comfortable as ye please on yon deck cargo below, and the winds a-drenching you with every gust. Mon, you're soaked through."

"Not quite," Jennifer laughed, "but that cloak wasn't much use coming up the companionway—oh, where's George?"

"Your dog? I had Budge take him along to quarters—no place for a fine large beast like that up here, ye ken. Crowded, sum'mat."

Jennifer glanced about the indeed crowded cabin, and agreed with emphasis. One swipe of George's tail would have soaked every person present.

"He'll be all right," the captain added reassuringly. "Budge is quite a hand with dogs."

The phrase reminded Jennifer of her new groom. "I've a man aboard who could take care of him," she began, but the captain was ahead of her.

"Aye, that'll be your man, Bates. Making himself right useful, he is. Best leave the animal with him with a wee blow like this about."

Jennifer laughed. "You call this a wee blow?"

"Aye, it's not up to much yet. The glass is still falling, nae doot it'll be worse afore it's better. You're enjoying it, perhaps?"

"I don't mind it," Jennifer admitted. "Not above deck, anyway. Down below it's rather bad. People sick all over the place, you know."

The captain nodded. "Aye, the passengers seldom seem to find much pleasure in a wee blow. But I confess I was surprised to see you this day, Your Lordship. I've not seen you about since we left England; have ye found your sea legs?"

Jennifer opened her mouth to say she'd never lost them, and remembered in time. "Yes, it always takes me a day or so to get them," she said.

"Your lady sister now, would she be still enjoying the voyage?"

Jennifer's lips twitched. "My twin is below, wishing for a quick end," she said solemnly, then her eyes met the captain's and they laughed together.

"Sure, it's really no laughing matter," said the captain a moment later. "I've seen the females carried ashore time and again after a poor passage. They be too weak to walk even a short distance. Takes it out of ye, seasickness does."

"Yes, it does," Jennifer agreed with deliberate emphasis.

"Ye've traveled before, I take it, m'lord," he remarked. "Rifles, eh? Used to know some of your fellows back in '12 and '14 when you were busy chasing Boney from the Peninsula."

She looked up at him quickly. "Indeed, sir?"

"Yes. In the navy then. First officer in one of the transports."

"But you left the navy, sir?"

He shrugged. He was a burly, grizzled man, with a heavily seamed face and eyes which appeared ever to be squinting off to the horizon. "Peace came. No need for a large navy. I had my mate's papers, now I have my own ship. Fortunes of war, fortunes of peace. So you're off to rejoin your regiment? The old 95th, weren't they? Thought I remembered it."

"To Halifax," Jennifer nodded.

"Aye, aye. Quite a town, Halifax. Changed a lot in the last few years. Remember it well during those war years, sailed into it often. Nice harbor. Lively place, then. Dead now. Still, understand the military men manage to have a good time, eh, m'lord?" He winked.

"No doubt. I'm not acquainted with it yet. The regiment was moved while I was in England."

"Well, well. It's a regular garrison town, m'lord. No better, no worse. You'll get used to it."

A sudden shift in the wind swung his attention abruptly from Jennifer to the steersman, who was suddenly fighting hard to keep the wheel steady. With the officer's quick assistance, the *Cambria* was brought back on an even keel and faced into the sea. Then the captain shouted orders to the visible crew.

"I'm in your way, Captain, I'd better leave," Jennifer got to her feet when he turned away from the steersman.

He looked at her but it was obvious his mind was far away. Then his gaze cleared. "Ye're not in the way, m'lord, not where ye are. Don't blame you for not wanting to stay about below. Welcome here whenever ye wish. Better have you here, where I can keep an eye on ye, than wonder if ye're washed overboard." He chuckled.

"Thank you very much, Captain," Jennifer said sincerely. "But I feel I should look in on my sister again. Our maidservant is ill, too, and the stewardess is rushed off her feet."

"Tell that man of yours to attend to them," the captain suggested. "Give him something to do." When he saw Jennifer hesitating, he added, "No Mrs. Grundy about, Captain. Not aboard ship in a storm!"

45

It was not exactly the proprieties of the situation which Jennifer was considering. Her lips twitched as she wondered what the captain would say if he knew he'd been entertaining Lady Jennifer instead of Viscount Welland. The captain, noting the glint of amusement and naturally mistaking the cause, said jocularly that he didn't suspect his sister would care who looked after her so long as someone did.

"Indeed, I think I'll follow your suggestion, Captain," Jennifer replied. "Only I must find Bates first, I've not seen him since we cleared England."

"I'll have Budge send him along to your cabin," the captain promised. "It's not necessary to go on deck, m'lord; you can pass this way. And I think perhaps some oilskins will be ready if you're set on a stroll about the deck. Budge will bring them to you. Come again, m'lord. Any time."

Chapter Five

Captain Walker had not been exaggerating: the glass had indeed fallen. The previous wind and rain were as nothing compared to a fury which mounted steadily until the storm reached a crescendo ten days out from England. By that time, Jonathan no longer cared who was attending to him. He had long since given up expostulating with his sister for peremptorily changing places and leaving him as a suffering female dependent on Bates's good graces. Instead, he lay supine in Jennifer's berth, white and stricken, too exhausted to brace himself even automatically against the sharp rolls and pitches of the vessel.

Katie had rallied slightly. She was able to partake of a little nourishment, and even ventured out into the ladies' saloon on the infrequent occasion when the *Cambria* did not feel inclined to stand bow down in a welter of wave. But she, too, had long since given up objecting to Bates's ministrations, and indeed accepted them with real gratitude.

"For I won't have you think I approve of this affair, m'lady," she said with a reproving shake of her head, "but I'll not deny that man's a mighty help."

He had been, too. From the time that he had appeared at Jonathan's cabin door and inquired diffidently of Jennifer if there was aught he could do to assist her, he had taken full charge of Jonathan and Katie, putting the cabin to rights, sponging Jonathan's face and hands, looking after Katie, and at the same time managing to keep a useful eye on Jennifer and her needs as well. He found food for George and disappeared regularly with the big dog, returning him to Jennifer's cabin fed, refreshed, and glad to see his mistress.

Without a lift of an eye, he had accepted Jonathan as Lady Jennifer, although it had taken Jennifer some peremptory commands to Katie and her brother to accept the deception.

"For there's no use your telling me it mustn't be, Jonnie," she said firmly. "I can't stay cooped up below decks all the time and I'm not allowed above decks in skirts. Besides, the captain himself is convinced I'm you, so everything's all right. When you get your feet under you again, I'll get back into petticoats." It never occurred to her that Jonathan would not recover before they reached Halifax.

"Jennifer, it's a damn-fool thing to do," Jonathan snapped with as much vigor as he could command. "If I didn't feel as weak as a sick cat, you wouldn't get away with it. God, Jenny, don't be such a fool."

"I'm not being the fool," his sister retorted. "You are. Nobody will know the difference, Jonnie, don't be so stupid. Katie, don't you forget and call him Master Jonathan—remember, now."

"Lady Jennifer, you get out of them trousers right away." Katie tried to sit up. "The very idea, going up on deck in the likes of that. Why, if the Duke were to hear of it..."

"Guardie won't have a chance to hear of it," Jennifer said impatiently. "I keep telling you, nobody will know the difference."

Apparently nobody did even begin to guess. From the captain down, one and all accepted Jennifer as Captain Lord Welland, and enquired solicitously after her "sister" who, even when the *Cambria* triumphed over the severe storm and settled down to cope with merely heavy winds, remained languid and ill while most of the other ladies regained their appetites and their desire to keep on living.

"M'lord," Bates drew her aside one evening. "I'm that worried about her ladyship. Nought will stay down, even now. I've tried broths and gruel and wines—the stewardess, she don't know what to suggest now, m'lord. She don't even seem to care."

"How about champagne?" Jennifer asked. "Is there any of that aboard?"

"I've tried everything else, sir," Bates said. "The stewardess didn't speak of champagne, but I'll ask her."

"I'll be in the cabin," Jennifer said, and Bates nodded and went off in search of the wine steward.

She thought she had become accustomed to the sight of her brother's white face, but nevertheless, his appearance shocked her this time. It seemed as if life itself had left him, and she touched his cheek in a panic.

"Jonnie, Jonnie, wake up."

Her brother moved his head slowly on the pillow and opened his eyes wearily. "Hello, Jenny."

"Jonnie, what's the idea of this?" Fear made her voice sharp. "Bates tells me you won't eat anything. That's stupid. You've got to."

"Oh, God, Jenny, I don't care," her brother said weakly. "Just let me alone." He closed his eyes and turned his head away.

"Jonnie, Jonnie!" She reached over and took his chin in her fingers.

"Go away, Jenny," her brother mumbled.

"Beg pardon, sir, the stewardess had some champagne." The creaks and groans of the *Cambria* had covered Bates's entrance, and she was startled to find him standing beside her, extending a glass with a very small quantity of pale golden liquid in it. "Best a little at a time, sir, she suggested," he said apologetically.

"Yes, of course," Jennifer nodded. She turned to her brother. "Jonnie, here's some champagne; do try to swallow some of it." She tried to get her arm under Jonathan's shoulders to raise him, but Bates was right beside her.

"I'll raise her, m'lord," he suggested. "Difficult to steady yourself against the roll." He bent and deftly slipped his arm under Jonathan's shoulders, raising him slightly and at the same time dexterously pressing another pillow into place behind him.

Jennifer held the glass to her brother's lips and tilted it. "Drink it, Jonnie," she said urgently, quite unconscious that for the second time in Bates's presence she had addressed her brother by his rightful name.

Jonathan tried valiantly to swallow, and managed to get a little of the liquid down before he gagged. Bates had a basin ready at once, but the expected paroxysm did not occur, and after a moment Jennifer held the glass back to his lips. "Try another sip," she urged. Once again Jonathan swallowed weakly. Little by little, the small quantity disappeared.

"I think that's enough for a beginning, sir," Bates said anxiously. "Too much would be bad, m'lord, she's nothing else in her stomach, see."

Jennifer nodded. Bates's persistent use of "she" had brought her warning at last. "Yes, you're quite right, Bates. Perhaps she'll go to sleep now. Do you want to lie down again, Jenny, or are you comfortable as you are?"

"I'm all right, just leave me alone," Jonathan breathed, and didn't stir when Bates gently removed his arm and let him relax against the pillows.

"I'll watch with her, m'lord," Bates promised. "With the rolling, 'twere best that I stay here, lest she fall out of the berth."

"Yes, much the best," Jennifer agreed. She got to her feet, but stood looking down at her brother's closed face. "Let me know if there's anything more I can do, Bates."

There obviously was nothing else necessary at that moment, so Jennifer left the cabin and, after a momentary hesitation, collected George and made her way to the open deck. The wind was blowing strongly and the *Cambria* was coping in a workmanlike fashion with the deep swells, but there were several people about on the deck and for the first time Jennifer felt odd at appearing on deck in trousers, without those borrowed and somewhat odoriferous oilskins as a protection. Further, not only was it broad daylight and a blue sky, but Jonathan's regimentals happened to be the only uniform aboard, and were consequently as conspicuous as a bright hat at a funeral. For England had been at peace some years now, and there were not as many officers in gay uniforms scattered about the country.

So to have a real, live officer aboard the *Cambria* sailing to rejoin his storied regiment—(for all regiments were storied in the England of the day)—was definitely something to be remarked, and indeed his arrival aboard ship at London had not gone unnoticed. Also, tales of the intrepid warrior's hardiness during the height of the storm had not gone unheralded. Consequently Jennifer found her passage about the deck interrupted by a steady flow of greetings from the numerous gentlemen who had regained their sea legs at last, and envied Captain Lord Welland for not having lost his.

Embarrassment made her curt, and her answers were short. Far from discouraging conversation, her brusque manner appeared to have the opposite effect. Clearly such curtness was taken as part of a recognized military manner. Affability and amiability were not expected.

With George at heel, she paced the deck with a measured stride. Common sense suggested that she retreat to Jonathan's cabin, but that never far from present devilment inherent in her persuaded her to remain and brazen it out. And, if her eyes were wary and a reckless amusement was not far below the surface, to all outward appearances she was a calm and assured officer in His Majesty's forces. So by the time she had circumnavigated the deck, her spirits were high and her sense of adventure fanned to a bright flame.

The days went by, unendingly to Jonathan and, in a slighter degree, to Katie, but swiftly and full of enjoyment to Jennifer. Again the glass fell, and the *Cambria* was stripped down, to deal with high winds, waves and sheets of rain. Jennifer buckled on her borrowed oilskins once more, braced the decks as long as the winds would permit, then found her way aloft to the pilot's cabin, where Captain Walker made her warmly welcome. She stood beside the captain on the open bridge and laughed as the spray swept across her face.

"Ye should have been a sailor, m'lord," shouted Captain Walker, and she nodded vigorously and laughed.

At night in her cabin she read Jonathan's drill book, which she had found among his luggage, apparently the only piece of reading material he had brought with him, barring several books of poetry which she tossed aside with a grimace. The drill book was interesting. Much of what it contained was already familiar to her from her careful attention to the tales of her guardian and his friends. She had even put many of the rules into practice some years back for the discipline and drill of the sons and daughters of tenant farmers and the staff of her guardian's estate, whom she had recruited into an "army" which she had generalled in quite a satisfactory manner. Indeed she had armed, drilled, and maneuvered her then "army" of twelve over some of the best natural hazards the country could offer. Now she noted with interest that a new type of drill had been formulated, carefully explained in detail in this book, complete with diagrams to make it clearer to an aspiring young officer, who probably would not have read so far in the first place. Jennifer studied it with care. It seemed to her that the drill would make for a good appearance on the parade ground, but she doubted if the maneuvers it advised would be of much value in the actual field. The noted instructors who were responsible, all unknowingly, for her tactical education had had much experience in actual warfare, and they had been most emphatic in their denunciations of certain generally accepted groupings and moves of the past. But this was all very interesting. Not for the first time she sincerely envied Jonathan.

"Well, we should be docking in Halifax come the morning after tomorrow," Captain Walker told her some days later. The *Cambria* had been at sea for four weeks and three days, well off her schedule, due to the storm conditions which had blown her many miles off course.

"So soon as that?" Now that the voyage was nearing an end, Jennifer found herself honestly regretful.

"Aye, so soon as that, though I've nae doot your sister will no think it 'so soon as that,'" mimicked the captain with a grin.

Jennifer agreed. "She doesn't appear to have strength to move from her bed," she said in a more worried tone than she realized.

"Aye, that's no surprising," said the captain. "It's no been so smooth a crossing for a delicate lady like your sister, though I've seen worse meself."

"And longer too, I'm sure," Jennifer said. The captain nodded.

"Aye, many days longer. Six weeks used to be the usual time, and once it took the *Mary Robert* ten weeks from Liverpool to Halifax, and bad weather all the way. Those were the days, m'lord, those were the days. Hardtack and no water and the passengers half-dead, and many of them full dead and buried at sea. Aye, things are different now. This *Cambria*, she's a good ship, fast, hardy. Aye, a good ship. A fighting ship, Captain." He passed his hand with unconscious pride over the mahogany of the rail. "A good ship, Captain."

"A very good ship, Captain Walker," Jennifer agreed, and sighed. "I shall be sorry to leave her." And it occurred to her that her days as "Captain Lord Welland" were numbered; now that they were nearing Halifax Jonathan would be himself again.

Only Jonathan was in no condition to take over. He still lay on his sister's bunk, looking at her from deeply sunken and shadowed eyes as he said weakly, "Jennifer, I don't care what you do. I just—don't—care. Get me off this boat, that's all I ask you. Just get me off."

"But, Jonnie," she was sitting on the edge of the bunk, "I can't very well get back into skirts now and pretend that I was sick all through the voyage, while you were hale and hearty. You'll have to get up."

"I can't," said her brother with weary finality. "It's up to you, Jenny. I don't care what you do. You've passed yourself off as me all the way from England, and I think you can carry on until we get ashore. I just won't report in until I can at least walk, I'm certainly not going to let anyone know that I had to be carried off this boat. No, it'll have to be you, Jenny." Then he closed his eyes with every appearance of being too utterly fatigued to talk any longer.

"Well," said Jennifer, a little uncertainly, "all right, Jonathan, I'll do my best." Then the sparkle came back to her eyes and she laughed aloud. "Jonnie, this is going to be fun after all! Fancy, I shall arrive in Halifax an honest-to-goodness officer of the Rifles! Oh, if only Guardie could see me now!"

"It's a very good thing he can't, m'lady," said Katie severely. "You ought to be ashamed of yourself, instead of standing there laughing with Master Jonnie so ill and all. Nothing funny about it."

Only to Jennifer, striding the deck with George obediently at heel, there was much that was very amusing about the situation.

Quite a lot that was somewhat nerve-racking, too. Her mood changed a little, but she refused to give in to any foreseeing of future trouble.

Chapter Six

Almost the entire passenger list of the *Cambria* was on deck as she sailed slowly into Halifax Harbor on the morning tide, after anchoring outside the harbor mouth for the night. Near the bow, Jenny stood, holding George on a short lead and surveying the approaching shoreline critically. The town did not look as large as she had pictured it, but of course it must extend beyond the citadel hill.

Certainly Halifax was prettily laid out from the waterfront. The streets marched straight and square with military precision back and forth along the shore and up and down the hill which dominated the harbor, and which was crowned at its peak by the impressive walls and revetments of Fort George. With the flag of Great Britain floating lazily from a tall flagstaff atop the Fort, a speckling of redcoats could be seen drilling on the far slope. The town looked clean and neat and tidy and prosperous and small—this last was not a welcome thought, for all of Jennifer's hasty calculations about their arrival had been based on Halifax's being at least as large as a town of similar importance in England.

There was little opportunity to dwell too long on the dubious prospects. Other passengers crowded around her, talking excitedly, grateful that the end of an uncomfortable voyage was at hand, promising to keep in touch with each other, exchanging all sorts of last minute messages, and pressing parting admonitions on any who would listen.

The *Cambria* was docked and secured. Husky longshoremen came aboard to unload the luggage, while cabmen argued and gestured heatedly about the disembarking passengers.

Jennifer had suggested that Bates go ashore ahead of their own party and arrange transportation before they attempted to land, and she noticed that he had been among the first to leave the ship. She saw him surrounded by cabmen, apparently arguing quite as fiercely with them as they were with him, and she turned away from the rail with a grin of satisfaction. The girl was sure by now she could rely on Bates to deal with such matters competently.

She made her way below, exchanging last good-byes with passengers who beamed admiringly at her, and found Katie in a perfect tizzy of excitement and last minute flurry and bustle. While Jonathan, tastefully arrayed in the simplest walking gown in his sister's wardrobe, lounged apathetically in the most comfortable chair the cabin boasted, one leg inelegantly crossed over the other.

"Jonathan, put your foot down," Jennifer admonished, coming into the cabin and hastily shutting the door behind her. "No female ever sits like that."

"I am no female," pointed out Jonathan, reasonably enough, but he uncrossed his legs. "Besides, I don't wonder no female sits so, these blasted skirts get in the way. I can't see why I had to get dressed like this, I could have been carried ashore as I was, quite as easily and far more comfortably."

"Where's your pride?" Jennifer scoffed, for this had been the cause of a heated argument with Jonathan, who had stubbornly demanded trousers and a stretcher. In the end, Jennifer had persuaded him into a gown. And, because in the long run it was always easier for Jonathan to give in to Jenny than to stand out against her, he had acquiesced. However, the actual business of getting him into that dress had required repeated coaxings, heated admonitions, much tugging, and a large amount of muffled giggles, for Jonathan's comments were acid and pungent. He really was not very strong, either, and the least exertion tired him, so that the feat of getting him into a whalebone corset, (ordered by Katie so that he wouldn't rip all the seams on Jennifer's gown), and then into petticoat and a bell-skirted dress, quite honestly wore him out. By the time the matter of a coiffure was discussed, Jonathan had had all that he could endure.

"No," he had said, with a finality which even Jennifer had to recognize. "You've got me into this rig, and that's enough. Tie a bonnet under my chin if you insist, though what you women want to do with bonnets I don't know, give me a shawl around my shoulders, and be hanged with the rest of it."

"But Jonnie," Jennifer began, then she stopped and shrugged. "All right, you'll pass now, anyway. I'll go up on deck and be down in time to let you know when we're ready to go ashore."

"It won't be too soon to suit me," Jonathan said grimly. "These stays are killing me. How the devil do you wear them, Jenny?"

His sister grinned. "I don't," she said. "Not often, anyway. Try and rest, Jonnie. I'll be down later."

She had left him then, and now, returning an hour later, she could see the unmistakable signs of exhaustion on his face.

"It won't be too much longer," she said reassuringly. "Bates will be here very shortly. Halifax doesn't look too large, Jonnie, so no doubt we'll be at the hotel quickly, and you can get out of that dress and lie down to rest again."

"Yes, and *you* can take off those trousers, m'lady," Katie said severely. "Displaying your limbs in such a fashion—fair takes the breath out o' me, it does! Shameful!"

"There's nothing wrong with my limbs, Katie," Jennifer objected, regarding her legs with a complacency guaranteed to arouse Katie's wrath. "Fine figure of an officer, if I say so myself."

Her brother grinned faintly, but Katie rose to the bait and scolded Jennifer firmly until Jonathan cut in on her expostulations.

"Did you say Halifax wasn't very large, Jenny?"

"It doesn't look too big from the water," his sister said frankly. "There's a hill right in the middle of it that I heard one of the passengers call Citadel Hill, and the Fort is atop it. Possibly the city goes back behind the hill a lot."

There was no time to say more. Bates's apologetic tap sounded on the door, to be followed, on Jennifer's "Come in," by Bates in person with two perspiring men behind him who had obviously been pressed into service by the enterprising Bates to attend to the luggage.

Under Bates's eagle eye, they did their duty speedily and he disappeared with them, saying as he left that he would return to assist m'lady as soon as he had seen their belongings safely stowed.

"We could go up on deck," Jennifer suggested as the door closed, but Jonathan shook his head.

"I'm staying here until Bates comes back," he said firmly. "Every time I stand up, this boat turns over, and I'm going to wait until he's here with a firm hand in support."

"Don't be silly," Jennifer scoffed. "The boat isn't moving now."

"That's a matter of opinion." Jonathan was grim. "I say it's moving. I'm staying here, Jenny." He turned a deaf ear to her coaxings and stayed in where he was until Bates reappeared and informed them that all was in readiness.

"I have made enquiries, m'lord. The Colonial Hotel on Hollis Street is the best you can ask for. So I stretched m'orders a bit and sent a boy there to see about rooms," he told Jennifer anxiously. "It seemed best, m'lord. Them ashore said as how good lodging is hard to find, owing to the military having taken over the Halifax Hotel for officers' quarters. Seems like part of the barracks was burned down a time ago. The officers of your regiment are staying there, m'lord."

"Bates, you are a mine of information," Jennifer said solemnly. "Excellent arrangements. Now, if you can assist Her Ladyship ashore, we can proceed to the Colonial—I think you said? yes? —the Colonial Hotel."

"And I shall be very pleased to arrive there," Jonathan muttered.

"It is but a short ride, m'lady," Bates said consolingly. "If Your Ladyship will permit, I could carry Your Ladyship ashore."

"No, no that won't be necessary, I'm sure," Jennifer said hastily, but "m'lady Jennifer" waved a suddenly regal hand.

"My brother is out of sympathy with me," "she" said languidly. "Really, Jonathan, you might allow me to conduct my passage in my own way. Your arm, I think, Bates, for the first, then we will see. I confess I find the floor most unsteady."

Rising slowly and with obvious difficulty to his feet, Jonathan leaned heavily on Bates's arm and proceeded at a snail's pace through the ladies' saloon to the companionway leading to the deck. Katie and Jennifer brought up the rear, carrying the few remaining items from the cabin.

The ladder-like companionway was, however, a different matter. Unused to skirts in the first place, hampered by a very real lack of strength as well as by his dress, Jonathan made heavy going of the first step. Then Bates said firmly, "With your pardon, m'lady," and picked him up as casually as if he had been a child, carried him up to deposit him gently and with his skirts completely unruffled on the scrubbed deck of the *Cambria* for his first view of Halifax.

"Isn't it delightful?" Jennifer gestured towards the town.

Jonathan looked ashore briefly. "Wonderful," he agreed. "Solid, too. Bates, how soon can we get there?"

"Right along here, m'lady," Bates guided him carefully towards the gangway which had been run aboard amidship.

Captain Walker stood at the head of that, taking a courteous farewell of his passengers. He bowed gravely over Jonathan's extended mittened hand. "I am sorry that we had no smooth a passage, your ladyship," he said in his gruff manner. "Nae doot ye'll no be sorry to leave m'ship."

"Not at all, Captain Walker," Jonathan said graciously, and somewhat ambiguously. "It is a most commodious ship, but I confess the thought of land is most attractive to me. Good day, Captain Walker. I trust we may meet again." Smiling and nodding graciously, "she" leaned on Bates's arm, and made "her" slow way down the gangway.

Jennifer, struggling with a laugh, shook hands firmly with the captain. "It's been a good voyage, Captain," she said heartily. "I shall indeed hope to travel aboard a ship of your command again."

"Aye, and ye'll be welcome aboard, m'lord," the grizzled captain returned. "Good-bye, and the best of luck to ye."

Bates had escorted Jonathan to a nearby cab, and he stepped into it with as much dignity as a duchess, relaxing with a sigh of content against the squabs and smoothing out his skirts with finicking fingers. "So fatiguing," he murmured, as Jennifer plunked down with no grace at all beside him. "So very fatiguing."

Jennifer bit her lips hard. "Jonnie, behave yourself," she muttered, and her brother turned limpid eyes on her.

"But my dear, I am," he protested, and resumed his scrutiny of the dockside. He shuddered delicately. "Water. Bates, let us proceed without delay to the hotel, if you please."

"Yes, m'lady, at once." Bates finished the bestowal of the last of the hand luggage, and swung himself up beside the driver, who gathered up his reins and clucked to his horses.

Jennifer looked about her eagerly as the cab rattled over the cobblestones. Everything was so new, so interesting. It was obviously a garrison town, for they passed several small detachments of soldiers on the short trip to the hotel. These were redcoats, Jennifer noted, with a thrill of excitement not unmixed with relief. Life in Halifax promised to be interesting, if even half of Guardie's tales were to be repeated.

"Not many Rifles about," she observed to Jonathan, who sat with a rather grim expression about his mouth and not looking too happy. "What's the matter? Aren't you all right now?"

"If this cab doesn't stop jolting soon," Jonathan said between his teeth, "nobody's going to be all right."

Jennifer glanced ahead anxiously. Jonathan was in a bad way, she could see that. If the hotel—ah! "It's just ahead," she said to her brother quickly. "Not half a block." She stiffened slowly. A tall figure in the dark green of the Rifles had crossed the road just ahead of their carriage and disappeared inside the Colonial Hotel. She turned quickly to her brother, but her words died away on her lips for Jonathan, obviously oblivious to the passing parade, was saying with taut vehemence, "Tell the driver to stop at once."

Bates half turned from his perch beside the driver. "The driver tells me this is the hotel, m'lady," he began, but he too stopped abruptly after a glance at Jonathan, ending quickly, "I'll see if the accommodations are ready, m'lord."

"No, you attend to my sister." Jennifer was peremptory. "I'll go in."

The cabbie had pulled his horses to a halt, and Jennifer jumped down from the cab and hastened across into the hotel. Anxiety for Jonathan made her forget her unease of the previous minutes, and she strode across the lobby with the purposeful air and set face of a person intent on his own business—which she was. So much so that the tall officer of the Rifles who had entered shortly before her, turned from his companion to regard Jennifer's entrance with approval.

Jennifer didn't notice him. The clerk was bowing to her, and assuring her that yes, indeed, his message had been received and a suite of rooms had been held for Captain Lord Welland and his sister, Lady Jennifer, and their servants. If the captain would just sign the register—?

Jennifer signed with a flourish, and the clerk once again almost succeeded in pressing his nose against the counter, while at the same time he rang a bell sharply and issued shrill commands to the porter who hurried to answer his summons.

"My sister has been most unwell on the voyage," Jennifer said curtly. "I desire access to the rooms without delay."

"But of course, m'lord. At once. At once."

Jennifer turned away from the desk and stopped short. A tall officer in green was lounging across the lobby and looking straight at her, with the obvious intention of speaking.

At that moment, Jennifer felt an almost overwhelming desire to turn and run. For only the barest flicker of a second, her eyes scanned the surroundings. The officer was between her and the street door, the desk clerk was at the counter behind her, the stairs went up to her left, but in full view of the lobby and of everyone in it. To turn her back would be an insult of the highest order and, worse, the most stupid action she could make.

All this flashed through her mind even as she was schooling herself to meet the oncoming officer—a captain like herself, she noted.

"Good morning, sir. My name's Dixon, "A" Company, 1st Battalion. I saw you come in, and I'm afraid I couldn't help overhearing you speak to the desk clerk. Allow me to welcome you to Halifax, Lord Welland."

"Thank you, Captain Dixon, very kind of you, I'm sure." Nervousness made her voice gruff. "Not sure what Company I'll be attached to, just arrived, y'know."

Captain Dixon nodded. "Yes, so I assumed. The C.O.'s been looking for you for almost a fortnight—oh, not you, personally," he added with a slow smile which lit up his pleasant, undistinguished features, "but a replacement for Captain Mitchell. Look, I won't hold you up now, I heard you say your sister had been unwell and I'm sure you'll want to see her to your rooms, but I'm due to report to the colonel at ten o'clock, and I'll be happy to show you to H.Q."

Again Jennifer hesitated only momentarily. What was it Guardie had told Jonathan just before he left? That he must report at once upon arrival? Before the day was out, Guardie had emphasized. It was a breach of military discipline to do otherwise. While to turn down this offer without adequate reason.... "At ten, you said, Captain Dixon? Very well, I shall meet you here fifteen minutes before. Would that be time enough?"

"Quite," Captain Dixon nodded. "Until then, Welland." He sketched a salute, which Jennifer acknowledged, and turned on his heel to rejoin his companion.

Jonathan had come in on Bates's arm as Dixon turned from Jennifer, but Jonathan wasn't noticing much of anything just then. All he wanted was a quiet place, alone, where he could get rid of this appalling contraption binding his middle, and where he could hopefully stay until the world stopped revolving.

He crossed the lobby and followed the porter up the stairs, negotiating his skirts with difficulty and with Bates's help. Jennifer, with Katie, followed him, and the hotel porters brought up the rear with their luggage. Even the desk clerk was in on the act, for he suddenly appeared ahead of them, flourishing keys and bowing.

The rooms were on the first floor, overlooking the street, and consisted of a comfortably furnished sitting room, two fair-sized bedrooms, and a cubbyhole off one designed for the maidservant's room. Bates would be accommodated elsewhere, the desk clerk informed Jennifer, and departed with another flourishing bow.

Jonathan allowed himself to be settled in a large chair and sank back with a large sigh. "I wish this floor would stop rolling," he murmured.

"It will," Jennifer assured him. She added meaningly, "It had better stop very soon."

Bates, who had followed the clerk from the room, returned now to supervise the bestowal of the heavy luggage, successfully coping with the cabdriver and his cohorts. After they had gone, and Bates was in one of the bedrooms sorting out the baggage with Katie's help, Jennifer said quickly in a low voice, "I met Captain Dixon of "A" Company downstairs."

"Oh?" Jonathan didn't open his eyes.

"I am to meet him again in half an hour to report to the colonel."

"What?" Jonathan's eyes flew open. "You are to *what?*"

"Captain Dixon has offered to take me along to H.Q. so that I can report to the colonel," Jennifer repeated, underlining her words so that, despite his very real weariness of mind and body, Jonathan understood her meaning.

"You can't," Jonathan began as Bates came back into the room.

"Begging your pardon, m'lord," he spoke to Jennifer. "I have laid out a clean shirt and stock, sir, and polished your other boots."

"Thank you, Bates," Jennifer said mechanically. Her eyes were on her brother's face, and she saw there the answer to her unspoken question. "I'll—wait a minute and you can brush up this jacket. Too bad, Jenny, to leave you right away, but remember what Guardie said about reporting first off? Wouldn't want me to make a bad impression, would you?"

"But—" "Lady Jennifer" opened her mouth, but "Captain Lord Welland" beat her to it.

"First impressions are very important, Jenny. You'll be all right. After all, Katie's here; she'll look after you." Then, without a backward look, she swung over to the door of Captain Lord Welland's room and closed it behind her.

Chapter Seven

Punctually at fifteen minutes to the hour, Jennifer descended the stairs to the lobby. Dixon arose from a chair and crossed to meet her.

"All set, Welland?" he smiled. Jennifer, resplendent in a well brushed uniform whose buttons had been polished until they shone, nodded agreement. Jonathan's credentials reposed in her breast pocket, his shako was placed squarely on her head, and his gloves were smoothed into place with a casual tug.

"All set, Captain Dixon," she answered, and swung out the door beside him. He was a good four inches taller than she was—Jennifer nudged five feet, eight inches—and well built for his height, but he moved easily and lightly on his feet.

Outside in the street, he hailed a passing cab and motioned Jennifer in ahead of him. "Never walk when you can ride, Welland," he advised.

She smiled. "Is it far to Headquarters?"

"So-so," he answered vaguely. "A mile, more or less. It's in the Citadel, you see. The poor old Rifles are scattered all over the place. The officers are quartered in the Halifax Hotel, the men are in South Barracks, and H.Q.'s in the Citadel. Bit of a nuisance, but there it is, and not too uncomfortable for us." He chuckled.

Jennifer smiled politely in return. She was noticing that the cab had proceeded back along Hollis Street towards the docks. However, instead of turning down to the waterfront, the cabbie now swung to the left up a hill to Barrington Street and along that towards a wooden-walled enclosure surmounted by a rail.

She turned to Dixon, but he forestalled her query. "This is Grand Parade," he gestured toward the enclosure. "We mount guard here at ten every morning, and go through the salute and troop before relieving the guard. Thought you'd like to see it first morning. Know what's done."

Jennifer thanked him and stepped out of the cab after him. They were not the only onlookers at a scene which regularly drew a crowd of strangers and people from the country, as well as passing townsfolk.

Drawn up on the Square was a small detachment of Rifles in their green uniforms. Drums beating, pipes squealing, along came a company of red-jacketed Fusiliers. "Billeted in the Citadel," murmured the helpful Dixon in Jennifer's ear. "That's 'C' Company of ours, Captain Thurston."

With military punctilio the drill was carried out. The relieved Rifles detachment marched off and were followed shortly by the Fusiliers. The show was over and the crowd dispersed. Jennifer followed him back to the cab. It occurred to her that the curtain was rising on her Halifax adventures against quite a different setting and with even a different cast of characters than she had anticipated. Or perhaps it would be more correct to alter that, truthfully, to the same cast of characters only viewed from a different angle.

The cab mounted the slopes of the glacis until halted by a sentry. Dixon got out, paid off the cabbie, and conducted Jennifer past the arms-pressing sentry and over a drawbridge spanning a deep dry moat, to the entrance of Fort George which was through a wide sallyport, with a guard room opening off the sallyport to the left.

Captain Dixon turned into the guard room, returned the salute of the sergeant on duty, and asked if Colonel Thompson were about.

"Yes, sir, I'll tell him you're here, sir," the sergeant prepared to hurry off.

"Tell him also that Captain Lord Welland is reporting from England," Dixon ordered, and the sergeant nodded, saluted again, turned on his heel to disappear into the farther office.

There was a barred window opening onto the parade ground and Jennifer crossed to it. Her eyes widened appreciatively. This was a fine fortress. She could count numerous casemates in the wall even from where she stood, while a stone cavalier was solidly built across the parade ground, a battery of guns surmounting it. A building to the left and a similar one to the right she surmised were magazines, and in this she was not mistaken, while atop the ramparts could be seen the revolving carriages of heavy artillery. A shiver of excitement trickled down her spine.

Dixon was standing beside her. "Of course it's not finished yet," he said, "but the engineers are doing a bloody fine job. Civilian contractors holding things up, of course, and the War Office keeps changing their minds, but it's a pretty tight place."

"The Warden of the north," Jennifer nodded, and Dixon cast her a shrewd glance even as he agreed with her.

Heavy footsteps marched back into the room, and they turned from the window.

"Would you go in, sir?" the sergeant said gruffly. And Dixon nodded and motioned to Jennifer.

"Come along, Welland," he said, and she followed him into the colonel's office.

They marched with military precision to a spot directly in front of the desk behind which sat the colonel of the regiment, and stiffened to attention, saluting smartly. "Captain Dixon reporting, sir. And Captain Lord Welland, from England."

The colonel returned their salutes. "At ease, gentlemen. Welland, welcome to Halifax."

He stood up and shook hands with a firm grasp. "We've been expecting you, my lord," he said. "Dispatches from the War Office in London stated you had bought Mitchell's commission and would be reporting as soon as passage could be arranged. What ship did you come on?"

"The *Cambria*, sir."

"Oh yes. Docked this morning, didn't she? Good, good. Got your orders?"

She extended her papers and credentials, and the colonel took them from her and examined them closely. She stood without motion before him, not a flicker of an eyelid betrayed her in her excitement, yet conscious of the colonel's approval of her promptness in reporting, and conscious also of Dixon's presence beside her. Jennifer felt herself stepping further and deeper into what might be a very embarrassing trap. She thought suddenly of Jonathan in her place now, and she knew, without knowing how she knew, that he would not have felt her sense of excitement, this sense of rightness, of approbation, of sudden glory, of belonging.

"Lord Welland, eh? Purchased Mitchell's commission, yes, yes. Sponsored by—who? Who's this?" He read the signature again, then he looked up with increasing interest and something else. For some strange reason, Jennifer thought it was dawning respect. "Burghley? Not the Duke of Burghley? Colonel March, as he was then?"

Jennifer nodded. "Yes, sir."

"Relative of yours?"

"My guardian, sir." She had been right. It was respect.

"Knew him well. Served under him for a spell. How is he?"

"Very well, sir, when I left him." This was an unexpected happening. Guardie hadn't mentioned that the O.C. was a Colonel Thompson. Probably he had not even known. Jennifer ran hastily through her memory to see if she could recall a Thompson among the many names in Guardie's tales.

"Probably wouldn't remember me." The colonel was almost reading her thoughts. "Years since I saw him. I was only a volunteer then. Quatre-Bras and Waterloo," and he shook his head. "Never seen such a battle since, thank God. Hope I never do. Just had to stand there to be pounded at. Nothing we could do." His mind was obviously far away.

Jennifer had it now. "Tiny" Thompson, the volunteer attached to Guardie's company.... Guardie had mentioned him often. Said he stood up to the fire as if he were a veteran.

"My guardian has spoken of you, sir, often," she said.

"Has he, by God?" the colonel was visibly impressed. "Well, old March. So you're his ward? Happy to have you serving under me."

"Thank you, sir," Jennifer returned simply.

"So you only arrived this morning, and reporting already. Well, well. Might have known you came of old regimental stock." He chuckled. "Overdue, weren't you? Ship, I mean."

"Yes, sir. Several days. We ran into heavy weather."

The colonel nodded. "Can be rotten. Found your quarters yet?"

Jennifer shook her head. "No, sir. I was just checking in at the hotel when I met Captain Dixon. I left my sister there, and came along to report."

"Left your sister, eh? Bring her with you?"

"Yes, sir, my twin sister. Lady Jennifer."

"Good, good. Good sailors?"

Jennifer's lips twitched. "I was, sir."

The colonel eyed her shrewdly. "Your sister wasn't, eh? Well, most women aren't. Takes a man to stand the sea." He fell silent, his eyes on the papers in front of him, then he said abruptly, "Lord Bradbury is here now. Does the Duke know that?"

Jennifer nodded. "Yes, sir."

"Sent you an introduction, eh?"

"Yes, sir."

"He and your guardian were good friends. Peninsula days, you know. I've heard Lord Bradbury speak of him often. Yes, indeed, speak of him often. Introduction to him, have you? You'll need to present that without delay. Wait—I'm sending dispatches along in a minute or two: I'll mention your arrival. What hotel did you say you were staying at?"

"The Colonial, sir."

"The Colonial. Yes. The regiment's all over the place since

the old North Barracks were burned out last December. Officers are messing at the Halifax Hotel, couple of blocks along from the Colonial. The men are quartered in South Barracks, four blocks up from the hotel. You're needed badly, or I'd say to take a couple of days off to get acquainted. As it is, you'd best see that your sister is settled today, and report for duty tomorrow. You'll have Mitchell's company. Don't mind telling you it's in poor shape. Digby's your senior lieutenant. I'll send for him, and he can take you around to the Halifax and you can arrange your quarters there." He raised his voice to a roar. "SERGEANT!"

The sergeant appeared on the double. "Yes, sir?"

"Have Lieutenant Digby report to me at once."

The sergeant saluted and disappeared.

"Mr. Digby can introduce you to your fellow officers at the Halifax and show you where the men fall in. Take the day to look around. You'll probably have a call to Government House this afternoon, but that shouldn't take long." He turned to Captain Dixon. "What was it you wanted to see me about? Oh yes, maneuvers. Want you to drill your men in that new order. See how it works. The C. in C.'s much interested."

"Yes, sir," Dixon was wooden-faced. The colonel eyed him shrewdly.

"Don't think much of it?"

"That's not for me to say, sir."

"Hmm." The colonel regarded Dixon speculatively for a moment, then he turned with a suddenness which Jennifer was to learn was characteristic of him. "Know what I'm talking about, Welland?"

"No, sir. Not unless it's the new order as diagrammed in the drill book, sir. Eight formations, sir."

The colonel's eyes glinted. "Know it?"

"I studied it, sir, on my way across."

"Studied it, eh? What do you think of it?" And, as Jennifer hesitated, he prompted, "Well, come on. What do you think of it?"

"My opinion, sir, is that it would depend largely on the terrain over which the action was to take place," Jennifer blurted frankly. Might as well be hung for a sheep as a lamb.

"Why?"

She gave her reasons. "Overmuch maneuvering, sir. Too much counterdrill."

"You know, Welland, I agree with you all the way." The colonel was beaming. "Excellent statement. Excellent. Should go far, Welland, far. Dixon, you and Welland study the drill, work it out together. That's all."

"Yes, sir." Dixon stepped back, saluted smartly, and withdrew, and the colonel sat back in his chair and regarded Jennifer.

"Like the army, Welland?"

"Yes, sir," Jennifer returned promptly.

"Evident, if you study the drill book coming across. Tell me, Welland, any news from England?"

Jennifer shook her head. "No dispatches, sir."

"No, no, not dispatches," the colonel shook his head impatiently. "What's happening in England? How's His Majesty?"

"Middling well, I believe, sir," Jennifer replied. "I'm not well acquainted with news of London, sir. I've been in the country."

"Ride?"

Jennifer nodded. "Yes, sir."

"Good," said the colonel. "You'll want horses?"

Jennifer nodded again. "Yes, sir." She added, "I've brought my groom."

"You have?" The colonel chuckled. "You must intend to set up a stable."

To Jennifer's relief, footsteps sounded in the guard room and a rap came on the door. "Digby, sir," said a bright, cheerful voice, and the colonel returned the salute.

"Yes, yes, come in, Mr. Digby. I want to introduce you to your new captain, Captain Lord Welland, Mr. Digby."

"How do you do, sir," Jennifer extended a steady hand and had a warm grasp in response.

"Welcome, m'lord," Digby was very proper.

"Carry on then, Welland," the colonel nodded dismissal. "Mr. Digby will show you about the station, I'm sure."

Jennifer and Digby stiffened to salute, and the colonel

returned it. They left together, young Digby carefully permitting his captain to precede him to the door.

"I suppose you'd like to inspect the Fort, m'lord?" young Digby was very polite.

Jennifer hesitated. If she were once shown about the Fort, it would look extremely peculiar if "Captain Lord Welland" forgot the layout too quickly. And she doubted if she could describe the entire setup to Jonathan with sufficient clarity to make him act as if he had already been over it thoroughly. No, it seemed to her that now was the time for Jonathan to take over. She could tell him enough about her interview with the colonel, as well as the other instances of the morning, for him not to make any obvious errors, but when it came to touring with Digby—she made her decision quickly.

"No, I believe I'd prefer to go back to the hotel first," she said. "If you wouldn't object to waiting for me for a short while before you begin to show me about, I'd like to see how my sister is faring. We had quite a rough crossing, and my sister was much indisposed."

"Your sister, sir? She came with you?"

Jennifer nodded. "Yes, my twin sister."

"Oh, good, m'lord." Young Digby had brightened remarkably. "I am sure we shall do all we can to see that she enjoys her visit here."

Jennifer's lips twitched. "I'm sure you will, Mr. Digby," she agreed with commendable gravity.

They walked down to the Colonial, which Jennifer estimated to be close to Dixon's mile, and Mr. Digby endeavored to pass the time pleasantly, and to a greater extent than he realized, he succeeded. Jennifer listened to him closely, carefully storing away such interesting items as the exact location of the commons, the married quarters, the ordnance yard, and sundry other points of interest. Mr. Digby's main tour was to come later; this was but a polite beginning.

At the Colonial, Jennifer, who had been considering the matter for several minutes, said apologetically that she regretted she couldn't introduce her sister this morning; she was sure Mr. Digby would excuse her. However, as soon as Lady Jennifer had recovered from her indisposition, she would see that Mr. Digby was presented. In the meantime, would Mr. Digby care to wait in the bar and she would ascertain the health of her sister and return shortly?

Mr. Digby signified his willingness, especially when Jennifer delivered him into the hands of an enterprising waiter and instructed him to procure what Mr. Digby desired, thus signalling obviously who would finance the tab.

Upstairs, Jennifer tapped quickly at the door of their suite and found Jonathan relaxing in the bedroom in her dressing gown.

"Well, where have you been?" her brother demanded. "Did you see the colonel?"

Jennifer nodded. She was busily unbuttoning her jacket and she talked quickly. "Jonnie, you've got to move fast. Downstairs, the senior lieutenant of your company is waiting to show you about Halifax and take you up to the other hotel where the officers are quartered, so that you can see where your billet is and meet the officers. The colonel has sent a message to Lord Bradbury saying that we're here, and you'll probably have to report out there this afternoon with our letter of introduction. Tomorrow morning you're to report for duty. You're taking over "B" Company, which is Captain Mitchell's old one, as you bought Mitchell's commission. The O.C., incidentally, is "Tiny" Thompson, the volunteer in Guardie's old company, and he knows Guardie well. I can tell more later, but in the meantime hurry up and get dressed and go about with Digby and keep your mouth shut. I'll fill in the gaps later."

"You mean right away?" Jonathan didn't move.

Jennifer nodded. "Yes, at once. Hurry, Jonnie. I've left Digby in the bar, told him I'd pay the shot, too. Said I had to check on how my sister was, and I'd be down shortly. It would be stupid for me to go around with him. I could never describe all the places and people to you so that you'd know them when you saw them—you'll have to take over now. Hurry up."

"Jennifer, I can't," Jonathan said flatly. "I tell you, I just can't do it."

Jennifer paused in the act of pulling off her boots. "Nonsense, Jonnie, of course you can. You're on land now. Perhaps you don't feel too bright, but you'll be all right once you get moving. Anyway, Jonnie, you've got to."

"I won't," Jonathan's voice was sullen. "It's all very well for you, Jenny, to say I've got to do this or that or the other thing, when you haven't any idea how wretched I'm feeling. I just can't do it."

Jennifer stared at him. "Jonnie, I can't go down to Digby and tell him I can't go around with him today, that I don't feel well enough. You just can't do that, and especially after reporting in to the colonel."

"Well, you didn't have to do that." Jonathan did not move. "Jenny, it's all your fault, and I tell you I'm not going to go out now. So there."

Jennifer was on her feet, staring at him incredulously. "Jonathan, have you gone mad? Do you know what you're saying? I know you don't like the army and you didn't want Guardie to buy this commission, but you know how Guardie feels and there's no use talking about it. You just can't leave now—you can't walk out of the army. You'd be courtmartialed, or worse. Jonathan, don't be yellow."

Her brother's face colored, but he only said furiously, "It's all right for you to talk. You've always liked everything about the army. I remember how you used to sneak down to listen to Guardie and his friends talking about the good old days. Disgusting." His lips curled. "Well, I tell you I'm not having anything to do with it. Why don't you take my place, as you're so keen on it?"

Jennifer's gaze didn't falter. "And what will you be doing while I am playing soldier?" she queried.

He shrugged. "Stay here, I suppose. Or else go on to Boston or someplace else. It wouldn't signify."

Jennifer after a long moment drew a single deep breath. "All right," she said evenly. "You'll take my place and I'll take yours. I've told Colonel Thompson my sister came over with me. I've told Dixon and Digby the same thing. You registered here as my sister. Guardie has written to Lord Bradbury that Lady Jennifer was traveling with her brother. So Lady Jennifer has got to be here in Halifax. I don't care if Lady Jennifer is too ill to show herself. She can remain in her rooms most of the time, but there may be occasions when

74

she'll have to emerge. She'll certainly have to make her bow to Lord Bradbury. That'll be you, Jonathan. You'll like that. You've always liked the female's role better than the man's. Oh yes, I've heard tales of your London exploits—don't worry. I've listened to more than Guardie's descriptions of his war experiences. And don't forget, you're my brother; I know you pretty well. I even know what you're thinking at times. And right now I don't like what you have in mind. But I'll make a deal with you, Jonathan, and you'll have to abide by it. Your place for my place; my skirts for your trousers."

Jonathan fiddled with the arm of the chair. "Jennifer, I don't think..." he began hesitantly, but his sister cut in.

"You're quite right, Jonnie, you don't think. You make a choice, now. Either you promise to stay in my skirts, most of the time anyway, or you get into this uniform right away. Which will it be? One or the other, Jonnie. There's no other choice. You're a Welland, and I don't propose to have to blush for the name."

"Oh, all right," Jonathan was goaded beyond his endurance. "I'll be Lady Jennifer and you can go on playing soldier. But what are you going to do about Bates? I tell you, I won't have him hanging around me."

Jennifer's gaze had not left her brother. "No, I'll take Bates," she said slowly. "You don't need to worry about him. You can have Katie to cover for you." She drew a deep breath. "I guess this is it, Jonnie. And it's a promise, remember?"

"Oh yes, I'll remember," her brother repeated testily.

"Good." Jennifer hesitated only a second longer, then she bent and pulled on her boots again, shrugged into the uniform jacket and fastened it snugly, picked up the shako and gloves and moved to the door. With her hand on the handle, she turned for one last glance at her brother. "Jonnie," her voice had softened, "you do know what you're doing, don't you?"

"It's not my fault," her brother began aggrievedly, but she cut him short once more.

"Jonnie, let's pretend that this is like old times; let's pretend it's all in fun, as it used to be. Because I don't think I could feel very happy if I thought all the time this was happening because my brother was a coward."

Jonathan attempted to meet her eyes. "Damn it, Jenny, you know it isn't that. If I were just feeling better—"

"All right, Jonnie we'll forget that. It's for fun, isn't it? All for fun?"

He hesitated, then he flung back his head and met his sister's eyes defiantly. "Of course it's for fun, Jenny. Just like old times."

Jennifer nodded. "That's what I meant, Jonnie. Good-bye, Jenny, look after yourself." The door shut after her, leaving Jonathan to scowl at the wall, as Captain Lord Welland, accompanied by George, went down the stairs steadily and purposely to enter on his first tour of duty with His Majesty's Rifle Brigade.

Chapter Eight

Mr. Digby's short personal tour of Halifax, undertaken in the hour or so remaining before messtime, was illustrative and educational. He was a fair-haired, fresh-cheeked youngster of close to Jennifer's own age, with a flip tongue and a bright eye for the ladies. And, as Jennifer was to discover, an inexhaustible fund of stories. He reminded her of the village schoolmaster's son whom she had bullied and teased for years past, and she found it difficult to be too stiff with him. Common sense told her she would have to be on her guard, that in order to carry out her masquerade she would have to hold herself aloof, be stern and unfriendly. It would not be too easy.

But Mr. Digby was a hard lad to suppress. Behind his round, fresh-cheeked, boyish face lurked the mind of a well-bred gutter pup, and Mr. Digby's innocent prattle, issuing as it did from full, babyish lips, would have caused a delicately-nurtured maiden to have blushed a fiery red, if not indeed to have swooned from shock.

Jennifer neither blushed nor swooned. She had heard such talk before from more experienced individuals than the youngster striding beside her. Although, to be truthful, those individuals were not aware that she was overhearing them, as such conversations had taken place in the small hours of the morning when, comfortably relaxed on innumerable bottles of port or other liquid refreshments, Guardie's friends and fellow officers relived the days of their youth, all unaware that behind the curtain shielding them from the draft of the great hall crouched a small figure busily listening to every word and savoring it to its fullest. Jennifer had had much more freedom than Guardie had realized.

However, it was one thing to have heard of such deeds from gentlemen of her guardian's vintage and another to listen of similar exploits from a younger gentleman with whom she consorted and who, with his like, would form the main body of her New World acquaintance. She listened with interest, aware that she was hearing much which would be of great assistance to her in the days to come.

"That's Mother Clark's," her guide pointed to a respectable-appearing house. They were on Barrack Street now, at the foot of the Citadel glacis. "If you can't get satisfaction at Mother Clark's, you won't find it anywhere," he chuckled and winked. Shops, pleasure houses, gaming palaces—he knew them all. And if his tour of the town neglected such points as the tourists were apt to regard with open mouths, it definitely included such points as many of the male tourists would have liked to have known about.

The location of the various barracks, the commons, the hospital, the military warehouses and offices were glibly tossed off, while most of the running commentary was directed to the pleasures which might be encountered in the town.

"It's a dead hole," Lieutenant Digby announced scornfully. "The civilians hate us worse than poison. Too bloody proper. Why, would you believe it, one of the poor bastards had the nerve to come up to the mess the other night demanding his daughter."

"Indeed," Jennifer remarked politely. "And was she there?"

Digby chuckled. "Certainly she was there. But the porter gave him such a run-around and Horace came out, that's Captain Thurston—he's Captain of "C" Company; regular chap—he came out and gave the old bastard a piece of his mind and sent him on his business."

"How about the daughter?" Jennifer enquired, fortunately mildly, for Digby's quick glance darkened with suspicion which she hastened to remove, "I assume she wished to remain?"

Digby's brow cleared. "Of course. No fun at all in this beastly town. A gal's got to have pleasure somewhere."

It sounded quite familiar. Nevertheless, Jennifer inquired in apparent innocence by what method the officers managed to dispose of their leisure hours.

"I've been telling you," Digby said, with a hint of indignation. "Of course, there's water sports and the like, and the races, hunting, fishing...that sort of thing, but it's a boring spot."

"Is this the main part of Halifax?" she queried cautiously.

"The main part? It's all there is," Digby said extravagantly.

Jennifer kept her face expressionless with an effort. All there was, and she had expected that the town continued behind the hill. It might be difficult for Jonathan to fade into the landscape. She said with a nonchalance she was far from feeling, "Of course, you can travel to other towns for leave?"

"What other towns?" Digby returned caustically. "There aren't any. No real towns, that is. Of course you can ride out to Rockingham and Prince's Lodge, Bedford Basin. And, if you're up to a fifty-mile jaunt, there're Kentville and Windsor up the main road.

"Of course, if you've a long enough leave you can take the boat to Boston—that's a proper town. New York, too," he added. "I've never been there but I've had reports."

"How often do the ships leave for—did you say, Boston?" Jennifer asked.

"Oh, every week or so," Digby answered. "There's a schedule but they don't stick to it very closely."

"How far away is Boston?"

"It takes three to four days to get there," Digby answered vaguely. "Something like that, I'm not quite sure. Look...here's The Bar and Gate—Honest John who runs it doesn't water the grog as much as the others." He slowed suggestively, but Jennifer was willfully misunderstanding and continued on. Digby, with a swallowed imprecation, followed her.

By a roundabout course, they eventually arrived at the Halifax Hotel, and Digby was, for him, almost silent for the last few blocks. Jennifer, who knew what was troubling him, was secretly amused and said gravely, "Walking is a dry business, Mr. Digby. Perhaps the steward..." she left her suggestion unfinished, but Digby brightened immediately.

"It certainly is," he agreed with fervor, and caught the steward's eye as he hove into sight. Without waiting for Jennifer to change her mind he gave a hasty order, and added, in spurious apology to his host that that was about the best they had in stock.

"Yes, I am sure it must be," Jennifer agreed, with such marked solemnity that once again Digby regarded her sharply, suspicious of a double meaning.

Her face told him nothing, it was smooth and expressionless as she looked about the room.

"Very comfortable quarters," she said in a tone of approbation, and Digby shrugged.

"It's not bad," he admitted.

The steward came then with a tray and two glasses and Digby chided him curtly for the absence of the bottle. "For you have to watch these fellows," he confided to Jennifer when the steward had withdrawn. "They pour out a couple of drinks and keep the bottle themselves."

Jennifer agreed gravely that it was indeed a serious state of affairs, and instructed the steward to put it to her account.

"I say, that's devilish good of you," Digby said with false gratitude. He had been afraid for a moment that the captain was going to let him pay for it, and his bar-bill was getting heavy.

The room was filling up, and Digby introduced her elaborately to all the officers. Drinks were clearly in order and Jennifer did her duty. She held herself slightly withdrawn while acknowledging the introductions with a firm handshake and a brief smile. She knew she was under scrutiny, new officers always were, but she preferred to give the appearance of a stiff militarist rather than a hail-fellow-well-met officer. She was polite but not cordial, and she was rewarded by observing the not supposed to be seen distaste of some of the flashier members of the mess. That suited her admirably, she had no desire to be drawn into a coterie of which young Digby was a part. She would have to feel her way carefully, and if the truth be known, had her guardian regarded her at that moment he would have praised her conduct even while condemning her presence.

The business of finding a room for her was somewhat more complicated. It appeared that the only room available was on the top floor and was not, said the porter carefully, a very large room.

"That's not the one Captain Mitchell had," Digby said briskly. "Who's in it?"

"Captain Dixon took it over, sir," the porter said respectfully.

"Dash it, can't very well turn *him* out," Digby chewed his lip.

"Let me see this vacant room," Jennifer took a hand in the debate.

"You don't want to be on the top floor," Digby protested.

"Why?" Jennifer demanded. "If there's no other room available."

"Well, turn somebody out," Digby suggested.

"What will that accomplish?" Jennifer asked. "No, let me see this room."

Digby shrugged, "Yes, sir." He took the stairs two at a time and Jennifer followed him. The vacant room was on the fourth floor at one end of the corridor. It was not a large room, to be sure, but there was a feature about it which pleased Jennifer more than added size would have done. The door opened into the chamber in such a way that it was possible for any occupant to see who was at the door before any visitor saw him in return.

Jennifer walked in and looked about. A wardrobe, a chest of drawers, a bed, a chair, provided the furnishings. The chamber was reasonably clean and the one window had an uninterrupted view over the harbor, a view which was appreciated by Jennifer. Not because of its scenic excellence, but because it meant that whatever went on in the room would not be visible from across a street.

"I see nothing wrong with this," she said with decision. "I'll have my man bring my bags up here this evening. I brought my groom across from England with me," she added to Digby, "as I shall be acquiring a stable shortly, but until I have attended to that, he can act as my batman."

"Believe me, sir, you can get another groom easier than you can get a batman," Digby said emphatically. "I give you my word, I have the laziest fellow. Half the time he forgets to black my boots."

There was a great commotion in the hall, and sundry deep growls. George suddenly appeared, with an agitated porter behind him.

"Beg pardon, m'lord," the porter gasped. "This beast insisted on coming in. I tried to hold him off, m'lord."

"You'd better get accustomed to him," Jennifer said coolly. "He'll be with me much of the time."

"He's your dog, m'lord?" the porter's eyes bulged.

Jennifer nodded. "I couldn't leave him behind, so I brought him across with me."

"I don't blame you, m'lord," the porter said gruffly. He eyed George respectfully. "Handsome dog, m'lord. Shouldn't care to be on bad terms with him. Looks like a man-eater."

"He's quite tame," Jennifer smiled. At that moment the tame one opened his mouth and yawned widely.

The porter was fascinated. "All those teeth, m'lord. Tame? Yes, m'lord. If you say so, m'lord." He touched his cap and withdrew, his gaze fixed with fascination on the big dog. "If you say so, m'lord."

Jennifer hid a grin. George was going to be handy to have around.

Chapter Nine

After luncheon at the officers' mess, Jennifer returned to the Colonial Hotel, to find Katie in a fine state of perturbation and a note addressed to "Captain Lord Welland," sealed with the Lieutenant-Governor's crest. Jennifer opened it quickly to find that it was, as she had expected a command, (in the form of a formal invitation), to appear at the Governor's Mansion that afternoon at half past three o'clock to present her credentials to Lord Bradbury. It was past two now, and hastily waving Katie aside, Jennifer sent for Bates and ordered that he have her uniform pressed and presentable for her call that afternoon. Then she turned to cope with Katie, who waited until Bates had left the room before she burst out with her opinion of the continued masquerade.

Jennifer heard her out in silence. When she began to repeat her arguments, Jennifer stopped her.

"Undoubtedly everything you've said is quite right, Katie," she said agreeably, "but unfortunately, it isn't going to do any good, because Jonnie and I have already decided that we're going to go through with this, for fun. Besides, I like the army and Jonnie doesn't. He'd be very unhappy in it, and I'll have a wonderful time. You wouldn't want Jonnie to be unhappy, would you?" she asked coaxingly.

She had Katie there. Katie adored the two of them, but she'd always had a softer spot in her heart for "her boy," and had invariably taken his part in any family fight. She wavered now.

"It's a daft plan, m'lady," she said with a show of her former indignation, which she spoiled by adding with a sigh, "but if it's what you and young Master Jonathan want, I suppose it's up to me to do my best to help you; though mind, I'm not for it."

Jennifer smiled. "I'm in no doubts about that," she added. She switched to a detailed commentary of her morning's expedition, and finished with a description of her quarters in the Halifax Hotel and George's reception. "I'm quite sure the porter is not convinced of his affability," she grinned. "I shall have to do what I can to encourage a feeling of respect towards George. He is going to be very useful."

"Aye, it's a daft plan," Katie muttered darkly. "Are you sure—"

"Yes, Katie, we're quite sure," Jennifer said firmly.

"Well, I've no more to say, then," Katie uttered in a resigned tone which indicated clearly that there was plenty more which she thought of it.

Jennifer smiled and left her. It was time to prepare for her call at Government House, and she had no desire to be late.

Bates was a good valet. Even in the short time at his disposal, her boots shone, her jacket was creaseless, her gloves were immaculate.

She left the hotel and turned south along Hollis Street. A short distance along, she recognized the impressive facade of Government House which, while nominally presenting its face to Hollis Street, had retreated so far from that thoroughfare that for all practical purposes its back had become its front, and the main entrance was generally accepted to be from Pleasant Street. Government House in all its glory was a fine and costly memorial to old Sir John Wentworth and his pretty, ambitious wife Frances, who at the turn of the century had ruled Halifax Society—civil, military, political and locally well-born—as Governor and Governor's Lady.

Tugging at her high collar with a suddenly nervous hand, Jennifer rapped smartly on the door and prepared to use her natural hauteur with whatever flunkey should open the door to her.

It was, after all, unexpectedly easy. A liveried servant had bowed formally, presented a silver salver for her letter of introduction to His Excellency, and showed her into the hall with a murmured request that she await His Excellency's pleasure.

It was an elegant hall, running from front to back of the building and it was easy to see why the custom had developed of using the back as the front, for the same wide double doors were at each end, and carved pillars reached from floor to ceiling, halfway down, dividing the length pleasingly to the eye. Gilt chairs lined the walls, and she disposed herself with as much ease as the seat of one encouraged under a portrait of the portly Sir John, whose wife had been responsible for such a magnificent edifice.

She had a very short time to wait. The butler returned noiselessly down the thickly-carpeted passage and, bowing even more deeply before her, requested that she follow him please. He preceded her down the hall to a door opening off to the right, where he announced her with solemnity:

"Captain Lord Welland."

A middle-aged, gray-haired man came to meet her, his hand outstretched, his face beaming. "My dear boy, this is indeed a pleasure. So you're Burghley's ward, are you? Come in and meet Lady Bradbury. Where's your sister?" he added, peering vaguely over Jennifer's shoulder.

"She's at the hotel, sir. I left her there when we arrived this morning." Jennifer shook hands firmly, and turned to greet the still handsome, gracious Lady Bradbury who, with a motherly smile, held out both her hands to her and insisted on kissing her guest on both cheeks. "For you are just the age of my son," she said smiling. "How nice of the Duke to send you to us."

"Sit down, m'boy, and tell me how you do. Commission in the Rifles, eh?"

Jennifer nodded, waiting until His Excellency had seated himself to subside onto the indicated chair. "Yes, Your Excellency. My guardian was most fortunate in discovering that a commission was available for purchase."

"Captaincy, eh? Pretty young for that, aren't you?"

Jennifer felt her cheeks color. "I'm twenty, sir," she said, with what she hoped was boyish dignity.

Lord Bradbury chuckled. "Yes, yes. And I've no doubt you feel you know more than the rest of us dodderers."

"Lord Bradbury," Lady Bradbury reproved gently. "That is not kind." She turned to Jennifer. "Your sister must come and stay with us. I will not hear of anything else. What hotel is she at now? You must go at once and fetch her. I will not hear of her staying at a hotel."

This was a contingency which had never occurred to either Jennifer or Jonathan. For a moment she was so completely taken aback that her mind went blank.

Only a moment, then she was floundering into speech. "Lady Bradbury, that's too good of you, but we couldn't think of it, my sister and I. Thank you very much, it's very kind of you, but under no circumstances whatsoever could we consider it, even for a short stay. I assure you I appreciate your offer most kindly, more than I can say. It's very good of you, very kind of you, but really ... we cannot consider ... cannot hope ... cannot impose on your hospitality in such a fashion. We couldn't hear of it ... no, thank you very much ... we just couldn't hear of it."

Her protestations and stuttering refusals had the very opposite result from what she had hoped for. Lady Bradbury was delighted by such boyish concern and consideration for her hospitality, but her mind was quite made up.

"Nonsense," she said briskly. "She will be company for my daughters. We should be delighted to have her with us."

This was worse and worse. Company for her *daughters!*

"My sister isn't very strong, Lady Bradbury," Jennifer said earnestly. "She has ... that is ... there is ... that is ... our old nurse has come over with us to be with her ... she, she stays with her. She, she even sleeps with her." There,

86

that should finish it. Jennifer had also a fleeting moment of how it would finish Jonathan, too.

Lady Bradbury's motherly heart was even more touched. "Why, the poor child," she said sympathetically. "I wouldn't sleep tonight if I were to think of her alone in that hotel. It will never do. And delicate, too. Tell me, is she very much younger than you?"

"We're twins, Lady Bradbury," Jennifer answered. "She...we thought, Guardie...that is...His Grace... it was thought the sea voyage would do her good, and as I was coming over here...he, we...the doctor...it was decided that my sister would come, too, for the trip and...for a visit here."

"How long did she plan to stay?" Lady Bradbury enquired.

Jennifer floundered badly. "It...it wasn't decided, Lady Bradbury." she said wretchedly. "We, we thought we'd see how the climate suited her and, well...we didn't know how long I would be here, and Guardie...the Duke, that is... well, we thought she could stay for the summer and then, well, then we'd see."

Lady Bradbury nodded her head. "Very sensible," she decreed. "Very sensible, indeed. The climate here is very salubrious and probably just the thing for her."

Lord Bradbury thought that he had been ignored quite long enough. "Did you have a good voyage?" he boomed.

Jennifer turned to him, grateful for the change of subject. "Capital voyage, sir," she said enthusiastically. "I enjoyed every minute of it."

"Did your sister?" Lady Bradbury inquired dryly.

Jennifer sobered. "She was most dreadfully ill all the way across," she admitted, and Lady Bradbury nodded as if in agreement with her own thoughts.

She rose. "I shall get my cloak and go back with you to the hotel immediately," she decided. "Your poor sister, alone in that hotel! It would never do."

Jennifer was on her feet. "Lady Bradbury, I cannot allow you..." she began miserably.

"Tut, tut," Lady Bradbury patted her on the arm in passing. "I can assure you, my dear boy, it will be no trouble whatsoever. No trouble at all. We shall be happy to have her staying with us." She swept from the room, and Jennifer resisted an impulse to run her finger inside her collar—it was suddenly very tight.

Lord Bradbury was watching her and he said dryly, "My wife is a very determined woman, my boy."

"It is altogether too good of her, sir," Jennifer said in a choked voice. "I cannot...I cannot express my feelings adequately to her. Why, sir, I never dreamed that she would be so, so hospitable, that you would both be. It is altogether too much, sir."

Lord Bradbury was beaming. "Not a bit of it, my boy. As my wife said, we shall be pleased to have your sister here. We shall be very happy. And my two daughters, I can assure you, would never have forgiven us if we hadn't insisted on it. They will be delighted to have a house guest, for you must realize that it is very difficult for them to find many friends of their own age in this town."

He spoke nothing but the actual truth, and yet Jennifer swallowed again as she realized the exalted circles in which Jonathan would be moving as Lady Jennifer. She had protested more than she dared—there was nothing further she could do except hope and scheme that in some way Jonathan could get away from there quickly. She chattered in a desultory fashion with His Excellency until Lady Bradbury swept back into the room, bonnetted and cloaked and gloved.

"I have told Alice and Marjorie that your sister will be coming to stay with us," she smiled at Jennifer, "and they are quite as elated as I knew they would be. Don't look so worried, my boy. Your sister will be well taken care of, I can assure you."

"Lady Bradbury, you are altogether too generous," Jennifer said fervently, and meant it even more than Lady Bradbury suspected.

The Governor's Lady beamed complacently even while she disparaged the compliment, for every woman likes to be told she's acting as Lady Bountiful, and Lady Bradbury, for all her excellent common sense, was no different from her sisters. She was good-hearted and generous and kind to a fault, but it was still nice to be told that she was so.

"You will come back with us, of course, for dinner," she

said. "Fortunately there are no other guests for this evening, are there, my dear?" she enquired turning to her husband. That worthy shook his head, and Lady Bradbury went on, "So it will be only a family dinner, informal. We dine early here, at half past five."

Jennifer followed her from the room, pausing only to utter a formal farewell to His Excellency, and collected her shako and gloves from the butler who produced them with the speed of a conjurer.

The vice-regal coach was waiting at the back door and Her Excellency was handed into the carriage tenderly. She tucked her skirts in and motioned to Jennifer to sit beside her, as she raised her parasol against the sun's rays and gave the direction to the coachman.

On the short trip to the hotel Jennifer thought frantically of some way to stall Her Excellency's entrance to the suite and finally said desperately: "Lady Bradbury, would you forgive me if I suggested that I hasten up to my sister's room to see that she is not indisposed?"

Lady Bradbury smiled. "Certainly, my boy. Your consideration does you credit. Don't hurry," she added, for they were drawing up by the hotel now. "I am quite comfortable."

Jennifer bowed low and disappeared into the hotel. She did not heed Her Ladyship's injunction not to hasten. Once out of sight of the lobby she took the stairs two at a time and rapped peremptorily on the sitting room door. "Katie, let me in," she called, and there was the sound of footsteps inside.

The door was opened cautiously and Katie's face appeared at the opening. "Is there anything the matter?" she queried anxiously.

"Everything's the matter," Jennifer said bitterly, pushing past her. "Where's Jonathan?"

Jonathan appeared at the bedroom door still wrapped in Jennifer's dressing gown. "What's wrong, Jenny?" His pale face suddenly mirrored Katie's anxiety.

"Lady Bradbury is outside in her carriage. She is coming up here. You are to go and stay there. I have done everything I can to stop it. I have said that you are delicate, I have said that Katie has to be with you all the time, has even to sleep with you, I've said no thank you, no thank you, and it was the wrong thing to have said—she is more determined than ever. She has two daughters, Alice and Marjorie, and you are going to be a nice companion to them. They are so glad to have a house guest to come and stay with them because they can't be very friendly with the young ladies in the town, it isn't possible.... Oh, Jonathan, it's a bloody awful mess and I don't know what we can do."

"You and your bright schemes," Jonathan said, and then, "*JENNIFER*, what will we do?"

"Do?" Jennifer turned from the window. "Do? There's only one thing to do, Jonathan. You'll really have to be Lady Jennifer now. You're delicate, you'll have to be careful, very careful, very delicate. You can't get away from here except by ship. This is all there is of the town. Just what we saw from the waterfront. There are ships to Boston from Halifax but they run on an irregular schedule, once a week or so, maybe more, maybe less, and it takes five days to get there, or so. Five, four, three days. I can get you passage there, but what's your excuse going to be? We're going to have to work on that, Jonathan, but right now you've got to get dressed, and you've got to get dressed quickly. Lady Bradbury is coming up and you are going to stay at Government House. And Jonathan....you're going to be a lady if it kills you."

Chapter Ten

His Grace, the Duke of Burghley, was enjoying a most excellent breakfast when the butler announced Lord Randall. The Duke glanced up from the platter of mutton, which he was regarding with serious intent, and said testily to show him in.

Rufus strolled in. "Good morning, sir. Sorry to interrupt your breakfast. I rode over to see Jennifer, and Collins tells me she isn't here."

"Sit down, sit down, my boy." The Duke nodded vaguely in the direction of a chair, and did not pause in his attack on the mutton. "You didn't know, eh? Jennifer's off—had a letter from her, too, want to see it? Somewhere around."

"Don't disturb yourself, sir," Rufus said easily. "Off where?"

"Canada," the Duke said between mouthfuls. "Didn't you know? No, you've been away, haven't you? Left two, three months ago. Begged me to let her go."

"Indeed, sir," Rufus was polite. Skillful questioning elicited the simple facts that Jennifer had gone over with Jonathan and must have left, Rufus calculated rapidly, a few days after he had gone to Walfram. "Sudden, wasn't it, sir?" he queried gently.

The Duke nodded. "Had to get the boy off sometime," he mumbled through a mouthful. "Getting to be a damned sissy, running around with company he was keeping. Poetry!" he snorted. "Just the thing, too. Got a letter. Got several letters—show 'em to you later. How's everything at your place?"

"Excellent, sir." Rufus was abstracted. It had never occurred to him that Jennifer would not be at Six Chimneys—she had been a fixture there for years, and riding over to see her had been as much a part of visiting his estate as living in the house itself.

Only unfortunately, a part can become detached. It had occurred only recently to Rufus that he missed that particular part.

"By the way, sir, thank you for sending Selim to my place," he said abruptly.

The Duke glared at him. "Send Selim to you? I did no such thing," he denied.

Rufus's eyebrows went up. "I beg your pardon, sir," he said politely. "I must have been mistaken."

"Horse should be shot," the Duke said. "Told Peter to get rid of it."

"I imagine that's just what he did," Rufus said gently. "I'll buy him from you, sir, gladly."

"No need, no need," the Duke said testily. "Keep him if you want him. Can't ride him anyway, horse is no good."

"He's not a bad horse," Rufus said tolerantly, and changed the subject. "Do you expect Jennifer back shortly?"

The Duke shrugged and wiped his fingers on his table napkin. "I don't know when she's coming back," he said. "Seems to be having a good time. Come on into the library—got some letters yesterday—show them to you." He rose from the table and Rufus sauntered after him.

The packet *Britannia*—eleven days Halifax to Liverpool—had, along with its other cargo and general passenger list, conveyed numerous letters addressed to His Grace, the Duke of Burghley, in varying slants of handwriting. The Duke, with difficulty, had read most of them and tossed them now at Rufus.

"Here, read 'em yourself. I tell you, the boy's doing fine. Proud of him—knew he had good stuff." The Duke settled himself into his winged chair with a grunt and lit up his pipe. "Take your time," he puffed around the stem.

Rufus had no difficulty in recognizing Jennifer's handwriting, and he picked her letter out of the pile first and read it through, his eyebrows drawing together as he reached the signature. Odd—it did not sound like Jennifer at all. It was a straightforward letter saying that the writer was happy and enjoying the good times at Halifax, that she was staying with Lord and Lady Bradbury. Their daughters Alice and Marjorie, were very delightful girls. They had been having many parties, and that she was in good health and hoped that he was, too.

Rufus picked up Jonathan's letter and the sense of bewilderment was even more pronounced. Jonathan's letter was bright and racy. He described the barracks, the Citadel, the drill, ending up by saying "We had a capital sham fight the other day. You would have enjoyed it, Guardie. With Dixon's help, I prepared some irregular cavalry by dressing some of our men in smocks with belts and arming them with lances, and we attacked the 1st Battalion. Our men behaved admirably and it was generally agreed that we'd carried the day." He added—"Jennifer appears in good health, as I am, and trust this finds you likewise. Your obedient ward."

Rufus shook his head—*that* did not sound like Jonathan. The army must be changing him.

The next letter was signed, "C. G. Thompson, Colonel Commanding," and was a brief note which read almost like a military report, informing the Duke that the undersigned wished to convey his respects to him, and to congratulate him on his ward, who has shown despite his youth marked ability as a leader of men.

The last letter was signed "Bradbury" and was a longer one, beginning—"My dear Burghley." It was a chatty letter, and spoke in glowing terms of the excellent manner in which young Jonathan had taken over his duties in the Rifles.

"Thompson tells me," wrote Bradbury, "that the Company of which he was placed in charge was the slackest in the Battalion. Mitchell, who sold out, was no disciplinarian and had little interest in the army. Your ward, by a marked display of ability, has developed a keen sense of responsibility among the men, and now they have become the crack Company on the station. The other day a sham fight was staged, and Thompson declared that it was owing to the ability of your ward that the reserve under his command quite carried the day. He is here with us often, and I must commend his gentlemanly manners and gaiety of spirit. His horsemanship, too, is beyond compare. He rode in the Officers' Handicap and carried all before him, a bruising rider.

"The health of Lady Jennifer appears to be improving. It is too bad she is such a delicate girl. Lady Bradbury is much worried about her. Her musical accomplishments are quite remarkable, and her charm is remarked by all the young gentlemen who call. My daughters are devoted to her, and we are hoping that you will permit her to stay for a long visit, but she insists that she must leave at the end of the summer. It would be a pity if you will not allow her to stay longer when the climate is so salubrious for her."

There was more in the same strain and Rufus read it quickly. An idea had occurred to him which was so impossible that he accepted it immediately. Indeed, knowing Jennifer as he did, it was the only answer to the mystery these papers had spun. He turned from the table. "Those are most interesting letters, sir," he said politely. "It is gratifying to read how well Jonathan is accepting his responsibilities."

The Duke nodded complacently. "Yes, I always knew he had it in him," he said puffing happily. "I told him that once he was in uniform he would feel differently about it. Of course, he didn't want to go, but you can see how much of a success he's making of it. I knew it would be all right," and he nodded several times and gazed benignly into the fire. "Fact is," he added confidentially, "I'm making the boy my heir. Saw old Andrews in London last week. Told him to fix my will up, signing tomorrow. Didn't have an heir, you know, after Willy killed himself. Rotten rider. Don't know why you want that horse. Brute. Still, up to you. Title's finished, of course, last of the line, but estates aren't entailed. Knew Jonathan had it in him. Took the army, that was all. Should have bought him a commission long ago."

"Yes, indeed," Rufus agreed in a faraway voice. He straightened. "I'm sorry Lady Jennifer wasn't here. I came to say good-bye for a while."

"Oh, are you going away?" The Duke turned to look at him.

Rufus nodded. "Yes, I'm making a short trip over to America—to Boston. My father has some relatives there, and I have decided to go over to see them."

"Boston isn't so far from Halifax," the Duke said. "You might take a run up and see Jenny there while you're on that side of the ocean. Give her my regards if you do."

"Thank you, sir, I might do just that," Rufus said gravely. He held out his hand. "Good-bye, sir. Thank you for telling me of Jonathan and Jennifer."

"Don't mention it," the Duke said. "Have a good voyage. Oh—don't tell the boy yet. About the will, I mean. Keep it a surprise. Almost forgot—thanks for allowing your groom to go over. Understand Jonathan has quite a stable now."

"My groom?" Rufus stood still.

"Yes—Gates, Jakes—Bates, that's it. Couldn't spare one from here. Good of you. Thanks."

"It was nothing," Rufus said solemnly. "Don't mention it." He got up to leave the room and the Duke followed him.

"Watch yourself on the roads these days," he cautioned Rufus. "Wouldn't believe it, but I travel with guards now. Necessary."

"Indeed, sir?" Rufus was polite but dubious.

"Fact." The Duke nodded. "Was held up few months ago. When I came up with Jonathan. Near here, too. By the Old Spinney. Fellow fired a gun, scared the horses."

"What happened?"

"Chap on a huge black horse—bruising rider—crashed down, took over, ordered me on my way. Tell you, Rufus, things ain't as they should be. Wonderful rider. Crack shot, too. Neat as you please. Knocked the pistol out of this fellow's grasp. Moonlight, too. Wonderful shooting."

"A black horse, sir?"

"Yes, fellow dressed in black, too. Probably up to no good himself, daresay. Still, can't complain. Took control, ordered me back to my carriage. Sent the coachman on his way. Would you believe it? The Great North Road, too." He shook his head glumly. "Pretty pass, Rufus."

Rufus rode home thoughtfully. Instead of dismounting before the Manor, he rode into the stableyard and tossed the reins to the boy who ran to meet him. Joseph, his head stableman, hurried to him, touching his forelock as he neared.

"Copper's in good shape, Joseph," His Lordship said approvingly. "Well exercised."

Joseph beamed. This was praise indeed.

"By the way," His Lordship added casually, "I understand one of my grooms accompanied Lord Welland to Canada. Now, who would that be? I cannot recall missing anybody."

Joseph showed signs of embarrassment. "He warn't nobody as you knew, m'lord."

"Oh?" His Lordship's eyebrows lifted. "Do you keep many grooms in hiding, Joseph?"

"Oh, no, m'lord, not that. Fact is, m'lord," Joseph was twisting his hands nervously, "old Peter—him that's head man at Six Chimneys, sir—he comes to me, m'lord. Then this man, Bates, his name was, he asked for a job and I gave it to him account of Peter, and then Peter, he comes to ask if he was any good, would he like to go to Canada. He was good and he would and he did, and that's how it was, m'lord."

"I see," Rufus was nodding slowly. "And just when did Peter come to see you first?"

"It was—it was, well, just after you was here last time," Joseph was trying hard to remember, and his eyes were blinking nervously.

"A great many things happened just after I left last time," His Lordship murmured. "His Grace was telling me today about being held up by a highwayman on the Great North Road just after I left. Did you hear of it, Joseph?"

"Yes, and indeed I did, Your Lordship," Joseph nodded emphatically, glad to be off the somewhat nerve-racking topic of the unknown groom. "Fair shook us all up, m'lord, that it did. Near here, too."

"Yes, so I understand," His Lordship nodded. He strolled

slowly towards the house, added casually, "Was it very long after I left?"

"Oh, no, m'lord, t'was the very same night, I remember so well. And it was the next day that old Peter, he was here telling about it."

"I see. The time he asked you take on Bates?"

Joseph swallowed and blinked hastily. "Yes, m'lord, I think so."

"How very interesting," His Lordship said blandly. "And *was* he any good, Joseph? This—this Bates?"

"Oh, yes, sir, very good, m'lord. Very good, indeed."

"I'm glad," His Lordship said gently, and went on into the house, leaving Joseph gazing after him with a dropped jaw. For what had His Lordship to be glad about? Joseph did not understand that.

But to Rufus, much was clear, and he was conscious of a new and peculiar sensation which he was considering from all aspects. His butler, who opened the door for him, commendably showed no signs of emotion when his master abruptly requested that his secretary should be found at once and sent to him, and that his bags be packed forthwith.

"Certainly, m'lord," he said, wooden-faced. "When will Your Lordship be leaving?"

"Tomorrow, I believe," Rufus replied, and strolled into the library where his secretary found him a minute or two later.

Admirably trained though that man was, and as accustomed to the whims of his master as he should be after six years' service, nevertheless, a startled expression appeared on his face when His Lordship calmly told him to take himself off to Liverpool with all possible speed and arrange passage on the first ship sailing for Halifax.

"For Halifax, sir?" repeated the secretary.

Rufus nodded. "Yes—it is a harbor in Canada, I believe. I shall leave here tomorrow and arrive in Liverpool the following day. I shall leave all arrangements to you. The fastest packet leaving. And, oh, Edward, you had better stop at my bankers and cash this draft for me." He sat down leisurely at his desk and scrawled off a note. "You might tell them I shall be in Halifax for some time, and suggest that they prepare a note immediately for their representatives there. You might even bring it with you."

"Yes, my lord." The bemused secretary, his face expressionless again, accepted the slip of paper from His Lordship's hand and walked to the door. He paused there. "Is there anything else, my lord?"

"No, I believe that will be all," His Lordship replied and the secretary bowed and withdrew.

Left alone, Rufus strolled to the window. Outside the fields were green with the fervent verdure of July.

In place of the lush growth, Rufus saw instead the freshness of a May morning and a straight-backed girl on a tall bay, riding across that meadow. His face creased in a slow smile.

"Trust you, Jenny," he said aloud. But what he was trusting her for he did not say, yet the smile was still about his lips when his butler came in to announce lunch.

Chapter Eleven

Two days of parade had been sufficient to convince Jennifer that the morale and discipline of the former Captain Mitchell's Company were both woefully lax, and when, on the Sunday as she marched at the head of the Company to church she overheard a child say clearly, "Look, Mama, that soldier's out of step," her jaw tightened and her eyes hardened ominously.

She glowered through the service and at its conclusion, after the men had been marched back to quarters and dismissed, she called the sergeant over and gave orders for the men to be paraded at seven o'clock the following morning.

The sergeant was a veteran and his face was blank as he saluted smartly and turned on his heel. She had been invited to dinner at Government House, or she might have been inclined to call the sergeant aside and find out something of his honest opinion. Jennifer was well aware sergeants had been the hard core of the British army for generations past.

While officers might come and go, your British sergeant remained in quiet power for near a lifetime.

His Excellency's carriage was waiting for her at the corner of Barrington and Sackville as she hurried down from the barracks. Lady Bradbury and her two daughters and Jonathan had watched the Company return from church parade, and Lord Bradbury commented on the fit appearance of the men.

"Yes, sir, they're a fine group," Jennifer said briefly, taking her place opposite His Excellency.

"A little lacking, perhaps, in crispness," murmured His Excellency, and Jennifer's eyes hardened.

"Extra drill at seven o'clock tomorrow morning, sir," she said shortly, and Lord Bradbury permitted a faint flicker of approval as he nodded.

"Very commendable," he murmured, and spoke of the mildness of the weather.

Throughout the family dinner which followed, Alice and Marjorie kept up a sprightly chatter with their parents, and Jonathan offered a demure word or two, while Jennifer exchanged pleasantries with Lady Bradbury and His Excellency's aide-de-camp, a young gentleman by the name of Irwin, who flushed easily and was made the butt of innumerable jokes by the two girls.

After dinner Jonathan excused himself to rest, and Jennifer went up to his room with him. Once inside, with the door safely closed, Jennifer collapsed on the nearest chair and stuffed her handkerchief in her mouth to stifle her roars of laughter.

"Oh, Jonnie, if you could only see yourself!" she got out, sputtering.

Jonathan sniffed. "Speak for yourself," he muttered.

"But however are you managing?" Jennifer sat up straighter to ask with honest curiosity.

Jonathan shrugged and allowed himself to be unhooked from his Sunday finery robed in a dressing gown by a grim-faced Katie, who proceeded to tuck him up on the bed.

"For you never can tell if Her Ladyship will drop in," she said warningly, and Jennifer went off again into paroxysms of mirth.

"Oh, not really truly an invalid, Jonnie!"

Jonathan nodded rather more than a little complacently. "I'm delicate," he said in a meek voice, and Jennifer again stuck her handkerchief into her mouth to drown her laughter.

"Stop it, you fool," her brother roused to growl, "they'll hear you if you're not careful."

She controlled her giggles with an effort. "Seriously, Jonnie, how do you manage?"

Jonathan shrugged again. "I couldn't do it without Katie," he said frankly. "She clucks over me and fusses at the door and won't let anybody in—'Lady Jennifer is resting'—she almost has to hold them out at times."

Jennifer cast a grateful glance at Katie who burst out resentfully, "It's all very well for you, m'lady, but I don't like no part of this. It's cheating, that's what it is."

Jennifer nodded. "Yes, Katie, I know it is, but..." she spread her hands. "What can we do? It's gone so far now that if we tell them what the truth is, it will only upset matters more."

"Oh, you've got to keep on," Katie conceded, "but I'm thinking you'd best get him away soon," she pointed at Jonathan comfortably ensconced on the bed. "Hot milk, eggnog...I'm letting out the dresses as far as I can."

Jennifer swallowed her laughter again. "Oh, Katie, if there was only someone we could share this with."

"How are you getting on?" Jonathan asked, but indifferently.

Jennifer shrugged. "Not too badly," she was noncommittal. "You'd probably hate it, Jonnie, but I like it."

Jonathan stretched. "If one of us has to be in the army to satisfy Guardie, I'm not sorry it's you. These skirts are a nuisance, but anything's better than the army."

As the days went and brother and sister slid more securely into their roles, Jonathan began to thoroughly enjoy his masquerade. Not too strangely perhaps, the accomplishments which angered his guardian so much were the very things that made him popular as a young lady. He could recite poetry, and that was considered quite the thing for a young lady; he could play the pianoforte with grace, another admirable accomplishment; his long white fingers could wield

101

a fan with dexterity, and his naturally fair skin encouraged the delicate aura which made him even more attractive. He fitted more and more into character, pressing into the background whenever possible with demurely downcast eyes, refusing to dance—it was too tiring—but refusing in such a carefully modest way that the young gentlemen continued to cluster around him, and even the young ladies were kindly disposed to him.

Jennifer, watching him in action at one of the balls, was overcome with admiration. He had far more graces than she knew she had ever had.

Meanwhile, Jennifer's own position was clarifying to her satisfaction. The Company had turned out for drill that Monday morning at seven o'clock as ordered. The sergeant had paraded them and, drawing a deep breath, she had proceeded to render them a complete account of their short-comings and general failings, delivered in such a language that there could be no lack of understanding among the men, and concluded with an admonition that things were going to be different, and that the Company was going to smarten up or enjoy the pleasures of His Majesty's detention cells. This, with a few extra well-chosen phrases, quite impressed the Company in question, and the drill showed a marked improvement by the end of the week.

Not, however, sufficient to satisfy their carping captain, who delivered herself of a few further well-chosen words and phrases and, when one or two of the hardier souls showed their disapproval by going over the hill, she imposed the strictest disciplinary measures allowable to her office and quite sobered their comrades.

Even the sergeant was impressed, and it takes quite a bit to impress a sergeant.

Jennifer was in her element. She thoroughly enjoyed the military atmosphere, the drill, the parade, the thousand and one rules and regulations. Life at the mess was something else again, and she had coped with that in a straightforward way, which had silenced several of the more loquacious officers whose sneering comments she did not allow to provoke her into any reckless action.

Jennifer had early realized that she could not hope to

match the steady drinking in which the officers indulged. Her stomach was not strong enough to stand it, and above all, she had to keep a steady head. She refused firmly and as casually as possible, but realized that that would not answer indefinitely. Already the grapevine had it that Captain Lord Welland was something of a prig. Such a reputation would ruin her authority, or at least undermine it severely, and she had no intention of allowing that to slip.

Accordingly, she settled herself in the mess one afternoon with a leather case opened on her knees.

Captain Thurston, the bosom companion of Mr. Digby, sauntered in, and observing her presence indicated it to another of his cronies with a jerk of his head. Joining forces, the two wandered in Jennifer's direction.

"Care to join us in a drink, Welland?" Thurston invited. The words were polite enough, but the tone was little short of a sneer.

The leather case held a pair of duelling pistols which had belonged to Jennifer's father. His Grace would have been much surprised to have seen them on his ward's knee at that moment; he was under the impression that they were reposing under lock and key at Six Chimneys. The case was one of the many useful things his ward had packed.

"Thank you, no, gentlemen," Jennifer replied civilly, engaged in cleaning one of the guns.

Captain Thurston brandished a bottle. "Come, now, Welland, a drink or two will be good for you."

"I'm very appreciative of your kind thought, Captain Thurston," Jennifer returned, "but, thank you, no."

Thurston exchanged a speaking glance with his companion who joined in the attack. "It's rumored, I believe, Welland, that you disdain strong drink?" he murmured.

It was not entirely the words, it was the manner in which they were uttered.

Without appearing to notice much what she was doing, Jennifer cocked the pistol and squeezed the hammer—a thread of gold fringe flew from Captain Thurston's epaulet and he staggered back, clapping one hand to his shoulder.

"I do not care to drink," Jennifer said coldly, and blew into the open breechblock.

The shot had the attention of everybody in the mess, and Captain Thurston's face was black.

"By God, Welland, you'll pay for that!" he snarled.

"I apologize, Captain Thurston," Jennifer's voice was calm, even nonchalant. "I'm afraid I startled you. I assure you, you were perfectly safe." She picked up the other gun and again without appearing to aim she pressed the hammer—a candle flipped from the candelabra on the long table.

Captain Dixon detached himself from the group at the other end of the room and strolled over.

"Duelling pistols?" he drawled. "A handsome pair." He stretched out a hand, and Jennifer extended one of the guns to him without comment. He took it and turned it over in his big hands, examining it with the ease of a man accustomed to all manner of firearms.

"Nice balance," he said in a congratulatory tone. He handed it back to her. "I judge you do not care to drink?"

"Not at the moment, Dixon," Jennifer amended.

He nodded. "The point is well taken," he agreed, and looked straight at Thurston. "Don't you agree, Thurston?"

Thurston hesitated, but Dixon outstared him. Thurston turned on his heel and marched away, and after a moment's awkwardness his companion followed him hastily.

"I should suggest that the next time you feel the need of a little practice, my friend," Captain Dixon drawled gently, "it would be less wearing on the mess if you were to aim perhaps at the window."

Jennifer grinned. "I'll try to remember that," she said and added inconsequentially, "Thank you."

Dixon nodded. "Don't mention it," he murmured and strolled back.

But Captain Thurston's face was black, and those who knew him best stayed far away from him for the evening, while one or two wondered uneasily what he would think of next and privately thanked the powers that be that they were not in Lord Welland's shoes. For Captain Thurston's temper was well known to be deep and vengeful, and his pride not readily assuaged.

Chapter Twelve

Lord Randall's secretary accounted himself most fortunate when, after traveling to Liverpool with all possible haste, he learned that the *Britannia* lay straining at her moorings prepared to sail on the morning tide for Halifax. He was further fortunate in that, by the spending of vastly adequate largesse, he was able to secure a private cabin for His Lordship, who enjoyed his creature comforts whenever possible, but did not cavil when, on certain occasions, any accommodations left something to be desired. He would have nothing to complain about this time, thought his secretary with satisfaction. The line was proud of the passenger cabins offered by the *Britannia*, and its pride was well-merited.

In his undemonstrative fashion, His Lordship expressed himself as well pleased with the arrangements, and ordered his baggage moved on board without delay. His secretary accompanied him to the dock to take leave of him and to receive whatever instructions His Lordship might care to give, and was slightly disconcerted when, in reply to his query as to when His Lordship would return, he was told His Lordship had no idea at all what that date would be, and that Randall would entrust the management of his affairs entirely to his secretary's hands, to do as he saw fit. His Lordship added that he was sure Edward would perform a noble job, and appeared to consider the matter settled. Indeed, his attention appeared wholly taken by the arrival at the dock of a large traveling coach, laden with all manner of bandboxes, trunks and that other paraphernalia recognized by all ladies as necessities of travel. His Lordship had recognized the crest on the door panel, and his secretary could have sworn that His Lordship muttered "Good God!" under his breath, but when he glanced hastily at his employer there was no sign of expression on his face.

The gentleman who descended from the carriage was middle-aged and worried. After him stepped a young lady whose eyes were sparkling and whose dark hair hung in proper ringlets under her much befeathered bonnet. She gazed about her with undisguised interest and paid no attention to the dowdily-dressed, resigned woman who followed her from the carriage and who now stood patting her skirts into place fussily.

"You see, Papa, we're on time," Rufus heard her say clearly. "I told you not to fret so."

"It wouldn't have surprised me at all if the ship had sailed," her father replied testily. "Come, come, don't stand there. Get aboard, get aboard." He propelled her forward and she tripped lightly across the rough planking and picked her way daintily up the gangplank. Almost the first person she saw when she stepped onto the deck was His Lordship, but her eyes brushed past him with the unseeing stare of the well-schooled young lady. When the dowdy woman following her looked about their surroundings in dismay and sighed lugubriously, the girl said impatiently, "Cousin Maria, you sound like a worn-out bellows."

Lord Randall's lips twitched appreciatively but he was looking to the middle-aged gentleman who now stepped heavily onto the deck and stared about him anxiously. His eyes fell on the watching Rufus, and his face lighted.

"Randall!" He advanced toward him with his hand out. "My boy, what are you doing here? Don't tell me...oh, don't tell me you...you're sailing to Halifax?"

Lord Randall shook hands. "That is my impression, sir," he said languidly.

"You don't know how glad I am to see you, my boy," said Sir Joseph Markham with enthusiasm "My daughter, Matilda, is going for a visit with Lord Bradbury, my brother; he's governor at Halifax now—and at the last minute I found I could not accompany her. Matters have come up—you know how it is. Matilda, my daughter, insisted that she be allowed to go—she said she was quite all right to travel alone, and she...well...she's very determined, Randall. And, of course, my wife's cousin, Mrs. Connell, is traveling with her. But, my boy, I would feel much safer in my mind if you would agree to keep an eye on her—you know, to watch her, to make sure everything is all right. The hazards of being alone without a father's hand to guard her she cannot comprehend at all. I simply could not make her understand. My boy, I realize it is a great deal to ask of you, but if you would consider it I would be forever in your debt."

"I would be delighted to take charge of Miss Markham," Lord Randall drawled. "I will undertake to see that she is safely delivered to the care of her uncle, Lord Bradbury."

"Good! Good, my boy," Sir Joseph sighed in relief. "My two nieces, Marjorie and Alice, have been writing repeatedly urging Matilda to come over. Seems they find it a bit dull there, I suppose, and they want some young company of their own age, and nothing would have it but Matilda had to go, and go now on this ship. I'll introduce you. Matilda...Matilda, my dear." He turned. Matilda was nowhere in sight. "Now, where has that girl gone to?"

"I believe she went below," Lord Randall murmured, having watched this maneuver from the corner of his eye.

"Drat that girl," Sir Joseph pulled his big turnip watch from his pocket and regarded it anxiously. "Ship's sailing in a matter of minutes. Look lively, my man," he adjured, as his servant went past laden with handbags of all varieties. "Look lively. Are you sure you have everything?"

"Yes, sir," the man said respectfully. "That's the last of it."

"Don't understand why women have to take so much stuff with them," Sir Joseph confided. "I don't need it—why, I used to get about with one bag. Not m'daughter. I didn't think there'd be space enough in the carriage for the three of us, but she assured me it's all necessary, all necessary." He shook his head. "Confound it, where is that girl? If I knew where her cabin was...."

Fortunately for his peace of mind, his daughter emerged from the companionway then.

"Papa, you must come down and see the cabin. It's lovely. Two little beds in the corner, one above the other—I'm going to sleep in the upper one because Cousin Maria says she could never climb up. And a sofa and chairs and a table. Really, Papa, you must come and see it. Hurry if you can."

"My dear, will you wait a minute?" Sir Joseph interrupted her. "I want to introduce a friend of mine to you, a son of a very old friend. Matilda, this is Lord Randall—Randall, my daughter, Miss Matilda."

Matilda curtsied politely and extended a gloved hand over which Rufus bowed formally.

"Lord Randall has agreed to look after you and see that you are safely delivered to your uncle," Sir Joseph went on. "I will leave you in his care."

"I am sure it's very kind of Lord Randall," Matilda said prettily, "but truly, Papa, it is not necessary."

Sir Joseph's lips tightened. "Matilda, you must understand that there are occasions when your father knows what is best for you. You will promise me that you will be obedient to Lord Randall, or I shall remove you from this ship at once."

"I wonder if you could, Papa?" Matilda's gaze was speculative but she added, "All right, Papa. I'll be good." She turned to Lord Randall. "It is very kind of you, sir, to put Papa's mind at ease in such a manner."

There was a twinkle in Lord Randall's eye, hidden by his half closed eyelids. He bowed. "I shall do my best to justify your father's trust, Miss Matilda," he said solemnly.

"Papa," Matilda turned back to her father and laid an

urgent hand on his arm, "Papa, you must come and see our cabin. Come along."

With a murmur of apology to Lord Randall, Sir Joseph allowed himself to be drawn away, and Lord Randall remained by the rail. His secretary was under the impression that something was amusing him, but as he himself could see nothing laughable he dismissed the thought.

"I had best be getting ashore, sir," he said respectfully. "That is, unless there is anything else I can do for you?"

His Lordship said not, and thanked him as he took his leave.

Shortly afterwards the warning cry of "All ashore" was heard, and Sir Joseph appeared hastily up the companionway.

"Good-bye, m'dear," he pecked at his daughter's cheek, and staggered slightly as she threw her arms around his neck and kissed him firmly. "Matilda!" he admonished, disengaging himself hurriedly.

"Good-bye, Papa. Take care, won't you, and don't forget to write me." His daughter appeared cheerful enough.

"You look after *yourself*," he said gruffly, and hesitated a moment longer. Then he awkwardly kissed her once more, and hurried to the gangplank.

Lord Randall had been watching from further down the deck. Now he strolled up to join the girl where she stood at the rail amidships. The gangplank was being pulled ashore, and the cries of the longshoremen mingled with the orders aboard ship. Sir Joseph remained on the dock, and Matilda waved to him from the ship until he was only a small figure left behind as the *Britannia* pulled out into midstream. Then she turned to Lord Randall. She was blinking.

"It's the wind, Lord Randall," she said determinedly. "I assure you, I am not crying."

"I'm sure you are not, Miss Matilda," he agreed solemnly and offered her his arm. "Would you care to stroll about the deck?"

Matilda Markham was eighteen, the only child of an adoring father who had in middle-life married a woman twenty years his junior, only to have his wife fade peacefully away when her daughter was born. Matilda was spoiled, pretty and willful, and had learned that she could get her own way almost every time if she went about it with due consideration for the foibles of her father or such of the servants and attendants who had had charge of her. To Lord Randall, accustomed as he was to another determined damsel, she was an amusing companion. She found him pleasant and affable, but oddly unmoved by her coaxings on the few occasions when she particularly wanted her own way.

"No, Miss Matilda," he said mildly on one occasion when she had expressed a desire to inspect the whole ship. "I think not."

"Lord Randall, it will be most interesting," she coaxed prettily. "And besides, Papa always said I should find out how things are run."

His voice was perfectly unruffled. There was even, although she didn't see it, a slow smile in his eyes. "No, Miss Matilda," he said again, and Miss Matilda, having well calculated her chances rapidly, surrendered.

"You're as bad as Papa," she observed crossly.

"Miss Matilda, I'm worse than your Papa," Lord Randall said solemnly. "Your Papa might have taken you." Then, as she looked at him in quick hope, he shook his head. "No."

So they got on famously, and by the time the *Britannia* was gliding into Halifax Harbor she regarded him as being quite on the same par with her father, only a lot more adament, and was on cordial friendly terms with him.

They stood together by the rail watching as the ship drew in to the wharf.

"Are all those people there just to watch us come in?" Matilda queried, almost awestruck for her.

Truly, there was a crowd of people about the dock and foremost were two booted and spurred horsemen, their mounts pawing restlessly at the planking.

"What are those doing?" Matilda wanted to know.

Lord Randall enquired of a passing sailor.

"Them's pony-express riders, sir," he was told. "Two companies, now. We carry dispatches. The *Britannia* is the fastest ship afloat, and they ride 'em over to Digby, and then the messages go by fast packet to St. Johns, last by special messengers to Boston and New York, sir. They race for it."

Lord Randall conveyed this information to Matilda and she watched eagerly as the gangplank was hoisted and the two horsemen dismounted to rush on board. Sure enough, two dispatch bags were waiting for them and they clanked down the gangplank again, ran across the intervening space, leaped into their saddles and spurred off, the crowd cheering vociferously.

"Well!" said Miss Matilda in a not-displeased tone. "I don't see why Alice and Marjorie think it's dull here, if that's the kind of thing that goes on all the time."

Among the onlookers on the dock who had come expressly to watch the departure of the pony-express riders, for the sailor had omitted to add that the citizens of Halifax were prone to wager heavily on the outcome of each race, were two officers of His Majesty's Rifle Brigade, who had ridden down to view the horsemen in question and to make their wager accordingly.

"Five pounds on the black," Captain Dixon declared.

"Done," said his companion promptly, "I favor the gray."

"I wonder," mused Captain Dixon thoughtfully, "if he'll still be riding a black at the end of the last relay?"

His companion laughed. "Probably not," she said cheerfully. "He'll probably have a gray and mine will have a black. I had a black in England," Jennifer added, for she was Captain Dixon's companion, "and I wish I had brought him over."

Her stable had grown rapidly since her arrival in Halifax. First had come a tall gray, purchased from a Mr. Compton. The gray was showy and looked well on parade, but he was a poor stayer. So a raking bay had joined him in the stable not long afterwards. The short-necked chestnut which she was riding today was her third acquisition, and displayed an aptitude for jumping which pleased Jennifer, but which also made her long more for the high-spirited if temperamental Selim. "I'd like to get Thurston's gelding," she added, steadying her mount with a firm hand.

Dixon laughed. "If he throws Thurston once more, you'll probably get him free."

"Thurston's cow-handed," Jennifer said scornfully.

"Better not let him hear you say that," Dixon murmured. "He's proud of his horsemanship."

Jennifer grunted. She was not impressed.

A newly arriving carriage caused a commotion in the rear ranks of the crowd, which pushed slowly aside to permit it to pass through.

"What's the Governor's carriage doing here today?" Dixon asked of his companion.

Jennifer shrugged. "I believe Lord Bradbury's niece is arriving for a visit," she answered.

"Shall we pay our respects?" Dixon murmured, and Jennifer shrugged again.

"I suppose so," she agreed, and twitched the reins against her horse's neck.

They drew up beside the carriage and bowed sweepingly.

"Good morning, Miss Marjorie, Miss Alice," Jennifer greeted them, and the two girls smiled prettily.

"Good morning, Lord Welland, good morning, Captain Dixon," they chorused in unison.

Both were pretty girls gifted with the dainty insipidness found in Dresden pieces. They were thoroughly genteel and thoroughly nice, and thoroughly without a thought in their collective minds. They enjoyed having two officers paying court at the carriage, and they engaged them in light conversation until the passengers began coming off the ship.

"We're meeting our cousin, Miss Markham," Miss Marjorie informed Dixon, "and look—there she is now! She's just coming down the gangplank—there's a gentleman behind her—that's not her father, although he was to come with her. I wonder what happened?"

Jennifer followed her gaze. The daintily descending figure she glanced at, but it was the man behind who speedily riveted her attention.

Her hand tightened unconsciously on the rein and her horse plunged in protest. She controlled him easily, but her mind was in a whirl.

Never in her wildest dreams had she ever imagined that Lord Rufus Randall would come to Halifax.

Chapter Thirteen

In the flurry and excitement attendant upon the Misses Marjorie and Alice descending from their carriage to greet their cousin Matilda, Jennifer's perturbation went unnoticed. She had plenty of time to pull herself together and, like Captain Dixon, to dismount and be standing by the carriage ready to be presented to the newcomers when they returned with the Misses Bradbury. The inevitable small boy had materialized from the onlookers to hold their horses.

The Misses Marjorie and Alice were genuinely pleased to welcome Matilda, not only because they had a very real, if cousinly, affection for her—which permitted them to criticize her with as much freedom as their genteel decorum allowed—but also because where Matilda was, there also was fun, gaiety and laughter. Matilda engendered all three, for those about her as well as for herself, and the Misses Marjorie and Alice looked forward with well-warranted anticipation to a round of summer amusements far superior to those encountered to date. Further, they were not at all displeased that Miss Matilda appeared to have produced a most eligible young man in the person of Lord Randall, and they beamed at him with all the ardor considered correct.

Chattering and simpering alternately, they drew Matilda over to the carriage, and there, with all the formality which her mother was wont to show, Miss Alice proudly presented Captain Dixon and Captain Lord Welland to "my cousin, Miss Matilda Markham," and if there was a tone of condescension in her voice, it was only because, after all, not every girl could introduce two handsome, uniformed escorts to a visiting cousin, with a hint that more would be available in due time.

Miss Matilda sketched a curtsey, and Captain Dixon and Lord Welland bowed in turn over her extended, mittened hand.

"And now pray permit me to introduce Lord Randall," Miss Alice went on officiously. "He has been kind enough to escort Miss Matilda to Halifax, in place of her father who was unable to accompany her. Lord Randall—Captain Dixon, Captain Lord Welland."

Firm handshakes were the order of the day.

"Welcome to Halifax, Lord Randall," Captain Dixon extended a large hand and a wide smile, and Rufus returned both the handshake and the smile.

Captain Lord Welland followed, if he was reluctant no one could have guessed. "This is unexpected, Rufus," she said steadily, extending her hand in turn, and looking him squarely in the face.

Lord Randall bowed gravely. "You are looking well, Jonathan," he drawled. "How is Jennifer?"

"Very well, thank you, Rufus," Jennifer answered unsmiling, her chin slightly raised.

Miss Alice looked from one to the other. "Are you gentlemen known to each other?"

"Yes, one of Lord Randall's estates marches with that of my guardian's," Jennifer explained briefly.

"I've known Welland since he was a boy," Rufus added.

"Well, my goodness, how nice!" Miss Alice was all aflutter. "Indeed, you must come to call upon us, Lord Randall. Captain Lord Welland's sister, Lady Jennifer, is staying with us, and I am sure she would be pleased to see you."

Lord Randall bowed. "I will be delighted to see Lady Jennifer," he said. "I have a message for her from her guardian, the Duke. Thank you indeed, Miss Alice. I shall be pleased to call upon you if I may. I must in any event present my card to your father, to discharge my duties to Miss Matilda's father, Sir Joseph. I shall call upon Lord Bradbury tomorrow. I shan't impose on your privacy today."

But Miss Alice would have none of that. "No, do call around this afternoon, Lord Randall," she implored. "Papa will be so pleased to see you."

Lord Randall bowed. "Thank you, Miss Alice," he said formally, and handed her into the carriage. When it had pulled away he turned back to Jennifer and Captain Dixon. "Well, Jonathan," he said, and he was not smiling, "I confess I did not expect to see you quite so immediately upon my arrival."

"I did not expect to see you at all, Rufus," Jennifer returned flatly.

He half smiled. "No, I daresay not. By the way—which is the best hotel? The captain said something about the Colonial."

"The Colonial is very comfortable," Jennifer said. "We stopped there when we arrived."

"Then I believe I shall repair to the Colonial," Lord Randall decided. He appeared to have lifted nothing more than an eyebrow yet a cabbie was suddenly beside him and was receiving instructions in Lord Randall's languid voice to gather up his baggage and transport it to the Colonial Hotel.

"Welland, if you'd like to go back to the hotel with Lord Randall I'll take your horse to the stable," Captain Dixon suggested.

"I wouldn't think of interrupting you," Lord Randall murmured. "No doubt I shall see you later, Jonathan. I shall be here for a while." His tone was cold.

Jennifer made up her mind quickly. Rufus had to be faced sometime. "I'll ride back to barracks and then join you immediately, Rufus," she said evenly. "The officers' mess is in the old Halifax Hotel, only a few doors along from the Colonial. The barracks burnt down last December."

Rufus nodded. "Very well, Jonathan. I shall look forward to having a chat with you."

He stepped into the carriage and the two officers mounted their horses. "Good morning, Captain Dixon," he added courteously. "It has been an honor to meet you and I trust I shall have the pleasure again shortly."

The cab rolled off and the officers followed. Jennifer was silent and Dixon said, with a slight cough:

"None of my business, of course, but that chap seems sort of patronizing, doesn't he?"

"Yes," said Jennifer, rousing herself with an effort. "He always is. I wonder what the devil brought him to Halifax?"

"Unexpected, I judge," Dixon murmured.

Jennifer nodded, "Very," she said flatly.

Dixon said no more and they rode in virtual silence up to the stables where their respective grooms took the horses from them.

"I'll see you in the mess, Dixon," Jennifer said in parting and Dixon nodded.

"If you need any help, let me know," he offered, and Jennifer smiled.

"I don't think any will be necessary," she said, "but thanks just the same."

Lord Randall's cab drew up as she neared the door of the Colonial and she waited for Rufus to step down. She felt his rather hard gaze sweeping her comprehensively as they passed into the lobby, but her face was impassive as she accompanied him to the desk. She had to admit that Rufus had an air about him which the clerk recognized immediately with his most servile attentions. A sitting room and a bedroom were immediately forthcoming for the guest, and another deep bow was produced for the captain, whom the clerk also recognized.

The porter was taking his bags upstairs, and Rufus turned to Jennifer. "I could meet you down here," he suggested shortly.

Jennifer shook her head. "I'll come up with you," she countered, and Rufus hesitated only a second then he nodded.

"Very well," he said.

They went up the stairs together and after the porter had withdrawn and the doors were closed, Rufus turned to Jennifer with as stern a look as Jennifer had ever seen on his face.

"Now, Jennifer, suppose you tell me what this is all about?"

Jennifer walked to the window and looked out unseeingly. It was an unconscious gesture, and one which to Lord Randall who knew her well was revealing. His stern glance softened a little as he picked out the most comfortable-appearing chair in the room and settled into it. Jennifer would speak in her own good time. He waited patiently.

At length she turned from the window.

"I don't know where to begin, Rufus," she said despairingly. "You're not going to approve of any of it, anyway."

"Probably not," Lord Randall concurred, "but I don't see that you have to regard me as a hanging judge, yet."

"Why did you come, here, Rufus?" she asked abruptly.

His Lordship's eyebrows rose. "Because I like to travel," he drawled.

"You're not *that* fond of travel, Rufus," Jennifer said impatiently. "Not to Halifax—there isn't anything to bring you here. The Continent, yes—France, Germany, Italy—not Halifax. Why did you come, Rufus?"

"Oh, come, Jennifer," His Lordship murmured. "I don't think you're in a position to ask too many questions, are you?"

"Rufus, don't beat about the bush," she retorted impatiently. "Why *did* you come? Did Guardie send you?" There, it was out, the crux of the problem.

His Lordship recognized her inner fear. "No," he said gently, "he didn't send me. As a matter of fact, he's quite proud of his ward's aptitude for the army. He has received some very admirable reports."

Jennifer's color deepened. "So?" she challenged.

"Reports mentioning the gallant young officer's ability in riding, for example," Lord Randall murmured. "Among other things, of course. Reports, too, which mentioned how much Lord and Lady Bradbury were enjoying the visit of Lady

Jennifer, and remarking on what a pity it was that she was so delicate."

His voice held the inflection of an enquiry, and again Jennifer colored. "You can guess most of the whole of it, Rufus," she said gruffly. "Why do you question me?"

"Because I thought it would be nice to gather some more pertinent details from you," Rufus replied quietly.

"But if you know the whole, why did you come?" Jennifer persisted.

"Shall we say—for old times' sake?" Lord Randall suggested.

"Why, Rufus?"

Lord Randall crossed a leg with deliberation. "Because it occurred to me," and his drawl was very marked, "that if my—suspicions, shall we say?—were well-founded, there might come a time when my humble assistance might—perhaps—be of some help. I am not without a certain amount of resource, you might say."

Jennifer turned suddenly back to the window. "That's kind of you, Rufus," she said and her voice was harsh from unexpected emotion, "but I can assure you, it's not at all necessary."

Lord Randall was smiling lightly. "No, I don't imagine it is now," he agreed. "The deception is better than I expected, Jennifer. Come, now, suppose you tell me when this started. Had you decided upon it before you left England?"

Jennifer shook her head. Her back was still to him. "No, not then."

"Perhaps after you arrived here in Halifax?"

Jennifer hesitated. "Well, in a way."

"In a way?"

"You see, Rufus, Jonathan was seasick, almost right away. And we ran into storms and I couldn't go up on deck—no females could—and Jonnie couldn't, so I—"

His Lordship nodded. "So you did. I understand perfectly. Jonathan was seasick. I should have thought of that, too. Was he still enjoying the discomforts of mal de mer when you arrived here?"

Unexpectedly, Jennifer grinned. "I don't believe he found the land too steady, either."

"No, I don't imagine he would. But I am still somewhat vague, Jenny. Who wore the uniform ashore?"

"I did." Jennifer was suddenly in a hurry to explain and get it over with. "You see, Jonnie couldn't act as if he'd never been sick when he was still falling all over the place, so he agreed to come ashore as me, and we were just going to the hotel and that would have been all there would have been to it, only that—" and again she hesitated.

"Only that what?" His Lordship prompted. "I must say, Jenny, you do pause at the most interesting places. What happened then?"

"Well, I met Dixon at the hotel as we were coming in, and he took me up to see the colonel, and there wasn't any time to change back because the colonel sent word to Lord Bradbury and I had to see *him* that afternoon. Then Lady Bradbury insisted that Jennifer come to stay with them, and brought me back to the hotel then and there, and took Jonnie back with her—so there we were! There wasn't anything else we could do, Rufus, really there wasn't." It was of a sudden very important to impress this point on Rufus, and she regarded him anxiously.

"I realize I'm only an individual of limited intelligence, Jennifer," His Lordship spoke with deceptive mildness, "but I am at something of a loss to understand how these things occurred within such a brief time limit. Am I to infer that Captain Dixon gathered you up willy-nilly and escorted you without an hour's delay to the colonel?"

"Well, no, not exactly," Jennifer admitted. "But Jonathan couldn't go, really he couldn't, Rufus."

"Funk?" suggested His Lordship, and Jennifer flushed.

"No, of course not," she denied hastily. This suggestion hit much too close to the truth. "He was still wobbly, Rufus. He was sick all the way over and couldn't eat a thing. Bates kept him going on champagne."

"Your brother has expensive tastes," Rufus murmured, stowing away the mention of Bates for future reference and continuing with the matter at hand. "I will allow that he was somewhat incapable of rapid promenading, but it still is a questionable point to me that he couldn't have managed to don his own attire at some time. There was no opportunity later, Jenny?"

For some reason, Jennifer hesitated, then made herself look Rufus straight in the eyes. "No," she said flatly.

"I see," said Rufus softly. He was smiling a little. "You know, my dear Jenny, I don't believe a word of this Banbury tale. Or perhaps I do, up to a point. But I'll wager a pretty penny that somewhere along the line of march you could have stopped. However, you can't now. I'll agree with you there. Tell me, how is Jonathan enjoying himself?"

Jennifer felt curiously let down, as if she had braced herself to meet a charge which never was launched. "He's doing all right," she said unexpansively. "Katie is with him, of course. He couldn't manage without her. I said my sister was delicate and had to have her nurse with her all the time, and Lady Bradbury accepted that." She swung back to the window and Rufus regarded her still with the half smile about his lips.

"Not as much fun deceiving Lady Bradbury, I take it," he murmured, and, as Jennifer made no reply, he went on, "How is the army?"

"Fine," Jennifer did not turn.

"Yes, I understand you've been making quite a success of your career. Do you propose remaining a soldier for the rest of your days?"

Jennifer shook her head. "Don't be silly, Rufus," she said crossly. "Of course not. Oh, I like the army part, and it's been capital getting the Company into shape, because it really was pretty ragged, you know. But it hasn't been so much fun in the barracks. It's not too bad now, because we're staying at the hotel, and I have a room on the top floor and George is with me and he's pretty good, but still—" she shrugged and left the sentence unfinished.

"I see," said His Lordship, and did indeed see quite a lot. He added, after a moment, "How do you propose getting out of it, Jennifer?"

She shrugged, "I haven't thought ahead that far yet, Rufus," she said truthfully. "Sell out, I suppose."

"After the excellent reports your guardian has been receiving?" Rufus asked.

"I tell you, Rufus, I haven't thought of it," Jennifer said again. "Something will happen."

"I see," Rufus said again. He regarded her steadily and his mouth was smiling. "You're a bit of a fatalist, aren't you, Jenny?" he said, and she looked up at him.

"A fatalist? You mean because I don't worry about tomorrow? I suppose so. Only we've got into this thing so deeply now, Rufus, that if I start to worry about tomorrow I'd be no use at all. I can't let Guardie down, and we can't let the Bradburys down. It can't come out—what we've done, ever. I know that. It wouldn't be fair to the Bradburys. But—" she shrugged again, "something will turn up."

Rufus' smile deepened. "I think it's a good thing I came, Jenny. By the way, although you haven't mentioned it, I must thank you for sending Selim to me. Very generous of you, I'm sure."

She colored. "Don't be an ass, Rufus."

"Not a bit of it, my dear. I'm really most appreciative. May I assume that Bates is proving his worth?"

Her eyes flashed up to his. "You're not angry, Rufus?"

"Not a bit, my dear. Not now. Of course, one usually likes to be consulted before one's staff is lured away, but as I believe I had little to do with the acquisition of Bates in my employ, I cannot find much at which to cavil. Might I congratulate you on a very fine shot?"

"Shot, Rufus?" She was uncertain how to take his remark.

"Yes, by moonlight, too. Very neat, Jennifer. I could be proud of you." His smile was mocking.

She rubbed a finger on the table. "Does—does Guardie know?" her voice was small.

"Who came to his rescue? Somebody on a large, black horse, I believe he said. Dressed in black, too. Probably up to no good, were his words, as I recall. Apt, I thought."

Jennifer's lip curved. "Well, it wasn't anything, Rufus. And I couldn't tell him, truly I couldn't."

"No, of course you couldn't," agreed His Lordship. "I quite agree with you. It would be far too great a shock."

Jennifer regarded him fixedly. "Rufus, you're not going to do anything drastic, are you?"

"Drastic, Jenny? It depends what you mean by drastic. I

don't believe so. But I'll be here. If you need some support for any of your activities, I trust you won't hesitate to call on me."

She looked at him for a long minute, then she said abruptly, "You're a good sport, Rufus. Thank you." She held out her hand, boy-fashion, and Rufus, with becoming gravity, got to his feet and shook it solemnly.

"My dear Jonathan," he drawled, "pray don't mention it, I beg of you."

Chapter Fourteen

The arrival of Miss Matilda Markham at Government House most assuredly stirred up social life to a gratifying degree. Less than a week after she had unpacked her bags, Lord and Lady Bradbury gave a Grand Ball, actually in her honor although officially merely a summer function. To this were invited all the officers of the garrison, as well as the social cream of the civilian population. Two bands were engaged to play for the evening, those of the Rifle Brigade and the 5th Foot spelling each other at intervals, and the attendant preparations had been on a high level.

The great ballroom of Government House was packed to suffocation on the night. All the public rooms on the ground floor were thrown open for the revelers, and candles gleamed brightly. Carriages drew up in front of the door in a steady stream. The ladies were ushered up the great curving staircase to a retiring room abovestairs to remove their wraps, and they swept down in all the glory of their ballgowns.

Lord and Lady Bradbury, with their daughters and Miss Matilda, received at the entrance to the ballroom, where their guest was introduced to each newcomer.

Miss Matilda, gowned in blue the color of her eyes, was well worth being introduced to, and, although Miss Alice and Miss Marjorie beside her were equally gorgeous in pink and pale green respectively, they lacked that entrancing glow which Matilda had in such abundance. Matilda's eyes were bright, her cheeks were becomingly flushed, her smile was gay and her laughter was near the surface. She could not be considered forward, but she made every young man believe that she was indeed glad to meet him personally. To do Matilda justice, she made the ladies feel the same way, a rare feat.

The dancing began, and the young ladies did not lack for partners. Even Lady Jennifer, sitting demurely in a corner, was besieged on all sides, but she rejected all requests with a gentle smile and a delicate sigh, which the well-mannered swains accepted with decorum.

All except her brother, Lord Welland, who came up to her when a waltz was announced, and said cheerfully, "Come along, Jenny, dance with me."

Lady Jennifer snapped her fan and her eyes, "No thank you, Jonathan," she said coldly.

"Come on, Jenny," her brother coaxed. He leaned over her. "Remember Taffy's Dancing School—one, two, three...remember? Come on, Jenny. For old times' sake."

Jennifer was in a gay mood that evening. Resplendent in the dress uniform of the Rifles—which could not compare in brilliance, of course, with the scarlet of the 5th Foot—she was a handsome and dashing figure, and her green eyes were alight with a vigor which was catching. "Come on, Jenny," she coaxed again, and Jonathan, looking up into those bright eyes, capitulated. He took his sister's hand and got to his feet gracefully.

"You'll see," he murmured, but it was strictly *sotto* voice and for Jennifer's ear alone.

She laughed aloud as she led her brother onto the floor and those around smiled in sympathy, for there was some-

thing very alive about the slight red-haired officer that evening, something bright and flashing and contagious.

The band struck up the waltz, and Jennifer bowed low to
her brother who curtsied in response and placed his hands
on his sister's arms. They were off then, swirling and dipping
in the rhythm of the waltz, and the abandon of the music
swept about Jonathan, too, so that he tossed his head and
met his sister's eyes and laughed with her, and swept and
dipped and swung lightly and expertly.

For there was a bond between these two far stronger than
the usual brother and sister attachment. Weak-willed and
somewhat effeminate though Jonathan might be, determined, strong-minded and tomboyish as Jennifer undoubtedly was, they shared a common gift of laughter and an
understanding of the other denied to ordinary brothers and
sisters. Some twins are like that, and these two were uncom-
monly close.

Watching them, Lord Randall, an honored guest, had a
sense of their oneness and his mouth was surprisingly half
a-smile. He was standing beside Lady Bradbury as they
swept past him, their faces as light as their steps, and Lady
Bradbury said quietly, "They're nice children, and very much
alike."

"Yes," Lord Randall agreed, "they are." And his voice held
a tinge of gentleness which would have surprised Jennifer
had she heard.

Lady Bradbury shot him a quick glance. "You've known
them a long time, I think, Lord Randall?" It was a question
and Lord Randall nodded.

"They were eight when their parents died," he answered.
"The Duke was appointed their guardian and he brought
them to Six Chimneys. She was always an independent child.
They both were," he added, though not too hastily, for he was
conscious of his slip.

Fortunately the music had covered it and Lady Bradbury
only nodded.

"He takes very good care of his sister," she said. "He was
very upset about her when he called on us immediately after
his arrival. Poor child, she's very delicate, isn't she?"

Lord Randall's lips twitched. Delicate was hardly the word

that he would have applied to Lady Jennifer, but under the circumstances he agreed that indeed Lady Jennifer was a delicate child. It was unfortunate but there it was, and, as Lady Bradbury had said, her brother took very good care of her.

"Quite touching," nodded Her Ladyship, and added in sudden anxiety, "Has that poor child now tried too much?"

For Lord Welland was escorting his sister from the dance floor solicitously, an arm about her shoulders.

"Forgive me, Lady Bradbury," Rufus said quickly, "I'll see if I can be of assistance." He bowed and slipped away on the words, threading his way with such ease through the dancers that his haste was not apparent. He came upon them in the anteroom leading to the ballroom. Jonathan was on a chair in the corner, and Jennifer was bending over him as Rufus came up behind them.

"Is there anything wrong?" he queried rapidly. Jennifer jumped.

"My lord, Rufus, you startled me," she said. Laughter which was very near the surface broke through.

Rufus advanced. "What on earth happened?" he asked, for Jonathan was hunched over in the chair.

Jennifer stifled a giggle. "Lady Jennifer has suffered a slight catastrophe," she said with great gravity, and Rufus looked past her to Jonathan. He saw what was happening and his face relaxed. "Shall we call it a slight heart affliction?" he murmured, for Jonathan was struggling desperately to replace his left bosom in the proper position; the vigorous measures of the dance had shaken it loose from its fastenings.

Jennifer was convulsed. Her shoulders were shaking, while none of Jonathan's muttered comments were conducive to solemnity.

There was an empty glass on the mantel beside him and Rufus picked it up. "In case someone else appears," he murmured, and just in time, for Lady Bradbury came down upon them anxiously.

"Jennifer, my dear, are you all right?" she asked, her kindly face worried. She found nothing more amiss than she expected. Lady Jennifer was relaxed in a chair sipping at a glass while, in properly sympathetic attitude, Lord Welland and Lord Randall hovered near her.

"I fear the exertion was too much for my poor sister," the captain murmured, and his voice shook ever so slightly. "My sister felt unsteady. I should not have urged her to dance."

"My dear child, are you feeling better now?" Lady Bradbury bent over the reclining Lady Jennifer.

"Yes, indeed, thank you, Lady Bradbury," Lady Jennifer sat up and kept her face down. "Merely a slight fluttering of the heart. It was my own fault, I should have known better. I shall be quite all right. Pray do not concern yourself about me."

"My dear child, you must lie down at once," Lady Bradbury insisted. "I shall call the doctor tomorrow."

"Oh no, truly, I am quite recovered," Lady Jennifer said hastily. "It is nothing."

Lady Bradbury hovered uncertainly. "Have you had such attacks before?" she queried, and Lady Jennifer assured her that she had.

"We did feel that perhaps the climate might be better for my sister here," her brother commented with concern.

"And indeed I think it has been," Lady Bradbury said. "This is the first attack that your sister has had since she came here. My dear, you must rest now. This has been too much excitement for you."

Lord Welland helped his sister tenderly to her feet. "I'll escort her up to her room, Lady Bradbury," he said, and tucked her arm through his and led her from the room.

Lady Bradbury watched them leave. "What nice children they are, to be sure," she said admiringly. "He takes such good care of his sister. I can understand his anxiety now."

"Yes, she is indeed delicate," Lord Randall said, and if there was a hint of irony in his voice Lady Bradbury didn't hear it.

"I wonder if I should send for Doctor Scott tomorrow?"

"I am inclined to agree with Welland, I feel it is not necessary," Lord Rufus said gravely. "Her nurse-companion will know what to do for her. I should not distress myself unduly, Lady Bradbury. I'm sure she will be quite recovered by morning."

"Well, I hope so," Lady Bradbury said doubtfully. "I shall see to it that the dear child has more rest." She turned to go back to the ballroom, and Lord Randall offered her his arm at once. "I am glad you have come over," she told him. "I am confident that it must be a great relief to Lord Welland to have such an old friend of the family close at hand, should your services be required."

Lord Randall's deep bow was indicative of his reply as he escorted her with great formality back to the ballroom.

Upstairs in the spacious, handsomely furnished bedroom shared by Jonathan and Katie, Jennifer locked the door behind her and threw herself on the reclining chair and no longer tried to control her laughter.

"It's all very well for you," Jonathan hissed, "but it's not as funny as all that. Jennifer...will you stop? Jennifer, shut up! Somebody will hear you."

His protests were to no avail. Jennifer laughed harder than ever, and tears were running down her cheeks as she rolled on the chair in a spasm of mirth. "Oh, Jonnie," she got out, "oh, Jonnie!"

"Yes...well..." Jonathan began, then "Jennifer...oh, Jenny!" his own lips twitched, and while his laughter was not as uncontrolled as his sister's, still it was genuine.

"Rufus and his 'slight heart condition,'" and Jennifer was off again. "Jonathan, I don't know what we'd have done if he hadn't come along. Good old Rufus, I didn't know he had it in him."

"Good old Rufus, my eye," Jonathan said inelegantly. "How long is he going to let us get away with this?"

Jennifer sobered slightly. "You don't have to worry about Rufus. He won't do anything."

"Well, it's about time something was done," Jonathan said grumpily. He got off the edge of the bed and paced about the room. His skirts were beginning to irritate him. "I'm getting tired of this game."

"What, tired of being petted and fondled and cared for?" his sister twitted. "Jonathan, I thought *that* day would never come."

But her brother was serious. "It wasn't so bad with Marjorie and Alice," he said irritably, "but now that Matilda has arrived, well...it's different."

"How is it different?" demanded his sister.

"I don't know, it's just different," her brother said lamely. "She tells me I shouldn't think so much about myself, for one thing, and she's always trying to get me to do something different. I don't know why she doesn't expend her energies on Marjorie and Alice and leave me alone." Acid as his words were, the expression on his face didn't quite match them. Jennifer regarded him with sudden interest.

"Not getting too fond of Matilda, are you, Jonnie?" she queried.

"Of course not," her brother returned hastily, but he averted his face from her scrutiny.

"Jonnie, you be careful!" Jennifer said with sudden gravity.

"Of course I'm being careful, what do you think I'm doing?" Jonathan demanded angrily. "But this is a devilish position, Jennifer, yes, it is. There's no use your laughing about it. It's not funny now."

Jennifer's eyes were serious. "No, Jonathan, I can see it isn't," she said slowly. "I'll have to think of some way to get you out of it."

"Well, think fast," her brother said ungraciously.

"Yes...yes, I will," his sister said thoughtfully.

Meanwhile in the ballroom the young gentlemen were vying with each other for the favors of Miss Matilda, and various plans were being put forward for her subsequent amusement.

"How do you occupy your free time?" Miss Matilda had asked, and the answers were varied. There was riding and boating, and of course horse-races, and the regatta, and hunting, and picnics.

"I say," suggested young Captain Hartford of the 5th, "how about some amateur theatricals? We could run over those plays we put on last winter, and if Miss Markham would be interested, perhaps she could play one of the ladies' parts. Privately, of course," he added hastily, for no true lady appeared on the stage in public. "Just for our friends. Miss Alice and Miss Marjorie could take part as well, and perhaps they would agree to a display of dancing in the *entr'acte*. We could ask Monsieur Lecompte to instruct for the dance."

His suggestion met with much approval, first by Miss Matilda, who received it gaily, and then by the young officers who had watched her anxiously to see what her reaction would be.

"And we could rehearse right here," Miss Matilda said. "I'll ask my uncle at once." She jumped to her feet and went directly across to her uncle, who, resplendent in all his badges of office, was talking to some high civic officials on very weighty matters when his niece interrupted him without apology.

"Uncle John," she smiled coaxingly at him. "These gentlemen have suggested such a pleasant thing, amateur theatricals—and Alice and Marjorie and I could take part. Now, couldn't we rehearse right here in the ballroom, just, of course, for our friends? Don't you think that would be fun? And they have suggested that a Monsieur Lecompte instruct us in a dance for the *entr'acte*—and, Uncle John, think how much pleasure it would be."

Lord Bradbury smiled indulgently at his vivacious niece. "I'm sure that it could be arranged to the satisfaction of all," he agreed. "Certainly, you may rehearse here. We could have a stage put up at one end—it won't be very large, of course, but go right ahead, my dear, go right ahead." He beamed at Colonial Thompson, C.O. of the Rifles, whose officers were very much in evidence that night. "A bit of innocent fun, eh, Colonel?"

The colonel agreed hastily. Amateur theatricals were usually indulged in during the long winter months when the troops were, of necessity, indoors much of the time, and were forced to find various amusements of their own making. But amateur theatricals in the summer was a different matter. However, when no less a person than the Lieutenant-Governor condoned it, there was little that a mere O.C. Rifles could say.

Jennifer, returning to the ballroom, was drawn into the ensuing discussion, and although she protested that she knew nothing of stagecraft, the following day found her solemnly proclaiming the words of Samuel Snozzle in the farce *To Paris and Back for Five Pounds* which, preceded by *The Captain of The Watch* and followed by *Used-Up* had composed the program of one of the winter's entertainments. For this event, however, *Used-Up* was being omitted, and *The Captain of The Watch* was being followed by a display of dancing by the Misses Alice and Marjorie Bradbury and Miss Matilda Markham, partnered by Captain Hartford of the 5th and Captains Dixon and Welland of the Rifles, the whole coached by Monsieur Lecompte.

In the middle of the ensuing days of rehearsal, the Rifles Brigade received orders to prepare to vacate the quarters which they occupied and move to the Citadel. The 5th, then in garrison at the Fort, were to occupy the quarters vacated by the Rifles.

Loud were the lamentations of the officers of the Rifles as their servants packed up their belongings, for life in the hotel was gay and unrestricted, and women and wine played a large part in their pleasure. Wine would still be present at the Citadel, but women were strictly prohibited under penalty of court-martial. Such was indeed a blow to the gay Rifles, although under the present circumstances not quite such a one as it would have been during the winter. Naturally, the officers of the 5th were equally loud in their glee, and on the appointed day the two regiments lined up and marched off in companies to exchange quarters, the Rifles opening their ranks as the 5th met them, to allow the senior regiment to pass through with military punctilio.

The transfer was observed by most of the Halifax citizens, who lined the streets to watch the regiments pass in formal parade, each Company preceded by its officers, and with the bands blaring gaily.

From the window of his hotel, Lord Randall watched the green-uniformed Rifles march past, and his gaze followed the straight, erect back of the captain of "B" Company as he rode his horse ahead of his men, and there was an expression on Lord Randall's face which would have been difficult for an onlooker to read.

Chapter Fifteen

The Rifles settled down very comfortably in their new quarters. Most of the casemates were finished and ready for occupation, although the Citadel was not yet entirely complete. The work had, after all, been going on for upwards of twenty years and would proceed, from all appearances, for another five or ten. The men were quartered in the Cavalier Barracks which stood in the northwest section of the parade ground, its parapeted roof bristling with guns. The officers' quarters were in the casemates in the redan, that point jutting out at the east front of the fort overlooking the barrack blocks. Just beyond the redan was the main gate, its drawbridge duly hauled up each night.

However, this was not as much of a drawback to a determined officer as might be imagined. Their casemates had windows opening into the dry moat, and although the windows were of course barred, bars have been known to be removable before now. Further, for the truly adventuresome, there was a large brick-lined conduit leading from the foot of the dry moat down under the glacis and connecting up with one of the main sewers of the town at the top of Buckingham Street on Brunswick Street, and by means of one of the six sallyports which led from the parade ground down to the dry moat and thence by lifting the perforated cover, at the head of this conduit, it was possible to pass through the brick-lined passage by stooping almost double and to emerge on Brunswick Street, again by the simple process of lifting a cover.

Of course, such a manner of egress was not intended for regular use, nor was it one which appealed to the majority of the officers, as the conduit had been built to conduct the sewage of the Citadel down to the city's system and across the town to the harbor, but still in times of emergency, if there was a particularly irate colonel pacing the ground, it could be used and had been known to have been so employed. All this was garrison knowledge, which led the thoughtful to wonder just how useful such an avenue of escape would be if the colonel knew about it from the beginning.

However, colonels are supposed to be notoriously blind, which is why they become colonels, and it is certain that the conduit featured at various times in the tales of various officers, and most certainly the exact whereabouts of the conduit was known to every man in garrison.

Much to Jennifer's relief, the officers were again quartered in private rooms, and their servants were allotted space in some of the adjoining casemates. Assuredly, they were not as comfortable as the chambers of the Halifax Hotel, but each casemate had its own fireplace for warmth, and was moderately dry and free from damp. With George as guardian Jennifer accepted her new surroundings with equanimity. Bates had developed into an excellent servant. She had followed Digby's youthful advice and secured the services of a local inhabitant for groom. She had wondered if Bates would be permitted in the fort as her servant, but no questions were raised, and Bates performed his duties as expertly as if they were still at the hotel. Her shirts were always smooth, her trousers pressed, her boots shining in their blackness, her quarters immaculate. Bates was something of a jewel.

It was, by and large, a very busy time for the officers of the two regiments, and most especially for those taking part in the amateur theatricals. Regulations for a new order of drill had been received by the Officers Commanding, and long hours were spent on the parade grounds instructing the men in the various maneuvers. This was work that Jennifer thoroughly enjoyed, and, with the able assistance of the sergeant, and the dutiful, if unappreciative, help of Mr. Digby, her senior subaltern, she drilled the men steadily, alternately praising and condemning them in language which they could easily understand. Jennifer's vocabulary had been peculiar for a female, to say the least, when she came to Halifax, and it had acquired even greater force in the course of her service with the Rifles.

Lord Randall, joining the ever present group of onlookers who had nothing better to do than watch the "sojurs" drilling, regarded her closely one day as the men paraded under her vigilant eye. He noted approvingly that their drill was smart and the men moved as one, and he waited until the troops were marched back to quarters. Jennifer saw him, and ordering Digby to dismiss the men, she walked over to him. She was looking tired, Randall thought. There were lines about her mouth and her eyes were heavy, but she smiled as she came up to him.

"Hello, Rufus, nice horse you've got there."

It was a greeting typical from Jennifer. Lord Randall nodded. He dismounted and stood with the reins over his arm.

"I bought her yesterday," he said. "Not bad."

Jennifer was walking about the horse. "Should be a good jumper," she commented. "Is she up to your weight, Rufus?"

"If you are hinting that you would like to acquire her, it won't do," he said. "She's not for you."

Jennifer's eyes glinted. "No?"

Rufus shook his head, "No."

Jennifer laughed. "Don't be so sure, Rufus," she said lightly, and he fell in beside her as she turned back towards the Fort, the horse walking at his heels.

"Lord, it's hot today," she added with a sigh, taking off her shako and rubbing her forehead with her handkerchief. "What do you think of our new drill?"

"Is that what it is?" Lord Randall said. "I thought the men had lost their way."

She grinned faintly. "Maneuvers are pretty stupid without a visible enemy," she agreed, "but the men are coming up nicely. We're to be reviewed next week by Lord Bradbury—full-dress affair. Bands and everything."

"Should be entertaining," Lord Randall said politely. "I'll have to try to be present."

Jennifer grinned. "You do that," she said cheerfully and stretched. "Lord, am I tired! I hope Bates has my bath ready. I have to see Monsieur Lecompte at four-thirty."

"Monsieur Lecompte?" Lord Randall murmured.

"He's instructing the dancing at Government House," Jennifer answered briefly, and did not appear inclined to discuss it further. Instead she asked, "How long do you intend to stay, Rufus?"

"I haven't decided," His Lordship said calmly.

"I should think you'd be bored stiff by now" Jennifer said frankly.

Rufus shrugged. "You underestimate the attraction of this town, my dear Jonathan," he said.

"I fancy it amuses you to watch us make fools of ourselves," Jennifer retorted shortly.

"Why, no, Jenny," Lord Randall said gently. "It doesn't, not in the slightest."

"Then why are you staying?" she snapped. She stopped short and faced him, and perforce he stopped, too.

"Because I want to," he answered calmly enough.

"I wish to blazes you weren't here," she said angrily. "Every time I turn around you're watching. I've never known you to stay in one place so long before."

Rufus's face was unreadable. "I shall try not to be in such evidence if my presence annoys you," he drawled.

"Oh, go to the devil!" Jennifer snapped, turning on her heel. She marched off with rapid strides.

Lord Randall looked after her thoughtfully, and if any emotion were visible on his face it was certainly not anger. Undoubtedly Jennifer, admittedly not always the most even-tempered of mortals, was displaying irritation. Now why?

Lord Randall remounted and cantered thoughtfully back to the stable.

Jennifer knew herself to have been unpardonably rude to Rufus, and the knowledge did not help to smooth her temper. She was in an odd humor these days. Nothing seemed to go right. She was in the blackest of moods one moment, and the height of elation the next. The men had felt the sharp edge of her tongue. She had snapped at Digby with quite unusual, although not unnecessary, vigor. Even Bates had come under her displeasure.

Now, as she wallowed pleasurably in the bath which Bates had indeed left prepared for her, her thoughts jumped from Rufus to Jonathan to Matilda, to the Government House, to the entertainment, and by this roundabout and insidious manner, to Monsieur Lecompte, the French emigré who to keep body and soul together gave dancing lessons. Her body suddenly felt on fire, as if the bath were a caldron and the blaze under it had been fanned to white heat. Even her ears flamed, yet the next moment she was shivering as with ague. All these strange sensations did not make sense. She could not, even to herself, account for the way she felt.

Nobody really knew who Lecompte was. He was a delicate, dapper, little Frenchman, dressing in finicking taste, with long white hands and a long white face, speaking with a suggestion of lisp. How he had arrived at Halifax was also unknown, but it was rumored that he had fled an abortive insurrection in Haiti, or one of the other French colonies to the south. He spoke mournfully of better days, and of his family, without going into further details, and hinted that he had once been the possessor of great wealth, but alas, it was gone, all gone. His manners were of the most meticulous. His French was fluent, his English graceful, his public behavior above reproach.

Still there were little rumors about that Lecompte's private behavior was perhaps not all it should be. Nobody quite dared to put such rumors into words, but mothers who employed Monsieur Lecompte's talents to instruct their daughters in the niceties of country dances and the waltz, and also in the art of the pianoforte, saw to it that those same daughters were never left alone with the elegant Monsieur Lecompte.

Though oddly enough, there were never any whispers as to the identity of any inamorata. The names of no ladies of either high or low station were ever connected with his, nor could even the most suspicious parent learn that any young lady had ever been seen at his lodgings night or day, unaccompanied, that is, by a chaperone, for Lecompte gave instruction at his rooms as well as in the homes of his wealthier patrons. Certainly he entertained, but young gentlemen mostly, collectively and individually. But, after all, there was nothing wrong in that, was there?

Yet curiously enough, rumors of some irregularity in the small Frenchman's life persisted.

Jennifer had heard all the current speculative gossip about the dancing master, for Digby gleaned scandal and retold on-dits with a relish. Having such a mysterious past paraded in her ears she had regarded the Frenchman with interested curiosity, not untinged with distaste. He appeared such a wisp of a man, a mere caricature of one, almost unreal, as if he could be blown away on a breath of wind. His voice, too, was thin and reedy on first hearing. However, as she became more accustomed to his affectations of speech, she caught a strange beauty in it. Not something you could put in words, it was rather a haunting thing, other-worldly in a queer way. Sometimes it even made her shiver without reason, for there were no drafts in the great ballroom where they were practicing.

"Now, gentlemen," Monsieur Lecompte was saying, "if you will just place your right foot so—and your hands so—and follow me—so—the music, please, Mrs. Connell," he addressed Miss Matilda's Cousin Maria who was obliging at the piano, as he placed his hands in Jennifer's the better to instruct her in the measures.

Something happened when his hands touched hers, something unaccountable. A hot flush swept through Jennifer, she felt light-headed, unsteady, and leaden-footed. Monsieur Lecompte pressed her fingers gently, encouragingly, and smiled up at her from under his heavy eyelids.

"Come, *mon capitaine*," he smiled. "The music, it is commencing."

Suddenly awkward and ungainly, Jennifer tripped over her feet, stumbled against the little Frenchman. "I beg your pardon, monsieur," she was covered with confusion. "I am so clumsy."

"Not at all, *mon capitaine*," the little Frenchman said politely. "Come, we will try again." His heavy lids raised momentarily as he smiled at her, and Jennifer flushed again at the strange beauty of the liquid brown pools so startlingly revealed, for he had beautiful eyes, deep, dark, and mysterious.

The girl remembered little about the rest of that first rehearsal. She exerted herself apparently to some effort, for the instruction proceeded. Lecompte professed himself as well pleased with the result.

Jennifer returned to the Fort that night with her mind in a whirl. She dreamed restlessly of warm hands, and a thin fluting voice, and deep eyes that were like pools, and she wakened drenched with sweat and trembling in the darkness. There was a feeling of danger which she did not understand and was oddly reluctant to think about.

She could hardly wait for the next rehearsal, and yet she dreaded it. The drill next morning was never ending, the play rehearsal was chaotic, but the dance rehearsal—she felt a wild ecstasy as she turned in at Government House. An ecstasy compounded of fear and excitement, and something that she could not, to her growing irritation, recognize. Common sense told her to turn and go back to the Fort, to make some excuse, yet something drove her on.

So it was no wonder that as the days went by her temper shortened. Lecompte himself appeared quite unaware of the emotion he was stirring up in her. His touch on her arm was gentle, oddly caressing, and yet not unduly so. Only occasionally, very occasionally, did he open to their full extent those heavy-lidded eyes. Yet, when he did, Jennifer went hot and cold by turns.

She fought with herself in the hours of the night, turning and twisting in bed, falling asleep at length from sheer exhaustion, getting up in the morning, heavy-eyed and un-rested. It was no wonder that she had snapped at Rufus.

The full-dress Review of the Troop came off the following week as planned, under a cloudless sky, and with the Lieu-tenant-Governor and his lady, his family, and his suite on the reviewing stand. All of Halifax turned out, too, to watch. The commons was bright with red and green uniforms and flashing gold braid, and swords and guns which glistened in the sun, and horses whose coats shone from repeated currying and whose saddles and bridles glowed with the results of saddlesoap and elbow grease.

It was a brilliant display, the men performed with disci-plined excellence, and the entire maneuver went off without a hitch. Still, Captain Lord Welland, sitting his horse easily and erectly, was conscious only of an overwhelming weari-ness and a desire to get this over and done with.

At length it *was* over, the troops marched back to barracks and dismissed, with the cheering news that a further issue of spirits had been allowed and would be served in the mess.

Jennifer dismounted stiffly and handed her horse over to her groom. She had returned with her company to the Citadel and now she walked slowly across the parade ground to her quarters, returning salutes automatically. There was a re-ception scheduled in the officers' mess at the hotel, which she had to attend, but she had little desire for it. Her head was splitting and the idea of mingling with a noisy crowd was almost more than she could endure.

George greeted her vociferously as she entered her room and she patted him absently, closing the door behind her and letting the heavy bar fall into place. She hung her shako on the hook, tossed her jacket and gloves on the nearby chair before throwing herself on the bed, her arm across her eyes, in an effort to shut out the noise in the parade ground. Jen-nifer was bone-weary, with an exhaustion which was not only physical but mental, and she was conscious of only one de-sire—to be alone and to be quiet.

George flopped down on the flagstone beside her bed, and the noise outside gradually receded. She dozed a little then, and wakened to a firm knocking. George was on his feet, shackles up, alertly facing the door.

Jennifer sat up groggily. "Who's there?" she called.

"Dixon," returned a familiar voice. "Aren't you coming down to the mess, Welland?"

"In a minute," she returned, and sat on the edge of the bed, her head in her hands until the room stopped whirling. She got to her feet and struggled into her uniform jacket before crossing to the door to swing the bar up.

"Hurry along," Dixon urged, lounging in. "We're all waiting for you—that was a capital show today."

She turned from him and brushed her hair quickly, then set her shako on at its proper angle and picked up her gloves. "Sorry to keep you waiting," she said soberly.

Dixon peered at her. "What's the matter—touch of sun?"

She shrugged. "Probably. I've a rotten headache."

"A drink will do you good," Dixon counseled.

The harsh sun on the parade ground slashed across her eyes, and she squinted sharply to lessen the impact. Her head had started thumping again, and she replied to Dixon's chatter in monosyllables and with a conscious effort.

The mess was as crowded and hot as she had thought it would be, and the noise and stuffiness crashed in her aching head. She drew a deep breath and, summoning all her will power, mustered a smile on her face and a light reply to the numerous loud and hearty compliments shouted to her. The Rifles were proud of Captain Lord Welland that day. His company had been so well drilled and maneuvered so flawlessly that the entire Brigade basked in its reflected glory.

A glass was thrust into her hands and she took a long swallow of the contents without thinking. Whisky burned down her throat and the room was suddenly blotted out by a wave of dizziness. She closed her eyes to steady herself, and felt the glass taken from her grasp. A hand on her elbow steadied her and a quiet voice in her ear murmured, "All right, Jonathan, take it easy."

It was Rufus, and for a moment relief overwhelmed her. Then she had pulled herself together, opened her eyes and said, with as even a voice as she could manage, "Hello, Rufus. What are you doing here?"

"What the rest of us are doing—celebrating a famous victory." Dixon was mellow. "Gentlemen, I give you a toast—to the Rifles, the best brigade in the whole of His Majesty's army!"

"And to "B" Company, the best company in the best brigade!" That was little Digby, far mellower than Dixon. Digby had not been letting any grass grow under his glass. The toast was duly drunk.

"To Welland," Dixon bowed solemnly, even owlishly, and flourished his glass in Jennifer's general direction.

"To Welland!" It was a popular toast, but there was one officer who did not honor it. At the bar, Captain Thurston crashed his glass to the counter and swayed to his feet, his face convulsed.

"Gentlemen!" he roared, but Rufus had been watching him.

"Gentlemen, the drinks are on me," he said clearly, and the cheer which followed successfully deadened Thurston's oration.

Under cover of the confusion, Jennifer sank onto the nearest chair, and Rufus glanced at her quickly. Her color was bad, he noted; even her lips were white, and her eyes were glassy. Her hand pawed at her collar, as if it were suddenly too tight, then she pressed her temples instead.

"Here, have a drink." Hastily, Rufus clasped her unresisting fingers around a glass. "Drink it, Jonathan, at once."

"No, no, Rufus," her voice was faint but determined.

"Don't you know Lord Welland doesn't like to drink?" Captain Thurston was alongside now, his heavy, florid face twisted in a sneer. "A toast to Lord Welland—in water." He raised his glass high, then with a quick, insulting action, dashed the contents in Jennifer's face and crashed the glass on the floor.

It was so sudden, so unexpected, that only a few officers saw exactly what had happened, but all of them heard Dixon's angry roar and a shuddering crash, as Thurston staggered backwards against tables and chairs, impelled by a swift, vicious blow by Dixon, backed by the whole of that officer's powerful frame.

"I'll, I'll—" Thurston was frothing in his rage.

"You're drunk," Dixon was scathing. "If you weren't, I'd smash you within an inch of your life." He turned to Jennifer, standing white-faced and dripping, slowly mopping the water from her face. "Welland, I shall see to it that Thurston apologizes when he's sober, you have my word on it."

"It's not necessary," Jennifer began, and swayed. The heat, the confusion, the sudden tension—her head was thundering and the room was a whirling diorama.

Rufus was beside her instantly, his hands sliding her into a chair again, his fingers at her collar, easing the tightness.

"Undo his jacket," Dixon urged, forgetting Thurston in his anxiety over Welland.

Rufus shook his head. "I'll get him back to the Fort," he said briefly. "Too hot here, I expect. He'll be better in the air."

"Pushed himself too far," an officer vouchsafed. "Doesn't pay—'tisn't worth it. Understand he had his men out drilling before the rest of 'em were up. Game chap."

Jennifer was steadier now. She got to her feet on Rufus's suggestion, and fastened her collar with fumbling fingers, at the same time attempting an apologetic smile at the hovering officers. "Damned sissy," she murmured, but Dixon would have none of that.

"I'd better go with you," he suggested, and came to the door with them, but Rufus shook his head.

"I can look after Welland," he smiled. "You stay here. Steward, another round, if you please." The steward, fingering the crisp note passed to him, smiled and nodded and hurried back to the bar.

Outside of the old hotel, Jennifer drew a deep breath and resolutely held herself erect. "I'm all right now, Rufus," she said gallantly. "Don't bother about me—I can get back to the Fort myself."

"I'll go with you," Rufus said briefly, with a firmness which brooked no argument.

Jennifer hesitated, then she shrugged and gave a little laugh which broke in the middle. "Yes, you said you'd be around if I needed any support, didn't you, Rufus?"

"I confess I did not think you would be quite so quick to take me at my word," he answered with mock solemnity.

He accompanied her to the Fort, and followed her into her casemate, accepting George's riotous greeting with a calm,

"Down, you monster." Then stood, looking about him casually. "Not bad quarters," he said.

Jennifer dropped the bar into place across the door then drew off her gloves and shako, before unbuttoning her jacket and throwing herself on the bed.

"Lord, my head's splitting," she muttered.

Lord Randall was wandering about the room. He came to a stop by the barred window opening onto the moat, turned, and said quietly, "Jennifer, you've got to get out of this."

"Yes, I know, Rufus, but let's not discuss that today," Jennifer pleaded. She pressed her hand against her temples. "If my head would only stop this thumping."

Rufus strolled back to the bed and looked down at her. "Is it very bad?" he enquired.

Jennifer moved her head on the pillow, then wished she had not. "Yes," she said honestly. "It is."

Uninvited, Lord Rufus took her uniform coat from the chair where she had tossed it, hung it on the nearest hook, then placed the chair behind the head of the bed. He settled onto it comfortably, and leaning over Jennifer began with slow even strokes to rub her forehead.

Her eyes opened in surprise. "What are you doing?"

"Shut your eyes and relax," His Lordship said briefly. "No, be quiet, Jenny, don't talk."

He sat there rubbing her forehead with slow even strokes until, under the steady pressure of his fingers, Jennifer relaxed and slept, her chest rising and falling smoothly. He continued massaging her temples for several minutes and then, certain that she was asleep, he arose noiselessly, picked up the chair and carried it over to the window and settled himself on it as comfortably as he could, until Jennifer should awaken again. George came and put his head on his knee, and Rufus patted him until George was satisfied and went to sleep, too.

Chapter Sixteen

Three nights later the grand theatrical entertainment went off with éclat, success, satisfaction, cheer and a great deal of laughter. The ballroom at Government House was packed with a very select invited audience, and the curtains on the improvised stage at the Pleasant Street end of the ballroom where the great round bay formed a natural setting, parted jerkily, despite the best endeavors of the master technician, a captain from the artillery, before the highly laughable farce *The Captain of The Watch* was performed with, as all were agreed, spirit. The entr'acte of period dances, arranged and directed by the well known Monsieur Lecompte, and executed with skill and artistry by the Misses Alice and Marjorie Bradbury and Miss Matilda Markham, partnered by Captian Hartford, Captain Dixon and Captain Lord Welland, was received with hearty applause. The final play, *To Paris and Back for Five Pounds* went off with admirable smoothness, and the curtain closed on a gale of laughter and much loud applause. Everyone agreed that it had indeed been a most admirable performance.

All the action had not taken place in front of the audience—much of it had gone on backstage. The last two days had been particularly hectic, because Miss Alice had developed a sore throat which threatened to keep her out of the cast completely, and Captain Hartford, already tearing his directorial hair, rounded on Captain Welland with instructions to learn Miss Alice's part in order to step into it if necessary.

"Nothing doing," retorted an unsympathetic Welland. "I'm already in the entr'acte and the *Paris* bit. No mortal man can get out of woman's rig into a uniform and out again into civilian attire and do a creditable job. Get someone else."

"But Welland," almost pleaded the director, "you can't imagine Dixon being 'Kathryn,' now can you?"

As Captain Dixon was six feet tall and built accordingly, Welland had to admit that it seemed a little incredible. "Try Digby," he suggested heartlessly.

"Digby can't remember two lines to save his neck," Hartford said despairingly. "Please, Welland, for my sake. For the sake of the cast—for everybody's sake."

Lord Welland capitulated, but with misgivings. However, Miss Alice recovered promptly, particularly when she discovered that the play was going to go on without her, and Welland relinquished his threatened role in *The Captain of The Watch* without noticeable regret.

'The Captain' in the first play skipped two lines, jumped back one, and missed his cue three times. 'Christina' played by Miss Marjorie, developed stage fright, and the play had to work around her until she got her voice back. Other than that it went off fairly well, except that the 'Officer' of the watch tripped over the prompter's stool coming onstage and very nearly precipitated his length at his 'Captain's' feet.

To Paris and Back for Five Pounds went off more smoothly. 'Sally Spriggins,' in the person of Miss Matilda, was pert and pretty, and if she was upstage when she should have been downstage, nobody, certainly not the select guests, was going to quibble about such a small error. She received a hearty ovation and curtsied prettily. 'Samuel Snozzle' declaimed with proper oratorial efforts, 'The Superintendent' was properly gruff, 'Lieutenant Spike' put in his small bit, and the whole went off with sprightly gaiety.

The entr'acte had been particularly well-received, for under the direction of Monsieur Lecompte the six performers had indeed achieved an excellence which imparted grace and charm to their dances.

When it was all over and the cast came out to receive the well-merited compliments of the audience, guests and players alike pressed through into the receiving rooms and the drawing room and dining room in the opposite wing from the ballroom, where servants hurried about offering refreshments and stimulants for the weary parties.

The evening's gaiety came to an end, and the last guest had shaken hands with Lord and Lady Bradbury at the door and been assisted into their carriages by the stately servants, while the cast were left to pack up their belongings, and take their assorted departures, leaving the Government House servants to clear up the mess and dismantle the stage.

Suddenly bone-weary, Jennifer slipped out alone. She had said good night to her host and hostess, declined the invitation of the other members of the cast to continue the evening at Mother Clark's, and now she walked quickly through the tree-shadowed streets toward the Citadel. She found she was wishing quite honestly that Lord Randall was with her. Since the night he had come back with her to the Fort after the review and had stroked away her headache, stayed there with her until she wakened in order that she would not be left with her door unbarred, she had felt differently about Rufus—about a lot of things, to be exact. Refreshed, even cleansed, she thought with a flicker of surprise, as if something ugly had been subtly vanquished. She could not understand what. Even the next dance rehearsal had been different. She had felt gay and lighthearted. Even when Lecompte had touched her hand again, opened his eyes wide, she had felt only happy, not hot and cold and hot again in turn.

She was pondering more about this, when quick, light steps sounded on the wooden walk behind her. Jennifer stiffened defensively. Holdups were not unknown in Halifax.

"Capitaine, Capitaine Welland," Lecompte's soft high voice called her name urgently. *"Mon capitaine,* would you not care to accompany me to my humble dwelling and partake of a glass of wine?" He was beside her now, his thin white hand on her arm, his face lifted very close towards hers in the moonlight.

She hesitated momentarily. Then it seemed churlish to refuse.

"Thank you, Monsieur Lecompte," she replied, without much enthusiasm, "I should be delighted."

"I am sure we will both be very happy," Lecompte answered softly, his slight suggestion of a lisp more apparent than ever.

As she walked on beside him along the dark street, Jennifer felt oddly puzzled and worried. There seemed to be something peculiarly clandestine about going to Lecompte's lodgings with him. Yet she could understand no reason for such a feeling. The uneasiness was there, though, suggesting all was *not* right. She shook herself mentally. This sort of imagining had got to stop.

As they walked up the steps to his lodgings it appeared to Jennifer that Lecompte cast a swift glance down the street, as if to make certain that there was no one about. But, of course, such a thing was ridiculous. Why should he worry? He unlocked the door and preceded her in rather quickly, too.

Lecompte's rooms were luxuriously, even ornately furnished. Jennifer had always had an odd sensation of stifling when she first entered. The same sensation enfolded her again tonight. Of course, the room was very warm, there was even a fire burning. She sank into a chair and stretched her legs out before her.

"I'm tired," she said frankly, and added, "my, it's warm here, shall I open a window?"

"I like it warm," Monsieur Lecompte said simply. "Where I came from, dear boy, it is always warm. This climate here, it chills me. I shall get the wine." He went into an inner room leaving Jennifer. The heat and the dancing flames, after the briskness of the night outside—for even in summer Halifax was fresh in the evenings—made her feel drowsy. She was struggling with a yawn when Lecompte came back into the room, a glass of wine in either hand.

"I'm sorry, monsieur," she apologized ruefully. "It's the heat, and the hour—I'm really not bored with your company."

The Frenchman smiled and handed her the glass. "Have some wine," he urged.

Jennifer did not care for wine actually, and especially not such potent wine as Lecompte poured. However she sipped it politely and yawned again. "Monsieur," she said, laughing apologetically, "I am so sorry."

Her host had seated himself beside her and his hand lay gently on her arm.

"Dear boy," he said softly, very slowly, now his eyes were wide open. "Why do you bother to return to your quarters this night? Come, I have a very comfortable bed. You could share it."

His eyes were very deep, very dark, very compelling. His hand was warm, gentle, soft. She felt the room pressing in on her. Her senses blurred dizzily. She sipped again at the wine. It seemed unusually potent, even for Lecompte's cellar.

"Monsieur," she faltered, "I...I am not...what I seem to be."

"Dear boy, we are men together," said the Frenchman softly. "What is there to question?"

He got to his feet and took Jennifer's hand in his, first putting the glass on the nearby table. "Come, my boy," he urged softly, coaxingly, "come."

As in a dream, seeming as if she had no strength to withstand his gaze, Jennifer allowed herself to be brought to her feet.

"The bedroom is over there," the Frenchman gestured. "You will be comfortable, I am sure."

Jennifer hesitated, trying to battle the overriding of her will, and the Frenchman persuaded her gently ahead. "Go, my boy. I will be—I will be along later."

As might a sleepwalker, Jennifer moved across the floor to the door which the Frenchman had indicated. She hesitated with her hand on the knob and looked back at him, shaking her head, trying to throw off the effect of the wine, the heat, the strange hold Lecompte appeared to have set on her. Why—?

"Make yourself comfortable, dear boy," he said again, his voice was peculiarly sweet. He turned and smiled across the room directly at her. "What are you waiting for?" he murmured.

At that moment a thunderous knock sounded on the outside door.

The Frenchman stiffened. Once more those heavy lids veiled his compelling gaze. His face changed in some indescribable way.

"Now who can that be?" he said, his voice harsh.

He set the glasses on the table and walked to the door. "Who is it?" he called.

"Lord Randall," was the reply. "Let me in, Monsieur Lecompte. I wish to speak to you."

"Lord Randall!" There was surprise in the Frenchman's voice. He undid the chain and opened the door. "This is indeed a pleasure, that you should honor my humble abode. Come, will you not enter?"

Lord Randall had already pushed past him. His hard eyes swept across the opulent room to Jennifer standing with a sleepy surprise and enquiry on her face. Some of his taut stance relaxed as he said, "I have come to congratulate you upon the excellence which your pupils displayed, Monsieur Lecompte."

The Frenchman bowed. "That is indeed kind of you, Lord Randall. Especially kind of you to call upon me tonight."

If there was a thread of irony in his voice it was not too open.

Lord Randall spoke across the room. "I must congratulate you, too, Jonathan. I regret I did not have the opportunity at Government House. I had not thought to find you here."

Jennifer released her grip on the knob and came back toward Rufus. His presence had brought a breath of fresh air into the overcharged atmosphere and, in some way that she could not recognize, a breath of sanity. Suddenly she wanted to be out of this place. There was evil here, she felt it, yet she did not know where it was or why. She just wanted away. She said hastily, "I was just leaving, Lord Randall. I . . . I had come to have a glass of wine with Monsieur Lecompte and to congratulate him as you have done."

"Fine! Good! I'll walk along with you," Lord Randall said, his voice still hard. He watched while she crossed the room and picked up her shako and gloves, then swung to the door and held that for her.

"Good night, Monsieur Lecompte," Jennifer said with an effort. "Thank you for the wine."

The Frenchman bowed low. "Good night, my dear boy," he said. There was no softness in his voice now. As he straightened to meet a cold, direct stare from Lord Randall, his eyes narrowed.

"Good night, Monsieur Lecompte," Lord Randall only said. However he looked the Frenchman directly in the face, and what there was in his expression was not pleasant. The door slammed behind him, not quietly.

Jennifer was trembling, yet she did not know why. She had only the sense of escaping something evil, evil beyond her comprehension. She cast a swift glance up at Rufus's face as he walked along the pavement beside her. His expression was hard; suddenly she felt cold.

She said in a small voice, "I would like to walk for a while, Rufus. Do you mind?"

"No," said Rufus briefly.

They walked. As they paced through the silent streets, turning up past the north commons and on out to the country lanes, the man beside her was silent. After a while Jennifer's trembling stopped. She said hesitantly, "Rufus...I...that is, thank you."

Lord Randall did not answer.

She said again, after a pause, "I'm glad you came, Rufus."

Still no answer from the grim man beside her, but he turned unexpectedly and headed back to town. She had to run a step or two to catch up with him.

Now that strange drowsiness had left her. The sensation of evil had vanished with Randall's presence. But the oddity of what had enmeshed her in the Frenchman's room grew more acute in her mind. His words and actions were so—so—

"Rufus?" she said hesitatingly. "Rufus, do you suppose he had...he knew...he guessed who I was, what I was?"

"No," said Rufus, not slackening his pace.

"But, but... what was wrong then, Rufus? I suppose you'll say I'm being stupid, but, but I felt something was not right. Only the wine and that heat—I couldn't think straight...."

They had reached the foot of the glacis now. A sentry paced the path just out of earshot—the shadow of a tree hid them from his sight.

Rufus stopped short, turned to face the girl, grasping her elbows urgently. "Jennifer," he said, and his voice had a harshness that hurt. "The next time a man asks you to get into bed with him, make sure that he knows you're a woman and wants you to be."

He pulled her to him with a force which hurt her arms, and pressed his mouth almost fiercely on hers, then thrust her away and, still gripping one arm, propelled her up the path towards the sentry.

"Good night, Captain Welland," he snapped, and left her in front of the saluting sentry.

Chapter Seventeen

Afterwards, Jennifer could never remember how she got up to the Fort. She stumbled along the path, ("Drunk," the sentry noted mentally, which was not unusual in officers returning at that hour), gained her quarters without conscious effort on her part.

"Shut the door," a voice said urgently from the darkness. "I thought you were *never* coming."

Still dazed, Jennifer pushed the heavy door to behind her. George pressed his nose into her hand and she felt his tail wagging, so she had no fear that the visitor was a stranger.

A match scraped, the oil lamp flickered.

"I've been sitting here in the dark waiting for you," the visitor said, and his voice was querulous. "What kept you? I expected you ages ago."

Jennifer advanced into the room. "Jonnie! My God, what are you doing here?" Despite her surprise, instinct kept her voice low. Strangers were not permitted in the Citadel at this hour, and if Jonathan were found.... She moved closer. "Jonnie, what have you got on?" For, as her eyes became accustomed to the half-gloom, she saw that her brother was not in skirts as she had feared.

"I found these things in one of the trunks," her brother said briefly. "Katie didn't know whose they were, but I thought they'd be useful sometime."

Jennifer gathered her scattered thoughts and feelings together with an effort. She recognized the outfit—it was the one she had worn for midnight rides at home. All that seemed so long ago. She remembered now—she had packed the garments in the bottom of a trunk thinking gaily, lightly, that she might be able to wear the clothes in Canada. It had never occurred to her that Jonathan would be the one to put on her night disguise.

"How did you get here?" she demanded. "Did anyone see you coming?"

"Don't be silly, Jen," Jonathan said crossly. "Certainly not. I came up the glacis under the fence and dropped into the moat, found the sallyport, the one you pointed out that day we came up with Lord Bradbury to visit the Fort, remember? It was unlocked, so I didn't have any trouble finding my way."

"And nobody saw you?"

He shook his head. "Certainly not. I tell you, I was very careful, Jen. Don't worry."

She heaved a sigh. "But what are you doing here, Jonnie?"

He looked at her. "Jen, this has got to stop. I...I can't go on as I have been. It's...why, it's impossible. I just won't. You'll have to change places now."

She shook her head. "That wouldn't do, Jonnie," she said quietly. "You don't know any of the military rules or regulations. It would be an awful mess. Worse than it is at present. No, we'll have to find some other way out." She added curiously, "Why so urgent, Jonnie? Why tonight?"

Jonathan got to his feet and paced the floor. "Jenny, I tell you, I've had enough, that's all there is. It just...well, tonight it just...well, it was too much. Matilda...well, I just can't keep skirts on any longer."

"What about Matilda?" demanded his more practical sister.

"She...well...she thinks I'm silly." In the darkness his sister couldn't see his flushed face but she sensed his embarrassment from his tone. "She doesn't say as much, you understand, but she...well, I know that's what she thinks," he ended miserably.

"Jonnie?" Jennifer's voice was very low. "Jonnie—are you—are you falling in love with Matilda?"

"That's just like a woman. Has to find some sentimental reason for everything," Jonathan attempted to bluster. "What an idea! Certainly not!"

"Jonnie?" asked his sister still in the same low voice. "Are you sure?"

Her brother came to a halt in front of her. "Yes, I'm sure," he said and his voice was defiant. "I tell you, there's nothing to that."

"But do you love her?" Jennifer persisted so he could not escape.

Her brother's head lowered. He sank down on the bed beside her. "Yes," he admitted gruffly. "I do, Jenny. That's the devil of it. She's...well, she's wonderful. Not just pretty, wonderful!"

"And just how do you propose to court her?" his sister enquired after a moment and with a certain amount of dryness.

"Well, I thought..." here Jonathan hesitated. "Well, you see, if I was...if I were you again...I mean...oh, dash it all, you know what I mean, Jennifer. I could, well, I could call on her as you, well, you know what I mean."

"And do you think that I, as you, have made such an impression that she might receive my, that is, your advances gracefully?" Jennifer enquired.

"Don't be difficult, Jenny," Jonathan said impatiently. "I...well darn it, I'd have a chance. I tell you, Jenny, you've just got to let me change back."

Jennifer shook her head. "Jonathan, it won't do," she said slowly. "You can see that as well as I. No...I think the only thing for us to do is to get away from here, and then, when Matilda comes back to England, you can call on her there."

Jonathan sprang to his feet. "Jennifer, I daren't wait that long!" He was so emphatic Jennifer stared in amazement. Gone was the lazy, easygoing manageable Jonnie she knew best. "Suppose she finds someone else? Suppose she accepts someone else? Suppose...."

Her chin rose a fraction as she asked, "Suppose she discovers that you, Jonathan, have been Lady Jennifer?"

Jonathan sent a desperate glance about the stone-walled room. "How could she?" he demanded, but his voice was uncertain.

"Very easily, if you insist on switching back now," Jennifer said. "I'm afraid the change would be quite obvious, Jonnie. Think a little seriously, will you? No, that's not the way. We'll have to plan something else. Now I wonder...."

George was on his feet growling—there was a slight tap at the door, and the door opened. "You back already, Welland?" There was Captain Dixon's voice, slightly blurred, to be sure, but still strong enough to carry. "Thought I'd come in and say good night." He straightway entered a few paces into the room beyond the door Jennifer had forgotten to bar. Then stopped abruptly, blinking owlishly in the lamplight. "Didn't know you had company," he added.

Jennifer rose swiftly. "Come in, Dixon," she said unnecessarily, as Dixon was in. "This is my—my brother, Captain Dixon."

"Brother, eh? Didn't know you had one. Glad to meet you." He offered a large hand which shook only slightly. "Say," his eyes opened, "how did you get in?"

"My—my brother came in here to wait for me," Jennifer improvised as best she could.

"Well you'd better get him out again as quick as you can," Dixon warned, swaying slightly on his feet. "The old man's on the prowl, and in a devilish bad temper. Seems one of the sentries reported seeing a figure crawling up the glacis, and the old man's practically turning out the guard."

In the emergency, Jonathan turned, as he always had, to his sister. "How will I get out?"

"The same way you came in," Jennifer answered quickly, then she hesitated. "No, it's down the sewer for you, I'm afraid, Jonnie, and fast."

Dixon was suddenly steady. "Wait—I'll look around and see if all's clear," he said and returned to the door. He was very light on his feet for such a big man. In a minute he glanced back over his shoulder. "Come along," he beckoned. Brother and sister followed him quickly, edging along the passage which would take them down to the moat, the sally-port through which Jonathan had entered.

It was pitch-black, so they felt their way down carefully. Jennifer's hand was on the last door when she heard voices along the dry moat.

"Door is barred," came the harsh voice of the sentry. And the sergeant who was with him said, "Try the next one."

Jennifer stiffened. She threw the bar over. "Down," she hissed urgently, and they flattened on the ground.

Heavy footsteps sounded outside the door—the handle was rattled firmly.

"This door is barred, too," said the sentry.

"Try the next one," ordered the sergeant, and they paced on.

"Damn it! That was close," breathed Dixon, getting to his feet cautiously.

Jennifer's hand was like ice as she raised the bar stealthily and pulled at the door. Fortunately the hinges were well greased—someone else had seen to that—and it opened noise-lessly. The two soldiers had disappeared around the angle of the redan, but there was the danger that at any moment they might return. She moved quickly. "Hurry, Jonnie," she breathed, and ran across to the grating of the sewer.

Dixon bent beside her and together they raised the cover quietly, then turned together and swung Jonathan down into the yawning blackness.

"Jonnie, see Rufus," Jennifer whispered, "and hurry." He nodded and ducked into the conduit. Jennifer, with Dixon's help, replaced the grating. "Whistle, Jonnie," she whispered, "whistle."

Dixon pressed her arm warningly. "Better not stay around here, Welland," he murmured. Hastily they made it to the back once more and barred the door.

Not a minute too soon. The sergeant's voice came from the moat. "All sallyports barred, sir."

It was the colonel who answered, "Very good, Sergeant. Detail a guard to search the casemates."

Dixon and Jennifer hesitated no longer. They sped up the stairs of the black passageway, into the parade ground. Fortunately, there was no one around, but the sergeant could be heard in the guard room ordering the men to fall in.

Jennifer's quarters were reached and Dixon followed her in.

"Oh—Lord! That was close," he breathed, and dropped onto a chair. "I could do with a drink," he added.

"So could I," Jennifer said grimly, and found a bottle which Bates had brought up when they moved. She had barely filled two glasses before there was a thunderous knocking on the door. "Open up, sir, Sergeant of the Guard."

Jennifer still feeling as if she had not drawn a really deep breath for hours now, threw the door wide open.

"What's the matter, Sergeant?" she demanded crisply.

The sergeant saluted. "Colonel's orders, sir," he said gruffly. "The sentry reported seeing a man sneaking up the glacis. Orders to search every casemate, sir."

Dixon lounged to his feet. "Well, come in, Sergeant," he invited, and his voice was blurred again. He gestured widely. "Regard our little abode. Comfort. Luxury. Have a drink, Sergeant."

The sergeant advanced and glanced perfunctorily around. "Thank you, sir. Good night, sir." he snapped a salute, turned on his heel and marched out. They heard him beating on the next door, his wooden-faced companions still a little behind.

Jennifer carefully closed her door, made a fumbling business of dropping the bar into place, and returned to the bed, to collapse onto it with a long sigh. After a moment she said shakily, "Thank you, Dixon."

"Don't mention it," Dixon's voice was airy but steady. "I heard voices and thought, well...I thought I'd better come on, and... well, I didn't know you had a brother, and, well...the colonel's awfully sticky about women in the Fort. Military discipline and all that sort of thing."

Jennifer looked up. "Thank you, Dixon," she said again, quietly.

"I didn't know you had a brother—" Dixon repeated. "None of my business, of course," he finished in haste.

Jennifer looked down at her glass. "Well...not exactly," she hesitated. "We...that is...well, we don't talk about him very much."

"Oh, I see," Dixon nodded knowledgeably. "One of those, eh? Looks a lot like you, too." He chuckled understandingly. "Got one in our family, too. My uncle's bit of fancy turned up a son. Pops up at odd moments—usually to touch the old man for a hundred or so. Trades on the relationship—all that sort of thing."

Jennifer had looked up quickly. "But..." she began, then she stopped, began to smile. What a perfect explanation! Luck still rode with the Welland clan. "Yes, Dixon, that's it exactly," she confessed. "I didn't even know he was in Halifax. He...well, he just pops up."

Dixon nodded again. "So does my—'cousin,'" he said dryly. He got to his feet. "Well, I'll see you in the morning, Welland."

Jennifer saw him out. "Thanks again, Dixon."

Dixon grinned widely. "Us captains have to stick together," he said, and went out, lurching obviously as he did so.

Jennifer once more shut herself in before she went slowly across to the window. Opening the casement she waited tensely. Then in the stillness came a distant whistle, the trill of a nightingale, sounding oddly sweet and restful in the quiet air. It came again, then there was silence.

A weight rolled off the girl's shoulders as she closed the window unsteadily. On her way to unfasten her jacket she stopped suddenly, for a thought had occurred to her.

Dixon had not been drunk. He had been perfectly sober, and she had told him....

She sagged down on her bed—first dismayed, and then laughing to herself a little hysterically. Without thought she had introduced a third—if highly disreputable Welland—and what if there came a need to manage the trio together? There was no use thinking of storming such a redoubt as that ahead of time.

Chapter Eighteen

The following morning when a hotel messenger brought a note, Captain Lord Welland broke the seal with a hand which was not quite steady.

It was from Rufus, as Jennifer had expected, and brief to the point of an order. Lord Randall would appreciate it if Captain Lord Welland would do him the honor of riding out with him that afternoon at an hour to suit the captain's convenience, and it was signed 'Randall.' One of Rufus's more curtly-styled communications, but she could expect little better.

Jennifer hastily scrawled a reply on a scrap of paper purloined from the guard room. Directing it, she passed the envelope to the boy.

Tucking Randall's note in a pocket, Captain Lord Welland went about her duties with an impassive face. The sight of Rufus's writing, as lacking in any friendliness as the few sentences had been, had somehow seemed more than ordinarily unsettling. When Jennifer rode down to meet him at four o'clock beside the common, she wondered for the hundredth time what she was going to tell Rufus, even how he might meet her. The scene with Jonnie had been startling enough to affect for awhile *all* her memories of the night before. Her hand unconsciously went up to her mouth.

Her lips were still sore—Rufus's kiss had been angry and his mouth had pressed hard on hers. But Rufus kissing her at all—and as if he wanted to punish her for something—that she still did not understand.

He was waiting for her, mounted on that handsome bay which she so admired. To her silent relief he greeted her casually, giving no hint in his face or manner of the events she recalled only too well.

She rode beside him easily, exchanging inconsequential comments while they passed groups of civilians and soldiers. Then, when they were in the country, she asked abruptly what must be her most important question now!

"Rufus, did Jonnie go to see you last night?"

He nodded, slowing his horse to a walk. Jennifer's mount matched its pace easily.

"Yes, he did," he answered. "He seemed somewhat agitated."

"What did he tell you?" Jennifer urged.

"That he wanted an end to this masquerade, and soon."

"Did he tell you he had been up in the Citadel?"

Rufus nodded. "Yes—ah, I believe he was discovered there."

"Dixon came in." Jennifer explained quickly what had happened. "I—I introduced him as my brother," she ended simply.

"Didn't it occur to you that *three* Wellands may be a little difficult to handle?" Randall suggested. She nodded unhappily. "Also—it is pretty well known there are only two of you in the stud book, as it were."

"Yes. I thought of that later," she admitted, and added gruffly, "but, Rufus, Dixon thinks—well, Dixon thinks—that is, he took it for granted that, well...."

"Are you trying to say that Captain Dixon believes your sister came in disguise?"

Jennifer shook her head vehemently. "Oh, no, not that. I'm certain he hasn't the least suspicion of that, but you see I—well, I hesitated before I introduced him as my brother, and so Dixon believes he's a sort of—well...."

"From the wrong side of the blanket, as it were," Rufus ended for her dryly. "A slight indiscretion on the part of your father—or was it your uncle? No, it would have to be your father. He looks too much like you."

Jennifer nodded more cheerfully. "That's it exactly," she agreed with a little sigh. Then she chuckled, "Rufus, isn't it silly?"

"No sillier than this whole thing has been to date," Rufus returned in so neutral and harsh a voice that Jennifer, sobered, rode on in silence. When she spoke again, her voice was tight.

"Rufus, why did you ask me to ride with you today?"

"Because I wanted to talk to you," Lord Randall returned promptly.

"About what?"

"About last night," His Lordship replied.

"Yes?"

"I believe," said His Lordship thoughtfully, seemingly unaware that his companion was taut in every nerve and muscle, "that three Wellands is one too many, that Lady Jennifer has overstayed her welcome at Government House."

"Yes," Jennifer agreed with some heartiness. Lord Randall turned to smile at her.

"My dear, I think the time has come," Rufus continued, "for Lady Jennifer to travel to—shall we say—Boston? To visit relatives there?"

"How is she going to get there?" Jennifer asked. Nothing would serve as well, but how Jonnie could be transported south—she was completely baffled.

"I believe I might contrive that," Lord Randall murmured. "A letter, perhaps an invitation. I would accompany her, of course. A letter from His Grace might even be produced to suggest a temporary guardianship on my part. I think this could be done. Then, once Lady Jennifer has been safely removed from Halifax, surely a method could be devised for Captain Lord Welland to follow his sister. You have no idea, m'girl, of the games I can also play!" There was a look about him which made Jennifer suddenly tense.

"Rufus, no doubt you mean to be kind, but you take too much upon yourself in the management of our affairs." Her voice was harsh and her face was very white. This was their own trouble, and she had no mind to embroil Rufus in it also. "I assure you, we are quite capable of looking after ourselves."

Lord Randall's mouth lifted slightly at the corners. "Jenny, my dear," he observed, "you haven't changed a bit. When you were eight years old, you were just as independent as you are now. I met you where the little river runs past the silver birches, and I was very condescending in those days. I said that as you were lost I would take you home, and you put up your stubborn chin, just as you are doing now, and told me with great firmness that you were not lost, that you simply did not know the way home. Jenny—won't you allow me to show you the way home now, as you finally agreed to let me do then?"

"Go to the devil, Rufus," she snapped. Digging her spurs into her startled horse, she lashed him into a gallop across the fields. Her eyes were so blinded with tears she did not see the wide stone fence beyond the brush. Her horse hesitated, then tried the leap gallantly and missed by only a few inches, falling awkwardly.

Unprepared, Jennifer went over the mount's head to land heavily, and lie without moving where she had fallen.

Rufus had seen the hurdle in time and his horse cleared it handily, to be jerked to a halt almost as soon as he landed. Flinging himself from the saddle the man raced to the crumpled figure in Rifle green.

"Jenny, are you all right?" he cried. He bent over her. "Jenny, are you hurt?"

He felt her shoulder move under his hand and Jennifer said huskily, "Go away."

Relief flooded him. "Are you sure you're not hurt, Jenny?"

"I'm all right. Don't call me Jenny, and just go away. Please leave me alone."

"Here—let me help you." Rufus attempted to raise her and she wrenched herself from his hands to hide her face more deeply in the grass.

"Go away, please—Rufus." Her voice broke over his name and her shoulders shook uncontrollably, as the tears could no longer be held back.

He let her cry herself out, kneeling quietly on the ground beside her, his hand gently smoothing her hair, while the horses grazed peacefully nearby. At length she pulled herself to a sitting position, wincing a little. Keeping her back to him she blew her nose defiantly, sniffed and mopped. Rufus got leisurely to his feet and, extracting another handkerchief from his pocket, wet it in the brook nearby and came back with it to her.

"Wipe your face," he commanded casually.

She took the handkerchief from him, vigorously rubbed her face, asking in a small voice, "Is my horse all right?"

Rufus nodded. "Yes. He picked himself up. He's all right."

There was a last sniff. Jennifer said, "I'm sorry, Rufus."

He extended a hand to her to pull her to her feet. "Come along over this way—it will be more comfortable under the trees."

This time she allowed his help. He caught the horses, tethering them in the shade of the clump of trees. This was a quiet spot, out of sight of the road behind, peaceful and serene.

Jennifer sank down to the ground, her back to one of the trees and brushed absently at the front of her jacket. "I'm sorry I—I said what I did. But, Rufus, you mustn't"—her head raised with determination and she looked earnestly up at him—"you *mustn't* get mixed up in our mess. Please—it's not that I think you're interfering, it's not that—but it's not fair to you. If—if anything happens, it's our fault, and we'll have to take the blame for it. You mustn't be caught in a scandal because of us."

"My dear," Rufus said casually, "didn't it ever occur to you that I knew I would be mixed up in your troubles when I chose to come here?"

She rolled over on the turf and plucked reflectively at the grass. "I didn't think, Rufus," she said at length. "I mean—I just didn't think." Jennifer knew she was not making good sense, but for the first time all her self-confidence seemed to have vanished, and she did not like the lost feeling which held her now.

"Seriously, Jenny, how long did you expect this masquerade to last?" he asked. She shrugged, but made no other answer, and after a minute, he added, "How long is it since you arrived here?"

"The end of May. Almost three months now."

"Good Lord!" said Rufus involuntarily. Then, "you've had a pretty good run for your money, don't you think?"

She nodded. "Yes." Then she looked up quickly. "Mostly it has been fun though, Rufus."

"No doubt," he agreed dryly.

Her smile faded.

"Rufus—do you think it was very—very bad of me?" she asked, and her voice was very low.

He looked down at her. "My dear, if I had been your brother I would have turned you over my knee and paddled you before I would have allowed you to undertake such a mad scheme."

"But—but—Jonathan didn't mind the idea," Jennifer said after a while.

"I know he didn't," Rufus said briefly. "He wouldn't."

Her eyes flashed up with some of her usual fire. "You mustn't blame Jonathan, Rufus," she said earnestly. "It was my idea entirely."

"I dare say." Rufus was blunt. "But if your precious brother hadn't been so much of a fool, you could never have gone through with it. My dear, don't try to stand up for your brother. I know you both too well. Answer me this—do you think for a minute that you could have got away with it with me?"

Her eyes fell again.

"Answer me, Jennifer. Do you?"

"I don't think I'd have tried," she confessed in so low a voice that he hardly caught the words.

"That's exactly what I mean. And how your brother could consent to passing himself off in your place at Government House for these three months—" he shrugged and shook his head. "I don't understand it."

"If you disapprove so completely, Rufus," Jennifer's face

was white but her voice was even, "why do you bother with us?"

"Because—" Lord Randall checked himself and looked down at the forlorn figure on the ground, for it was forlorn despite the steadiness of the voice. He drew a deep breath and finished in a lighter tone, "Because somebody has to, and I happen to be at hand."

Jennifer's eyes were on the ground. She said, after a minute, unsteadily, "Thank you, Rufus." Then later—"What can Jonnie do?"

"Lady Jennifer will leave as soon as I can learn of a ship sailing for Boston, and I will escort her and her chaperone there to visit some distant relatives of yours."

"Jonnie won't want to go."

"I'm not much concerned with what Jonathan wants or doesn't want." Rufus said tartly, his eyes narrowed. "What do you mean, he doesn't want to go? He seemed quite eager to me last night to get away from Government House."

"He wanted to change places," Jennifer said simply. "He wants—well, you've met Miss Markham?" Rufus nodded. "He likes her, Rufus. He says—he says he loves her."

"Good God!" said Rufus blankly.

"So he doesn't want to leave Halifax," Jennifer ended quite simply.

Rufus's eyes were twinkling now. "How does he propose to court her?" he inquired with interest. "Or did you offer to attend to that?"

Jennifer smiled faintly. "I did, as a matter of fact," she admitted. "I also told Jonnie that the best thing to do would be to wait until she got back to England. But he's afraid that someone else will come along in the meantime, and that will be the end of his chances." She looked up at him. "I think he's really in love with her, Rufus. And I'm sure it would be much the best thing for him if he were out of Halifax, because I don't think she's good enough for him, do you?"

"He's not good enough for *her,"* Rufus retorted, then his face softened. "Now, don't fly up in arms about your brother again, Jenny, it won't do you any good. Besides," he added, and he was grinning, "she'd probably be very good for your

165

brother. I should think she'd make him toe the mark quite respectably. She's very like you, you know."

"Like me?" Jennifer sat up in a small blaze of sudden anger. "I've never played so missishly and prattled like a pea hen in my life! You can't mean that, Rufus, how could she be like me?"

"In many of the ways that matter," His Lordship continued. "She has your determination and a sense of humor. She's not as much of a tomboy, that I will agree. But she's thoroughly spoilt—even more than you are, as you didn't have a doting parent to give in to your every whim—and she's always been accustomed to having her own way. Yes, all in all, I think she would be quite good for Jonathan. I believe if she caught him languishing about idly, she'd give him a piece of her mind and see that he got started on some worthwhile employment. Meanwhile the situation *is* a little awkward." He pulled at the tip of his ear. "Well, one thing at a time. Lady Jennifer will have to leave, and if this questionable third Welland remains in Halifax, at least there'll be only two of you to worry about. I suppose *he* had better remain, seeing that Captain Dixon has already met him and has remarked, you say, on the resemblance." He chuckled. "Seeing that you have hastily acquired a bastard relation, you might as well let him exist for a while."

Jennifer stretched out on the ground. "I'm glad you're here, Rufus," she said irrelevantly, and added inconsequentially, "I like Halifax."

Rufus looked down at her inscrutably. "Thank you," he murmured, "I don't see the connection, but no doubt there is one. However, I trust you will not acquire such a fondness for Halifax that you will want to stay here indefinitely."

"Don't be silly, Rufus," Jennifer murmured. Her eyes were half closed—it was very pleasant there lying in the shade of the tree. She was tired and strangely drowsy and completely relaxed. For the moment it was nice to be able to shift her problems to Rufus's shoulders. He had a way of making trouble ease away. She heard Rufus's voice at a distance, as the tree above blurred and wavered. Then the sky faded out. She slept blissfully.

Jennifer blinked and stretched, and groaned—she discovered she was exceedingly stiff—and opened her eyes dazedly. The shadows were long on the grass and she was alone. She sat up and looked about her—no question of it, she was entirely alone.

"I must have a peculiar effect on you," Rufus's voice came from behind her. She turned quickly. "That's the second time you've gone to sleep when I've been with you."

"Rufus, I am sorry!" She was conscience-stricken. "I didn't mean to—did I go to sleep? What time is it?"

"To the best of my knowledge you did, and it's nearing seven." He got up from the ground and came over to her.

"Nearing seven!" Her eyes widened. "Rufus, why didn't you waken me?"

"Short of picking you up and dumping you in the nearest brook, I couldn't figure out any other way that would accomplish that feat," he said calmly. "I tried kicking you—if you're black and blue in certain spots you can always blame me—but it didn't seem to work."

She looked at him uncertainly. "Rufus, you're jesting, aren't you?" She moved, and grimaced. "Maybe you're not," she added ruefully.

Rufus grinned. "That's right, give a dog a bad name and you might as well hang him," he said cheerfully. "Have a sandwich." He extended a plate and her eyes widened again.

"Rufus, where did this come from?"

He nodded his head. "Down the road. There's a farmhouse there, so I rode over and begged some food and milk from them. Experience has taught me on previous occasions that you're likely to be famished when you waken up—I seem to recall your first words inevitably being, 'I'm hungry.'"

"Rufus, you dear," she said gratefully, and bit into the sandwich. "I *am* hungry! How clever of you!"

"Well, I'm not averse to something to eat myself," he confessed. "And, as it's probable that you will have to dine with me when we return to town, I believe it's past mess-hour—I thought I might as well feed you now and save myself the necessity of explaining to the waiter that I had really not been starving you, as you proceeded to your seventh helping."

She laughed. "Rufus, you are an ass." Her eyes were very bright. "This is such fun."

He smiled but said nothing, and presently they finished up the sandwiches and drank the milk, dividing it scrupulously between them. Jennifer got to her feet, groaning a little as she straightened, and put her shako on her head, patting it into place with a practiced hand. She mounted her horse and sat easily in the saddle, sweeping the countryside with her wide gaze.

"I shall always remember this place, Rufus," she said simply. She brought her eyes back to him and urged her horse over to his. She held her hand out, "Friends again, Rufus?" Her face said more than her words.

His eyes were very gray. She had a notion his gaze was probing deep into her. He took her hand and his grip was warm and firm. "Always, Jenny," he said quietly, "not just again."

Chapter Nineteen

Lady Jennifer left Halifax quite suddenly a few days later, bound for Boston to visit some distant kinsmen of her guardian's.

"My dear, we are sorry to see you go," Lady Bradbury said kindly. "Your departure seems very hasty, but I can understand that your cousin is anxious for you to come. It is most opportune that Lord Randall has to travel to Boston on business, and has undertaken to escort you there since your guardian has agreed to this."

"And I am most sorry to be leaving you, dear Lady Bradbury," returned Lady Jennifer, quite untruthfully. "I have so enjoyed my visit here." Which *was* true, to a point.

"We have been glad to have you," continued her hostess determined to have the last word as was usual with that lady, "and we do hope you will come back again."

Lady Jennifer smiled, murmured polite things and, on a bright August morning, was driven down to the dock with

Katie in attendance. Lord Randall met them there and, having already arranged their passage, saw to it that her trunks and cases were carried on board while Lady Jennifer bade a last farewell to Lady Bradbury, who had come down to the dock to see her off.

"Pray don't wait, Lady Bradbury," she begged, "for I will go straight to my cabin and lie down. I know I shall be miserably unwell as soon as I set foot upon the ship, and I desire nothing more than to be in my bunk."

This Lady Bradbury could understand only too well—the sea had much the same effect on her. So she patted Lady Jennifer's hand understandingly and agreed that such a precaution was much the best thing, and waved to her from her carriage as Lady Jennifer climbed the gangplank, with her brother—who had received special permission to be present at that hour—assisting her.

Lord Randall paused by Lady Bradbury's carriage to assure her earnestly that he would take the best of care of Lady Jennifer, and Lady Bradbury nodded and smiled and said that she was certain of that, and that she had no hesitation whatsoever in commending Lady Jennifer to his custody.

Captain Lord Welland went down to the cabin with his sister and came on deck again at the last minute to take farewell of Katie, and to shake hands firmly with Lord Randall, before he hurried off the gangplank and stood on the dock to wave good-bye.

In the bustle and confusion attendant upon the departure of any ship, nobody had noticed a slight youth clad in dark attire slip down the loading gangplank and disappear swiftly into the crowd.

The "All Ashore" was called, and the hawsers were cast off, the inevitable good-byes were cried. As the ship moved slowly from the dock, Lord Randall and Katie stood at the rail waving to Lord Welland on the wharf.

The captain turned slowly away and walked up toward the city. Some acquaintances spoke sympathetically of Lady Jennifer's departure, and he replied a trifle soberly to such as wished her a quick return. He was indeed such a devoted brother, several of the ladies assured each other.

In this they were, of course, sadly mistaken. For Lord

Welland was not in the least regretting the absence of his sister. Instead, he was feeling a strange overwhelming sensation of loss at the departure of another, and that sensation occupied him to the point of nearly dour absentmindedness now.

Even as the *Cambria* cleared Point Pleasant, and the Sambro Light, the late Lady Jennifer was sitting in front of the mirror in Lord Randall's hotel bedroom, impatiently snipping off locks of hair which had grown far too long. Supervising the procedure was the captain, who sat with both hands laced about one bent knee and a most critical eye for the shearing.

"I must say, you and Rufus together have given me a fine character," the ex-Lady Jennifer complained bitterly. "Born on the wrong side of the blanket, a libertine, a ne'er-do-well, gambler, general scoundrel, up to no good. Fine reputation you two have cooked up!"

"We didn't say all that," Lord Welland protested.

"You didn't have to," Jonathan grunted. "All you needed to do was say that I was your 'er, brother,' and for Rufus to murmur that the best of families had one, and the lady cats did all the rest and enjoyed every rumor they spread."

"Well, at least you're still here in Halifax," Jennifer pointed out. "And I think it was decent of Rufus to arrange for you to occupy his rooms."

"Oh, it was decent enough of him, I dare say," Jonathan conceded grumpily, "but how the deuce do you expect me to court Matilda with a reputation such as that? She won't have anything to do with me."

"What else did you expect us to say?" Jennifer countered, reasonably enough. "There had to be some reason why we didn't discuss you."

Jonathan grunted. "Well, I think the quicker you get out of that rig the better it will be," he decreed, and as Jennifer had been thinking the same thing there was nothing for her to answer.

Instead she shrugged and moved to the door. "I've got to be getting back to the Fort, Jonnie," she said. "Look after yourself and don't try to meet too many people. You've all the money you need, haven't you?"

Yes, her brother had everything he required. He had

clothes—Rufus had seen to that—and money—Rufus had also seen to that—and a place to stay—also thanks to Rufus. All he needed was an introduction to Miss Matilda, but that not even Rufus had been able to accomplish for him. The future was gray, but not solidly black. He adjusted his high stock and combed his hair carefully into the latest mode, then he shrugged into his coat, picked up his top hat and a cane, and sallied forth to look over those parts of Halifax which, as Lady Jennifer, he had certainly not been permitted to view.

Life went on. That the masquerade had lost much of its savor for Jennifer was not really anybody's fault. Nobody knew that she checked days off her calendar wistfully, nor that when a howling storm blew in from the Atlantic and all shipping was delayed, Captain Lord Welland's heart was anxious. Meanwhile, he performed his regimental duties meticulously, and in his free time he escorted his "brother" about the city, introducing him to such of the officers as they met and taking him out to the North-West Arm, where they hired a small craft and went sailing. Sailing was Jennifer's speciality, but Jonathan was willing enough to go along for the trip—small craft in inland waters didn't upset him as a large ship on the ocean did—and he was satisfied to leave the manipulation of the craft to Jennifer and loll on the cushions at the back. Then he met Matilda again.

To put it more correctly, Matilda met him. Walking downtown with her cousin Maria for protesting company, Matilda spied his red hair through the windows of one of the shops and turned in promptly, thinking it was Lord Welland and intending to enquire after his sister. She was somewhat taken aback to discover that facing her was a strange gentleman who doffed his hat quickly and politely, and apologized for not being Lord Welland.

"Although my name is Welland," he added with a smile. "You see, Lord Welland and I are—er—related."

Matilda cocked her head. "There is a strong resemblance," she commented.

Jonathan bowed with a flourish. "So it has been said."

Matilda had heard the gossip—there was little that went on that Matilda did not hear sooner or later, via the servants and maids and ADC's scampering about Government House. Now she readily placed this young gentleman.

"I know your—your brother, and sister, quite well," she explained. Again Jonathan bowed.

"I am sure you have not heard of me from them, Miss Markham," he said daringly. Her eyebrows went up.

"You know my name?" she asked, not quite pleased at his rather forward manner.

"Who is there in Halifax that does not know Miss Markham?" he murmured, and Matilda laughed.

"Very prettily put, Mr. Welland," she said and, as her cousin came fussily into the shop in search of her, she added hastily, "I trust you will do me the honor of calling upon us at Government House some time."

Jonathan shook his head, allowed a faint expression of sorrow to cross his face. "I do not feel that I will be welcome there, Miss Markham. Indeed, I fear I shall not have the privilege of meeting you again."

"Nonsense," said Matilda briskly. "I dare say you may be right that you shouldn't call at Government House—I don't understand these things, but it seems to be the way of the world. But I can't see any reason why you can't see me again. I shall be riding tomorrow morning at eleven o'clock along Pleasant Street, and I shall be very pleased for company."

"Miss Markham, you should not be seen with me," Mr. Welland replied honestly.

Miss Markham's rounded lips set together mutinously in a way her father would have at once recognized. "Stuff and nonsense," she said briskly. "Yes—I'm coming, Cousin Maria. Good afternoon, Mr. Welland." She inclined her head gravely, and the young man bowed as she swept from the shop to join her cousin on the sidewalk.

Jonathan returned to the hotel in the highest spirits, and only recollected when he got there that somehow, somewhere, he would have to find a horse. That did not perturb him too greatly. He remembered Lord Welland numbered three in his stable, and he hastily dispatched a note asking for the loan of one for the following morning.

The captain, who was on duty that afternoon, sent back word to help himself, and wondered fleetingly just what had got into Jonathan, who was certainly far from inclined to such exercise as a rule.

By the time Lord Randall returned to Halifax on the tenth day—the ship on which he had secured return passage being a slow tub which had taken five days to accomplish what the *Cambria* had done in three—the courtship of Miss Matilda by the scandalous Mr. Welland was progressing rapidly, and was the best on-dit of the town. For, as Lord Randall had observed succinctly, Miss Matilda was a determined miss who had been accustomed to having her own way all her life, and the only thing necessary to make her decide that Mr. Welland was a desirable young gentleman was a show of opposition from almost any person. Furthermore, Miss Matilda fancied herself in the role of reformer, and lectured Mr. Welland most severely on the general weakness of his character.

"It's all very well to admit openly that you were born on the wrong side of the blanket," she said severely, and Jonathan hung his head unhappily, "but that's no reason for you to conduct yourself in such a reprehensible manner. Just because you're...you're...", (even Matilda couldn't quite bring herself to say 'bastard'), "you're a natural son of your father's is no reason why you should not follow a respectable career. Gambling and traveling from one town to another endeavoring to pick up some short manner of livelihood is not sensible. It is perfectly ridiculous that you should consider your birth a valid excuse for such behavior. You are entirely capable of finding yourself a reputable place in the world—others in a like case have. Why, there have even been kings—look at William the Conqueror!"

Mr. Welland was heard to murmur that a person in his sad state needed some encouragement.

Quite properly, Miss Matilda decided that she was the encouragement that he required, and assured him that she intended to devote some of her time and attention to such an end.

Lord Randall, to whom Jonathan reported part of his success—for Jonathan had to have a confidant, and at that moment was very pleased with himself—was mildly amused.

174

"You'd better watch out, Jonathan," he warned, "she'll turn you into a useful member of society yet."

Jonathan grinned. "She's wonderful, Rufus!" he said fervently. His grin faded. "But, golly, Rufus, what's the use?" He sank into the nearest chair. "This is all very well but where can it end? Oh, if only I hadn't let Jennifer rush me into this mess! Just because I was too sick to report for duty— I didn't ever want to be a soldier—I'm not the soldiering kind. If she hadn't started this crack-brain scheme, I could have asked Matilda to marry me and everything would have been settled. Confound Jenny anyway, it's all her fault! I've a notion to tell Matilda the whole story." He jumped to his feet.

"Jonathan," said Rufus, and his voice was very soft, but it was anything but pleasant at that moment. "If I were to suspect for even one minute that you harbored any serious intentions of going to your beloved and mentioning anything about this present and past masquerade, I believe I would be very cross. I might even find it incumbent upon me to remove you bodily from this town." Then he added, as Jonathan turned to stare at him astounded, "Do I make myself clear?"

His gaze was very steady. Jonathan swallowed and ran his finger around a neck cloth which was suddenly tight. "I won't say anything," he promised thickly. "But it's all Jenny's fault."

"Jonathan, I find it extremely difficult to believe that Jennifer forced you into the role which you have been playing. Yes, you were seasick, but you used that opportunity to get out of something you disliked. Jenny must have thought she needed to cover up for you—reckless as she is, there was more behind it. If you're truthful you'll admit it." Lord Randall's voice had not risen above the soft level tone which he habitually employed.

Jonathan refused to meet that level gaze.

"Well, maybe she didn't force me. But it was *her* idea."

"Yes, I am quite certain it was her idea, just as I am equally certain that you were much in favor of it at the time. Or at least the part which savored of avoiding any form of unpleasantness on your part, such as you might perchance come across in army life."

"Jennifer likes what she's doing," Jonathan protested sullenly. "I didn't ask to be shoved into a uniform. I'm no soldier."

"I am very well aware that Jennifer has enjoyed her experiment," Lord Randall agreed. "And I am equally well aware that until this moment you were quite satisfied that you were not Captain Welland; therefore, I would consider it little more than just that you refrain from any remarks concerning your sister's conduct in the future."

Jonathan stared at him openmouthed. "What's it to you, anyway?" he demanded.

"That is not a matter which need concern you," Lord Randall replied coldly, and got to his feet. "I find you quite tiresome at times, Jonathan. Not the least of those instances being when you are busily engaged in finding excuses for your own weak will."

He strolled to the door. Pausing with his hand on the knob, he turned once more to face the disgruntled youth. "Remember what I said, Jonathan. I mean it."

He passed out into the corridor, closing the door behind him quietly.

Jonathan surveyed that closed door with a bemused expression on his face, then he dropped into a chair as understanding came to him.

"Good Lord! He's in love with Jenny!" he said, the sound of his voice was loud in the quiet room. "I wonder if she knows?"

Chapter Twenty

Summer was fading fast—August was near over. With the last week of that month came an event which the sporting circles of Halifax had discussed with vigor for weeks past. Three days of horse racing wound up what was generally regarded as the summer season. For, although September might be a gay, warm month, summer was officially conceded to have gone with the three-day meeting.

As the sporting circle comprised all the officers of the garrison, who were quite naturally sporting-mad, together with the elite of Halifax society, plus several hundred others, it was not surprising that racing was a topic which held a principal place in every social conversation. And it was still less surprising that, at a picnic instigated and arranged by Captain Lord Welland as a means of saying thank you for the hospitality which had been extended to him that summer, and to which had been invited certain fellow officers and some of the prettier belles of the town, including the Misses

Marjorie and Alice Bradbury and their guest, Miss Matilda Markham, the forthcoming horse races should have been discussed avidly.

The picnic had gone off very well. Two open carriages had called for the young ladies and their chaperones, and they had been escorted out to the grounds at Point Pleasant by young officers mounted on their handsomest steeds. Lord Randall and Mr. Welland were also included in the gathering, and Mr. Welland paid particular attention to the desires of the demanding Miss Matilda. As the culinary arrangements, together with the mechanics of the picnic proper, were under the supervision of Bates, Lord Welland's eminently able servant, all went off with dispatch. Bates had commandeered the servants of Captain Welland's fellow officers who were also guests, and under his supervision they had set up tables and provided hampers which had been transported to the chosen area long before the picnickers made their appearance.

It was a gay party and a happy party, not the least of it being due to the solicitude which Bates showed for his duties.

"Are you entering any of your horses in the races, Lord Welland?" Miss Alice asked prettily, and the captain nodded.

"Most certainly. I'm looking forward to it."

"Will you be riding, Lord Welland?" Miss Majorie queried.

"Certainly," Jennifer returned promptly. "I wouldn't miss it for the world."

"I hear the courses are to be stiffer this year," someone else observed, and there was a general discussion concerning the height of the jumps in the steepleraces, and the condition of the ground for the flat races.

"Which do you prefer, Lord Welland," Miss Marjorie asked, "flat racing or jumping?"

"Jumping," he replied promptly. "There is a thrill in taking your horse over a jump that cannot be found in flat racing."

Miss Marjorie shivered delicately. "But it's so dangerous," she objected.

Lord Welland laughed. "Lots of things are dangerous," he said cheerfully, "but they don't all have the same sport to them."

"Of course, you won't be riding, will you, Lord Randall?" Miss Alice turned to the gentleman beside her.

"I haven't quite decided, Miss Alice," Lord Randall answered, and the captain put in, "I've been trying to talk him into entering his bay, Miss Alice—I'm sure Lord Randall would make a good showing."

"There's only one horse I'd back against yours, Lord Randall," Captain Dixon said thoughtfully. "Thurston has a strong chestnut gelding."

Lord Randall nodded. "So I understand."

"Of course he can't ride the beast properly," Dixon added. "The animal's thrown him three times that I know of, but if he could stick on, I think he would give you a good run for your money."

"I'd like to have that horse," Lord Welland said wishfully, and Captain Dixon murmured callously,

"Wait until the races are over—you'll probably be able to buy him cheaply."

Bates had seen to it that sailboats and other watercraft had been secured for the pleasure of Lord Welland's guests. And those same guests, having eaten all that they could possibly contain, wandered down to the shore where the ladies allowed themselves to be helped into the craft of their choice. Bates was again present, seeing that all was in proper readiness, and he was seldom far from his master on whom he seemed, to Lord Randall's observant eye, to be keeping a careful watch. Indeed, at one moment when Lord Welland caught at a boat to pull it up on shore, the easier for Miss Alice to step, Bates was right there with a murmured, "Excuse me, m'lord," and a firm tug on the gunwale. Lord Randall's glance became thoughtful.

By devious machinations, Mr. Welland had maneuvered Miss Matilda into a well-cushioned canoe for two, and settled himself in the stern with the air of a man well pleased with the world. One or two of the young ladies decided they would rather stay on shore, but the remainder of them were only too happy to be paddled or rowed about the bright waters. Two others declared themselves to be much in favor of a sail, and Lord Welland, with Captain Dixon, promptly helped them aboard the waiting dinghy.

"You'd better come along, Bates, as crew," Lord Welland called out, and Bates hopped aboard with alacrity to set about raising the mainsail and generally making himself useful aboard the craft as he had on shore.

Lord Randall watched without expression. Mrs. Milloy, whose daughter was one of the passengers in the sailboat and who had come along as chaperone, sighed gently.

"I used to so enjoy boating and sailing in my younger days," she said rather wistfully, and Lord Randall smiled down at her.

"Madam, I should be delighted to act as motive power if you would entrust yourself to me and a canoe."

"At my age, Lord Randall?" she scoffed, but she gave in without much entreatment and settled with a sigh of content in the last canoe. "This is very thoughtful of you, Lord Randall," she said as he pushed off shore, and Lord Randall assured her that the pleasure was entirely his.

He kept fairly close to shore and within the small cove, for the established custom was that, while the young ladies were permitted on such an occasion to be unaccompanied in a canoe, it was unwritten law that they should stay under the eyes of the chaperone—only those in a sailboat were exempt from the proviso, and even they were not expected to go too far afield.

It was a beautiful afternoon, with sufficient breeze outside the little cove for the sailboat to handle easily and skim the waters gracefully, while the curving shore of the cove protected the smaller craft.

"You were acquainted with Lord Welland in England, were you not, Lord Randall?" Mrs. Milloy murmured, and Rufus nodded.

"Yes, I've known the Wellands for years."

"Lord Welland is a charming officer," Mrs. Milloy said, and added thoughtfully, "There is a delicacy about him which one does not often find in army men. I understand Mr. Welland is a cousin?"

"He is a relative," Lord Randall acknowledged, and Mrs. Milloy nodded.

"Yes, so I have heard." She was watching the white sail and she said sharply, "Lord Randall, that other boat, what's it doing?" She sat up so quickly that the canoe rocked. "Lord Randall, don't they see the dinghy—don't they see them— why it's going straight for them—why—it's doing it deliberately! Lord Randall, they're over!"

The canoe was very close to shore. With one savage stroke, Lord Randall beached it and said urgently, "Mrs. Milloy, would you step out, please?"

Mrs. Milloy struggled out as quickly as she could move, and Lord Randall shoved off and paddled with deep, powerful strokes to the overturned boat.

He was not the first there. Almost everyone of the picnickers had been watching the two craft approaching each other, but the second sailboat was already far down the Arm.

Captain Dixon was supporting one of the girls clinging to the bottom of the boat, while the second girl was being helped into one of the rescuing boats, but of Bates and a bright red head there was no sign. Lord Randall spoke sharply.

"Where is Welland?"

"He dived after Bates, Randall," one of the officers answered. "Apparently the man couldn't swim."

Even in the few minutes since the boat had overturned they had drifted several yards, and Lord Randall scanned the water with a face that was hard, the mouth stern set.

A head broke surface some feet away—he paddled there swiftly.

It was Jennifer, one arm clutching the unconscious form of Bates.

Rufus shot the canoe to her and, kneeling on the bottom, leaned over and grasped the unconscious man's arm.

"Grab the canoe, Jenny," he ordered briefly, and Jennifer, very white of face, did as he bade her.

The others had come up now and Lord Randall handed over the unconscious Bates to be hauled aboard one of the rowboats, while he gave his attention to Jennifer. For above all, she must not be pulled into one of the other boats with her wet clothes clinging to her body.

He balanced the canoe expertly, and helped her aboard with a strong pull of his arm. She collapsed in a sodden heap on the bottom of the canoe and lay there gasping for breath. Rufus peeled off his coat and tucked it about her, then picked up his paddle and headed for shore. Someone else could look after the sailboat. He had more important matters to attend to.

The girls and Captain Dixon had already been put ashore and, wrapped in blankets, were being plied with wine. One of the girls was having hysterics. Mrs. Milloy had her in her arms comforting her.

Willing hands pulled up the canoe and Jennifer, who had struggled into Randall's coat in the canoe, gratefully accepted the outstretched arms and the proffered blanket. She swayed and might have fallen, but Lord Randall had his arm about her swiftly, and Captain Hartford whipped out a flask of brandy.

"Have a swig of this," he urged, and Randall took it from him and held it to Jennifer's blue lips. The stimulant seemed to steady her, for she straightened and drew back from Rufus's protecting arm.

"Thank you, Rufus," she said with a ghost of a smile. "I'm all right now. Where's Bates—is *he* all right?" She looked anxiously along the beach.

"Peters is working on him," Captain Hartford said, "he was still unconscious when they got ashore. What happened, Welland?"

It was a question that everyone was asking, and no one could answer.

"I don't know," Jennifer said. "We saw this other boat, but we were keeping on our course which would have cleared him nicely. Then, suddenly, he seemed to veer and come straight for us. I don't know what happened. Next thing we knew he'd crashed into us and we were over."

Substantially the same story was repeated by Captain Dixon—who added forcefully, "If it hadn't been for Welland we'd have been run down. He twisted the tiller at the last second and the fool caught us a glancing blow on the stern, enough to send us flying, but at least the boat didn't sink and we were able to hang onto it. Welland, if Bates lives it will be due to you. I never saw anybody act so quickly. One minute you were there holding Miss Margaret and I said 'Where's Bates?,' and the next minute you weren't there."

Faint color came into Jennifer's cheeks. "Don't talk rot,

182

Dixon," she said roughly, and went down on her knees beside her unconscious servant.

Under the administrations of Mr. Peters, Bates was coming around. His face was gray, but his head moved wearily on the sand.

"Bates?" Jennifer spoke urgently. "Bates, open your eyes. Bates, are you all right?"

With an obvious effort the man blinked and turned his face towards his master's. "Aye, m'lord," he spoke huskily. "I'm—I'm all right." Then—"What happened, m'lord? That—that boat...."

"Yes, yes, Bates, You're safe now." Jennifer said soothingly. "We overturned, but you're all right now."

"That—that man—" Bates struggled to sit up, and willing hands helped him. "'Twas that captain, m'lord. I saw him—he did it deliberate."

"Who did it deliberately, Bates?" Captain Dixon's voice was sharp. "Who was in that boat?"

"That—that captain. Captain Thurston. I saw him. He—he saw who was in the boat. He—he turned his rudder. I yelled, sir, but he came right on."

"Yes, I heard you, Bates," Jennifer said quietly. "But I'm sure you're wrong, Captain Thurston wouldn't do a thing like that."

Dixon's eyes were hard. "I'm not so sure about that, Welland," he said grimly. "Thurston's had it in for you for a long time. It would be just the kind of thing he might do. Here—you stay where you are," he added to Bates, who was trying to struggle to his feet. "You've had a rough time. Have another drink." He held a flask to the servant's lips, and Bates drank eagerly.

"Lord Randall?" Mrs. Milloy spoke up clearly. "I think the best thing now is to get these young ladies and Captain Dixon and Lord Welland, with his man, back home and into dry clothes as quickly as possible. It was a delightful picnic, and it's entirely due to the efforts of Lord Welland that it didn't end tragically. Captain Dixon has already told us of your bravery, Lord Welland, and I assure you it won't be forgotten."

The captain flushed and shook her head. "It was nothing,"

she said briefly. "Captain Dixon and I can ride back, but if you would permit Bates to travel in the carriage with you and the Misses Margaret and Patricia, I would much appreciate it. I'm worried about him—I feel he should get back to quarters as quickly as possible."

"Most certainly," Mrs. Milloy said promptly, "but I think you and Captain Dixon should come along in the carriage with us, too. You can't ride in those wet clothes."

Captain Dixon was an unexpected ally of Lord Welland's. "I'm partially dry already, Mrs. Milloy," he said. "Certainly, Welland and I can ride back. Pray do not concern yourself about us. Indeed, I'm upset for the young ladies."

"I think they will take no harm," Mrs. Milloy said. She rounded them up expertly and bundled them into the carriage, and a feebly protesting Bates was tucked into a corner.

Randall held Jennifer's horse a little apart. "Jenny, are you sure you can manage?" he asked in a low voice.

She nodded, not quite meeting his eyes. "Yes, of course, Rufus. Thank you for coming out. Are you sure you'll be all right without your coat?" for she was still wearing it.

"Quite all right," he said firmly. "Jennifer, I'll call on you this evening."

"Look after the rest, Rufus," she entreated, and Rufus nodded.

"Yes, I'll look after everything," he promised, and watched her ride away behind the carriage, the sag of her shoulders telling him more than she had wanted him to know. His face was hard as he turned back to the remaining picnickers. Captain Thurston again. Why the devil should Captain Thurston display such a hatred of Captain Lord Welland? Lord Randall had a few questions he wanted answered.

Chapter Twenty-one

The Halifax races began two days later, with the flat racing occupying all day Thursday and Friday morning, and then the course being set for the steeplechase Friday and Saturday afternoons.

All the town was buzzing, not only with racing gossip, but with rumors about the unfortunate boating accident on the waters of the North West Arm Tuesday afternoon, and the bravery of Lord Welland. For the tale had spread through Halifax like a forest fire and lost nothing in the retelling. Lord Welland, by reason of his red hair, was easily recognizable as he went about the streets of Halifax, and many were the officers and citizens who stopped him to shake his hand and offer warm and sincere congratulations.

Barring an almost overwhelming feeling of lethargy, Jennifer was fully recovered the next morning, while Dixon suffered no ill effects whatsoever. Bates was determinedly about on Wednesday morning, but his face was pale, and Jennifer ordered him to lay up for a while.

He point-blank refused to do so, and Jennifer, who did not feel inclined to force the issue, let him alone. She admitted ruefully to herself that she would have missed his services, for he had developed into a most excellent personal servant. Her quarters were always spotless, her uniforms immaculate, and her morning tea hot and fragrant. He never intruded, yet he was always there if she needed him. Also he looked after George with the same care and attention, securing food and tasty bones from the cook, seeing to it that the dog was properly exercised and groomed at all times.

On occasion, Jennifer wondered if he perhaps suspected the true identity of the officer he was attending, but his manner was impeccable and above suspicion and Jennifer asked no questions.

As he had promised, Lord Randall called at the officers' quarters Tuesday night to see for himself how Welland had got over his unexpected swim in the chilly waters of the Arm. He found Jenny rather heavy-eyed but otherwise apparently recovered, entertaining Captain Dixon and several of the officers of the regiment in quarters, while Captain Dixon regaled them with a fairly accurate description of the afternoon's exploits.

"But are you sure it was Thurston?" one of the officers objected. "I can't see why he'd do a thing like that. Bates must have been mistaken."

"I wish you'd forget it," Welland pleaded. "None of us saw him—and I agree with you, I'm sure Thurston wouldn't consider such action. It was a mistake—even if it were he in the boat. Don't talk rot, Dixon."

Dixon was not convinced. "Well, if it wasn't deliberate why didn't he come back?" he demanded of the room at large, which was a question that Lord Randall, who entered at that moment, would have liked to have had answered, too.

Most of the officers present knew Lord Randall, and Welland introduced him to those who had not met him. He sat down prepared to await his chance to have a word with Dixon, grasping that opportunity when that officer went in search of more whiskey.

Unobserved by the others present, Lord Randall slipped out after the young man and had an enlightening chat with him before returning to Welland's quarters with food for thought. For Dixon's memory had served him well in regard to the incident in the mess at the Halifax Hotel shortly after Welland had arrived on the station.

"Thurston's a queer fellow," he said slowly. "He's a bully and he doesn't like people who face up to him. He got his hooks into Welland from the start—I don't know why, he just didn't like him, and he was determined to get him drunk. That's the way Thurston is. I think Welland acted commendably. He isn't big enough to battle Thurston physically, but he nicked Thurston on the raw with his shooting. You see, I don't suppose Welland knew it, but Thurston's a touchy devil about firearms. He can't hit a barn door, and when he first got his commission he was the butt of every mess joke. I'll wager that's what back of this—or maybe Bates was wrong, maybe it wasn't Thurston. I'll wager it was, though—and if so I'll bet you that's at the bottom of it. Thurston goes off on blind drunks, and he was probably in one then. You remember what happened in the mess after the review. He doesn't think, he just acts."

"I see," said Lord Randall thoughtfully, and indeed he did see more than Dixon has told him, for he knew more of the background. He added, "I'm inclined to agree with Welland—nothing useful can be obtained from bandying Captain Thurston's name about in connection with this episode. I would suggest that you omit further reference to him. After all, it is only supposition."

Dixon looked at him closely. He had been inclined to argue, but something in Randall's face stopped him—he paused, then he said quietly, "Yes, Randall, undoubtedly you're right." He stretched out a large hand and Lord Randall grasped it firmly.

"I believe there are other means of dealing with Captain Thurston," Lord Randall murmured, and again Captain Dixon nodded.

"Quite, sir," he agreed, and they returned to Welland's quarters on terms of mutual understanding.

But the rumor had already spread, as indeed Rufus had

known it would, and Captain Thurston was on the receiving end of numerous hard stares and some cold-shouldering. Thurston, who was not a patient man at the best of times, was more uncertain of temper—while his dislike of a certain Lord Welland increased with each rebuff. He cast about for some means of returning the insults and humiliations which had been directed at him onto the person whom he held responsible, but it was not until the finish of the steeplechases Friday afternoon that an opportunity presented itself.

There had been three steeplechases that afternoon for purses of varying sizes. The officers of the Rifles were jubilant because one prize had been won by a fellow officer, and another by a civilian whom the mess had more or less adopted. The third had fallen to a professional rider, so did not count.

Thus the mess was holding a party for Lord Welland and Lord Randall, for Welland had won the first race, open only to officers of the garrison, and had come in second in the third race, open to gentlemen-riders and/or officers, when Lord Randall and his bay had beaten him to the post by a full four lengths. It had been a good race, that last one, and Jennifer had enjoyed every jump of it. She had known that her horse did not have the power to keep up with Rufus's but the pleasure of a race was not necessarily in the winning of it. So she had taken the jumps with a light heart, and showed a broad grin when she trailed in second. The mess liked a good loser as well as a good winner, and spirits were accordingly high.

"Now, if we can just clean up in the relay race tomorrow," somebody said, "we'll have the cup for keeps."

"I wonder if Thurston would let Welland ride his gelding," a subaltern said thoughtlessly. "Then it would be in the bag."

"It's well enough in the bag as it is," Dixon said curtly, and the subaltern flushed, for he remembered too late the current gossip.

"So somebody thinks Welland could ride my horse better than I could myself?" Captain Thurston's harsh voice came from the entrance to the mess. He shouldered into the room and glowered about him.

The young subaltern who had said the wrong thing, muttered nervously, "I didn't mean that, Captain Thurston. I meant..."

"I heard you," Thurston growled. He looked about the room, noted the carefully averted faces and heads, and his eyes flamed. Jennifer was perched on the edge of a table, one leg swinging, gazing intently down at the glass in her hand. Thurston stalked across the room to halt some six feet away from her.

"Welland," he snarled, "I challenge *you* to a race tomorrow over a course to be set by the stewards, the prize to be my horse which you so obviously desire—you to be mounted on whatever nag pleases you."

Jennifer's face was a little pale. However, as she turned slowly to face him, she put her glass down with a steady hand.

"I think your stakes are not quite even, Captain," she observed coolly. "I should like to add five hundred pounds."

There was dead silence in the room. Captain Thurston's face flamed scarlet. He did not answer as if he could not trust his voice at that moment.

Jennifer continued evenly, "Dixon, will you arrange with the stewards so that such a challenge race will not interfere with the racing card? I accept your challenge, Thurston. Captain Dixon will notify you of the hour at which the race will be run."

Her eyes were very steady. Thurston's gaze dropped first. He muttered something unintelligible, swung on his heel to stamp from the room. Jennifer lifted up her glass and sipped slowly.

"My God! What a blackguard!" breathed one of the officers, and Captain Dixon said urgently,

"Welland! You're not going to meet that crazy challenge?"

Jennifer shrugged and nodded. "His horse is at stake, Dixon," she reminded him. "And I have said I'd pay almost any price to own it."

"But it's not just a race," Dixon said. "Thurston has something else in his mind—I'll swear to it."

Jennifer's eyes were clear. "I'm confident, Dixon, that the course will be a fair one, and that the race will be honorably run." She turned to Lord Randall. "Rufus, may I ride your bay?"

Their eyes met, looked. For a long minute Randall held her with his gaze. He knew, as Jennifer did, that there was nothing else she could have answered in reply to Thurston's challenge. It was the rankest insult the man could have offered, and yet, had she not taken it up as she did, it would have been her honor which would have suffered and the honor of the brigade. He saw, too, that Jennifer understood the risks as well as he did—that there was unspoken question and answer in her gaze. At length he nodded shortly.

"Yes," he said, "you may ride him."

"Thank you," Jennifer said simply, and lifted her glass. "Gentlemen, to tomorrow."

She dined later that evening with Rufus and Mr. Welland in Lord Randall's private suite, and there was a fourth guest at the table—a primly clad middle-aged woman who, heavily veiled, had returned under Lord Randall's protection from Boston and settled in rooms at the hotel. Katie might inwardly condemn the behavior of Lady Jennifer and her Master Jonathan, but she regarded it as her duty to be where they were, and she had returned unprotestingly with Lord Randall in the guise of "Mrs. Adams," a respectable widow in moderate circumstances. She was worried in her mind about sitting at the same table with Lord Randall, but he had put her at her ease so kindly that such grand company no longer upset her.

Jonathan was in a sullen mood and the cause was soon forthcoming. "Matilda wouldn't see me today," he cut in sulkily, crumbling his bread with restless fingers.

"Wouldn't, or couldn't?" Jennifer asked.

He shrugged. "Couldn't possibly, I suppose—I guess. She was at the races. When I went to speak to her, she turned away."

"I must say I am not at all surprised," Mrs. Adams declared roundly. "In my opinion, Miss Matilda has been behaving in a manner not at all befitting a properly brought up young lady. Consorting with a gentleman whom she believes to be, well—not what he should be. You brought *that* upon yourself, Master Jonathan."

"Don't blame him, Katie," Jennifer said with a little laugh. "It's my fault—I thought of it."

Katie sniffed. "As I have been given to understand," she said firmly, "this present arrangement was none of your doing. Had it not been for the thoughtless behavior of Master Jonathan, creeping into the Fort that night, such play-acting would never have been necessary. Your suggestion that Master Jonathan go back to England and await the return of Miss Matilda, was right, sensible and practical. All this botheration is no good, and nothing good will come of it, neither!" For strangely enough, Katie was even more perturbed about Jonathan passing himself off as a base-born son than she had been when he was masquerading as Lady Jennifer.

"Well, what's to be done now?" Jonathan said sulkily.

"I would suggest that you begin by behaving like a gentleman instead of—of what you've made people whisper about you being!" Katie said tartly. Lord Randall's lips twitched.

"Katie, you are a great support to me," he said solemnly. "Such a straightforward view is particularly praiseworthy at this moment."

Katie was not quite certain whether he was laughing at her or not. She glanced at him a little uncomfortably, but he was smiling at her. After a moment she smiled uncertainly back at him.

"And of course, m'lady, it's time *you* finished up this masquerade," she said in a softer tone, "it's gone far enough."

"Yes," Jennifer answered soberly, "it has." She pushed back her chair and got up from the table. "I think it will very soon be over," she added slowly. Lord Randall was watching her from under lowered lids as she crossed the room to halt by the long window. "It's quite time it was over," she repeated.

She gave herself a little shake and returned to the table. "Rufus, I hope you will excuse me now. I feel I had better return to quarters—there are some duties I have to attend to."

Rufus got to his feet. "I'll go along up with you, Jenny," he said quietly, and followed her to the door.

They walked without speaking through the quiet streets until, as they were nearing the path up the glacis, Rufus stopped his companion by a hand on her arm. "Don't do anything without discussing it with me first," he said quietly.

She kept her face turned from him. "It's got to end, Rufus."

"Yes," he said, "I agree with you. Will you promise what I've asked?"

She hesitated, and his grasp tightened on her arm.

"Promise? Please. I'm not asking much, I think. But this I do ask of you."

She sighed. "It is easy to be wise when it is too late."

He nodded. "Very easy," he agreed. "That is why I ask this of you. Will you promise to do nothing until you have spoken with me?"

She turned to him then. "It is only because I do not wish you to be drawn into any trouble," she said earnestly.

"But I am in," he said a little grimly. Then he added in such a way that there was no mistaking his meaning, although it was said in so low a voice that it could not have been heard a foot away, "If you do not promise me this, I promise *you* that you shall come back to the hotel with me tonight, and I will stay with you until you agree."

She smiled then. "I think you mean that," she said. "All right, Rufus, I promise." She held out her hand. He took it and smiled a little as he did.

"You won't forget?"

She shook her head. "You have my word, Rufus."

He let her go then and watched as she mounted the path past the saluting sentry and on out of his vision, then he turned and walked briskly back to the hotel. He had certain matters to attend to that evening, and not the least of them was dealing with a rebellious Mr. Welland.

Chapter Twenty-two

Saturday dawned clear and fresh. Jennifer, who had returned to the Fort in a strangely light frame of mind after giving her promise to Rufus, whistled cheerfully as she dressed. In the mess at breakfast Dixon sought her out.

"Your challenge race will be run at twelve o'clock," he told her, "over the same course as you rode yesterday. It has to be altered for the relay race in the afternoon, but the stewards have agreed to leave it until you have raced it."

She nodded. "Thank you, Dixon."

He hesitated. "Watch it, Welland," he said abruptly. "Thurston is in the devil of a mood today. Nobody can go near him."

She smiled a little. "I'll keep away from him until twelve o'clock," she said.

A messenger came up to hand her a note. She took it and,

turning it in her fingers, frowned at the crest. It bore a Government House seal.

She broke the seal and smoothed out the folded page. The message was very brief.

> "Captain Lord Welland, it would be appreciated if you would call upon the writer at eleven o'clock of this morning, at Government House. Yours, etcetera, Elizabeth, Lady Bradbury."

Jennifer's eyebrows knitted together. Lady Bradbury! Now what on earth was amiss? Eleven o'clock. That was cutting it rather fine. Still, perhaps it would not take too long.

She performed her necessary regimental duties that morning, then hurried back to her quarters and changed into a fresh uniform. Her groom had her gray ready for her and she mounted and rode off for Government House.

Lady Bradbury was obviously awaiting her, and she was shown without delay to the Chinese Room, where the Governor's Lady received her formally and bade her be seated.

Jennifer sat warily near the edge of her chair. More than ever she was certain this interview would concern Jonathan, and she was not mistaken, for Lady Bradbury opened by coming directly to the point.

"Lord Welland, I am aware that you have been placed in an awkward situation, but you must understand that this is a difficult position for me, too. I have under my care Miss Matilda Markham, for whose welfare I am responsible to her father. It has come to my ears that she has been consorting with a young gentleman who is described as being a relative of yours. It is not that there is a question of lack of decorum, or that this gentleman has not displayed the most excellent of manners and correct conduct—it is rather that as Miss Markham is, as I have pointed out, under my protection, I must know more about this young gentleman and his family."

Jennifer frowned. She did not answer at once, and watching her, Lady Bradbury read the trouble in the young face and her voice softened.

"Lord Welland, believe me, I know how trying this is for

you. You do know this young gentleman in question, of course. The family similiarity is too great to be denied."

Jennifer nodded. "Yes, I know him, Lady Bradbury." Her voice was low.

"Is he your—your—cousin?" Lady Bradbury persisted.

Jennifer drew a deep breath. "No, Lady Bradbury," she said evenly, "he is not my cousin. He is my brother. His father was Colonel Viscount Welland and his mother was Lady Mary Welland. He is not a—a bastard, as I am sure you have heard. He is a legitimate son of his parents."

Lady Bradbury's face was a study. "But—but I never heard that your father had more than one son," she said blankly.

"Nobody did," Jennifer said, and she spoke the truth. She looked across at Lady Bradbury rather desperately. "Lady Bradbury, if you will—will only trust me for another few hours. The story is not mine to tell—not just now, believe me. Mr. Welland is an eminently respectable gentleman, free to court Miss Markham. His fault has been that he has not called upon you as he should. I cannot condone it—and just now, this minute, I cannot explain it. But Lady Bradbury, if you will give me leave to come back later, tomorrow, I promise you the explanation will be a truthful one."

Lady Bradbury regarded her steadily. What she saw in Jennifer's face obviously decided her, for she nodded abruptly and got to her feet. "Lord Welland, you have always proven yourself a gentleman whom I could trust," she said, and held out her hand. "I shall await your explanation tomorrow."

Jennifer had scrambled to her feet and bowed over her outstretched hand. On impulse she lifted it to her lips. "Thank you, Lady Bradbury," she said huskily, and turned to hurry from the room.

In the Chinese Room, Lady Bradbury was blinking thoughtfully after her. "Another son?" she mused aloud, "I don't believe it. I wonder—?" Her face creased in a frown, then she shook herself. "No—it isn't possible."

But her wonder had been closer to the truth than she had known.

As she hurried through the hall, Jennifer glanced at the clock in passing. It was twenty-five to twelve and her eyes widened in horror. Twenty-five minutes to get up to the race course and be ready to ride did not allow her much margin. She sprang into her saddle and urged the gray up the hill.

Captain Dixon and Lord Randall were awaiting her together.

"Good Lord! Where have you been?" Dixon greeted her. "I hunted for you everywhere. Thurston's been hinting that you're not going to show."

"I'm sorry I'm late," Jennifer answered briefly. "Is everything ready?"

"Oh, certainly. Carr will start you, and Henderson will check you in at the finish line. You'll find you've quite a lot of spectators," he added. "I don't know how they all heard about it, but look," and he gestured widely to the field, where, although there had been no races that morning, the grandstand was half filled. Dixon added with a grin, "You carry the popular money, although the experts are backing Thurston's horse."

"The experts can't know the horse I'm riding," she said, and turned to Lord Randall. "Wish me luck, Rufus."

Rufus had been regarding her gravely. "Is there anything wrong?" he asked in a low voice, as Dixon turned away to check with the stewards.

She shook her head briefly. "Not really," she answered, "but I'd like to see you after the race, Rufus. I promised, remember?"

"Where were you?" he demanded in the same low voice.

"At Government House," she answered. "But I haven't time to tell you more now, Rufus. You'll be here afterwards, won't you?"

He nodded. "Yes, I'll be here."

Dixon came back to them. "Carr is setting up the race now," he said. "I told Bates and he's bringing out your horse."

They walked over to the enclosure. Bates had not allowed the regular groom to look after the bay. When he had heard of the race the night before, he had gone directly to the stables and posted a guard of his own choosing about the mount's stall. For Bates had his own opinion about Captain Thurston, and one not complimentary to the captain. Now he led the bay out, saddled and bridled, and helped his master to mount, adjusting the stirrups carefully once she was in the saddle.

Jennifer gathered up the reins and smiled down at the two men standing beside her. "Don't look so grim," she said cheerfully. "It's my neck."

"Yes," said Dixon, and there was an undercurrent of steel in his voice. "That's exactly what I'm thinking of."

She raised her whip in salute and walked her horse to the starting line. Dixon and Lord Randall moved off to the rail and Dixon nodded about the track, "There are officers at each jump," he said quietly. "I hope I'm mistaken, Randall."

"I hope you are, too, my friend," Lord Randall agreed, and glanced over his shoulder, for Bates had come up with a saddled horse.

"You, too, Bates?"

Bates touched his hat. "Beg pardon, m'lord. I thought I'd have one ready in case you needed it."

Lord Randall smiled grimly.

At the starting line, Captain Thurston did not look at Jennifer. Mr. Carr, who agreed to call the start of the race, walked over to them. "Gentlemen, you know the course—one complete round is the agreement. Are you ready, gentlemen?" He pointed his pistol in the air and pulled the trigger, and a roar went up from the grandstand, as the two horses took off almost simultaneously.

It was the first time Jennifer had ridden Lord Randall's bay, but once she had cleared the first jump her nervousness disappeared and she settled down to the excitement of the ride. The insult of the challenge, the problems of the intolerable situation in which she had become involved—all these were swallowed up in a surge of pleasure, the feel of the horse beneath her, jumping in perfect co-ordination and regaining his stride with not a break in his rhythm. She settled down to ride with her hands and her knees, her whip tucked out of the way, for there was no need for it. The bay's ears pricked forward as he covered the ground with a long, effortless stride and rose smoothly to clear the jumps.

A length ahead of her, Captain Thurston was using the whip mercilessly and his big chestnut was running hard. Jennifer pressed her knees and urged the bay on. He responded nobly. She was beside Thurston at the second to last jump, slightly ahead of him as she came up to the last one.

She had not noticed Thurston's mottled face, nor the rage which consumed him as she passed him, nor did she see the sudden hate that distorted his face when, as her horse gathered himself for the last jump, Captain Thurston suddenly swung his own horse off stride and whipped him at an angle over the jump.

The chestnut tried to swing away, but Thurston's hand on the bridle and the whip was merciless, and the mount crashed into the bay in mid-air.

That officer whom Dixon had stationed beside the jump had seen Thurston's maneuver too late to do more than yell, for there was no mistaking the deliberateness of the collision.

A drawn-out cry of horror came from the grandstand as Jennifer was flung off her horse, while the bay, caught off balance, fell heavily on top of her. The chestnut kept its feet with an effort, and Thurston lashed him down the course, to be met by a furious crowd of onlookers who caught at his horse's reins and half dragged him out of the saddle.

For what had been obvious to the officer stationed beside the jump had been as plain to everybody in the grandstand, and Colonel Thompson shouldered his way through the crowd to fix Captain Thurston with a hard stare.

"Return to your quarters, Thurston," he thundered, "and remain there until I send for you!"

Captain Thurston's lips curled and Colonel Thompson waited expectantly, but the furious man collected himself in time, and throwing his whip aside, saluted contemptuously and passed through the crowd, looking neither to the right nor the left.

The officer who had been stationed at the jump was first at Jennifer's side, but Lord Randall, seizing the reins of the led horse from Bates and vaulting into the saddle, got to her almost at the same time. The bay was struggling to its feet neighing pitiously, one leg hanging useless.

Dixon and Bates arrived together. "Is he dead, m'lord?" Bates cried anxiously.

Lord Randall shook his head. "No, he's not dead," he said briefly. "I think an arm is broken, possibly the leg."

Jennifer stirred and opened her eyes. She blinked up at

Rufus. "My—my horse—" she whispered. "Rufus—the bay—?"

"The front leg's broken," Rufus said briefly.

Her eyes closed and she bit her lip. "Has—has anyone a pistol?" she whispered. "Please, Rufus—"

Lord Randall glanced up at the surrounding officers. "I have, m'lord," Bates answered.

"Rufus—will you—will you—" Jennifer's voice was very low. She tried to move and caught her breath on a moan of pain.

Lord Randall looked up at Bates and nodded, and Bates cocked the pistol and walked over to the agonized bay and pulled the trigger.

Jennifer turned her face into Rufus's shoulder when the shot came and tried to move again. Pain swept through her and she mumbled frantically, "Rufus—" and fainted in his arms.

Bates was beside them again and Lord Randall glanced at him quickly. "Help me get him up," he ordered, and between them they lifted Jennifer from the ground and carried her from the racecourse.

"Better take him to the hospital," Dixon said anxiously, walking beside them, but Lord Randall shook his head.

"No, I'll take him down to the hotel," he said. "I'll look after him, he would prefer it, I know."

"As you say, sir," Dixon said doubtfully. "I'll send the doctor."

He hurried ahead and commandeered a carriage and had it driven up to the track. Bates got in and helped Lord Randall prop his master on the seat, and the driver touched up the horses and drove off to the hotel.

The jolting roused Jennifer and she moaned and moved her head.

"Lie still," Rufus commanded. "Don't move—I'm taking you to the hotel."

She opened her eyes then and looked up at him, and something close to a smile touched her lips. "Dear Rufus," she murmured, "thank you."

"Yes. Now be still," Rufus said. Obediently she closed her eyes, but the little smile lingered on her lips.

He carried her into the hotel and up the stairs to his rooms, to lay her down gently on the wide bed in the bedroom. She had fainted again, he saw, and was glad of it, for he knew her uniform had to come off and that the pain would be severe. He said over his shoulder to Bates, "Go to Room 16 and ask Mrs. Adams to come here immediately."

"Yes, m'lord," said Bates, and left on his words.

Carefully, with the gentleness of a woman, Lord Randall eased the uniform jacket off Jennifer, and with it off, his fingers pressed expertly up her left arm—the lower bone wasn't broken, neither was the elbow—it was the shoulder, but it wasn't broken, as far as Rufus could judge. It was dislocated, though, and his jaw tightened. That joint would have to be slipped back into place and such treatment was an ordeal.

Katie had hurried in and Lord Randall looked past her to Bates who was standing at the door.

"Close the door, Bates, and wait in the sitting room. If the doctor comes, let us know."

"Yes, m'lord," Bates said without question, and closed the door quietly.

Katie's face was aghast.

"Lord Randall! What's happened?" she cried.

"Help me to get these trousers off," Lord Randall said shortly. "She was tossed from her horse and the beast rolled on her. Her shoulder is dislocated, and I'm afraid her leg is broken."

"Oh dear! Oh dear!" But Katie wasted no time in moaning. Instead she set to work to help to get Jennifer undressed, and Lord Randall produced a voluminous nightshirt from his bureau drawer and handed it to her, turning away until Jennifer was encased in it; then he came back and bent over the bed.

He felt her leg carefully. It was broken all right, but it felt like a clean break to him, and he had had some experience in broken bones. As a boy he had worked with a bone-setter out of curiosity and compassion.

"It's that shoulder I'm most worried about," he muttered, and he thought aloud. "If the doctor starts working up there, he'll know at once. He can set the leg, but—" his fingers were busy about her shoulder.

Jennifer's head moved again and her eyes opened.

"Rufus! You're hurting," she whimpered.

"Lie still, Jennifer," Rufus said, and went on poking.

"Rufus! you're hurting. Oh-h-h!" the cry was wrenched from her as she involuntarily jerked under his hand, and her right fist went up to her teeth.

"It's not broken—it's dislocated," Rufus said evenly. "I've got to get it back, Jenny." He was prodding tenderly, and, although she did not cry again, her jaw was clenched hard and her forehead was wet.

He stopped, took her chin gently in his fingers and turned her face to him. "Jenny—this is all for the best," he said, and she did not see his right fist as it smashed up against her jaw. She collapsed limply, and Rufus set to work to do what had to be done. He threw off his coat and his face was white with effort as he wrenched the shoulder back into position. Suddenly the bone slipped into the socket with a click, and Rufus let his breath out in a sigh of relief.

"That's going to be very sore and stiff, Katie," he said, "but it's in place. I'll send Bates for some plaster and bandages to hold it so that she can't move it."

Just at that moment Bates rapped on the door. "The doctor's here, m'lord," he said, and Rufus looked quickly at Katie.

"Remember, Katie—there was nothing wrong with the arm," he said, almost in a whisper, and Katie met his eyes.

"Nothing at all," she agreed.

Rufus opened the door then and went into the sitting room.

"I'm afraid Lord Welland has broken his leg," he said gravely. "It appears to be a clean break, however."

"Dear, dear! Most unfortunate," the doctor shook his head. "These jumping accidents—dear, dear!" He clucked and picked up his bag and went across to the bedroom door.

Lord Randall beckoned Bates to him with a jerk of his head and said in an undertone, "Get some plasters and bandages, Bates, as quickly as you can." He hauled out some notes and pressed them into the man's hand and nodded to the door, then followed the doctor quickly.

In the bedroom the doctor was bending over the bed, poking firmly at the leg and clucking professionally.

"Yes, indeed, a clean break," he announced with satisfaction. "Lucky I brought some splints along. Good thing the young man's unconscious. These things are a little painful to set."

He opened his case and fussily extracted splints and some bandages, and turned back to the bed.

"Now—if one of you will hold the captain's foot and the other sit on the leg, above the knee, so that the captain can't move. Where's your man?"

"I'm sorry. I sent him off on an errand," Lord Randall apologized. He glanced at Katie. "However, I'm sure Mrs. Adams will assist. She could sit on the captain's hips—I believe her weight would be sufficient to keep him from sliding down, and I'll pull the foot."

Katie, her face white but determined, did as she was directed and sat gingerly but firmly on Jennifer's hips, grasping her thigh tightly.

At the foot of the bed Rufus took hold of her foot, and at a sign from the doctor pulled slowly but steadily.

There was an anxious moment and then the two ends of the bone ground into place with an indescribable sound, and the doctor nodded his satisfaction and proceeded to splint it up firmly and, as Rufus noted, expertly.

"Now—if we can just keep a tension on that leg," the doctor grunted when he had finished, "there shouldn't be any trouble. I've got just the thing in my carriage—just the thing. I'll go and get it."

Rufus had heard the outer door close. "Perhaps my man could get it for you," he suggested.

"Good! Good! Excellent idea. Meanwhile—hold the foot there, will you? Don't let the pressure go—much better not to." He hastened out to the sitting room and Rufus heard him directing Bates down to his carriage, with instructions to look in the back for an old weight which he had there.

"Used to have to put it on my horse," he said when he came back to the room. "Don't need it with this one, now. He stands." He walked up beside Jennifer's bed and flicked her eyelid. "Still unconscious. All to the good."

He hunted in his case and produced some cotton which he proceeded to wind about the ankle before he fastened a piece of stout cord to act as a rope. Bates had returned meanwhile with the prescribed weight, and the doctor took it from him and fastened it to the end of the rope. He placed a chair at the foot of the bed and arranged the weight to hang over it in such a way that the pull on the leg was straight.

"You can let go now," he said, and Rufus released his grip slowly, allowing the weight to take effect. Katie got up and pulled the bedding into place as best she could.

"Nothing more I can do now," the doctor said. "Bound to be some fever—lot of pain, too; discomfort. If it gets too bad I'll give you some laudanum. Here—better leave it for you, anyway. Don't give it to him unless it's necessary—it loses its effect if you give too much."

He shook out some pellets into an envelope and Rufus took it with a murmur of thanks.

"I'll be in to see how he's getting along," the doctor said, and picked up his hat as he went through the sitting room. "Meanwhile, keep him as comfortable as you can. Not much else I can say." He shook hands with Lord Randall and beamed at the pressure of the crisp note that passed into his fingers. "Thank you very much, m'lord," he said. "Very kind of you, I'm sure."

He thought it was even kinder when he glanced at the note as he was going down the stairs and found it was for a hundred pounds. His eyes opened a little in surprise, then they narrowed thoughtfully. Yes—well, Lord Randall could be certain that his professional discretion would be maintained intact.

Chapter Twenty-three

The doctor had hardly disappeared down the stairs when Jonathan came rushing in.

"What's happened to Jenny?" he burst out, as soon as he was in the room, not stopping to notice that Bates was nearby.

Lord Randall, on his way back to the bedroom, stopped and turned. "Where have you been?" he countered.

Jonathan's face reddened. "At Government House," he said gruffly. "I went to—I determined to—well, that is, I thought I'd better see Lady Bradbury."

"And did you?" Rufus queried.

Jonathan nodded. "Yes. She was quite decent to me—said that she'd been speaking to Lord Welland, and she had great confidence in his integrity, and that he had told her suspicions of me were unfounded, and she allowed me to see Matilda. But what's happened to Jenny? As I came into the hotel, Captain Dixon stopped me and asked me what the doctor had said. I didn't even know what he was talking about."

Lord Randall was regarding him steadily. His words had brought back to mind what Jennifer had said so urgently before the race. "I've been to Government House"—she had said—"I want to talk to you about it afterwards, Rufus." He had almost forgotten.

"What's happened to Jenny?" Jonathan said again.

"Welland was crashed at the last jump and his horse fell on him. His leg is broken and a shoulder dislocated."

"And you brought her here?"

Lord Randall's eyes flickered to Bates, but there was no sign of amazement, or of expression, even, on Bates's face.

Jonathan was too distraught to notice the side glance. "You brought her here, Rufus?" he repeated. "Why, Rufus, she can't stay here; it's not proper."

Lord Randall's eyes narrowed, his voice was very soft, very silky. "Jonathan—that is a matter which I shall take up with you in great detail at a later date. Meanwhile you will oblige me if you will inform Captain Dixon that Welland has a broken leg and is in much pain, but the doctor has declared it is a clean break and will heal in time. And Jonathan—you will say nothing more; do you understand?"

"But—but, Rufus," stammered Jonathan.

"I am sure Captain Dixon will be anxious to hear your report, Mr. Welland." Lord Randall's gaze was steely and under it Jonathan swallowed, dropped his head, shuffled his feet, stammered, "Yes—well, but—" then, "Oh, very well," and turned to fling himself out of the room.

As the door closed behind him, Lord Randall let his gaze travel to Bates. "Bates," he said, in the same soft voice, "I'm quite sure that none of this need go further than this room."

Bates met his eyes squarely. "No, m'lord."

Lord Randall held his gaze. "It is—perhaps—no surprise?" he hazarded, and Bates, after a moment, shook his head.

"No, m'lord. Not—not really, m'lord. I had—well, that is, I—I had my suspicions."

"I'm sure you kept those suspicions to yourself?" Lord Randall murmured.

Bates eyes were level. "Lord Welland did a lot for me. I

could never repay him, m'lord—and not—not just this week, m'lord. Anything he wanted to do was all right with me."

"Then I am sure I can count on your assistance?" Lord Randall said quietly, and Bates nodded.

"Whatever you say, m'lord," he said simply.

Lord Randall's face relaxed. "Perhaps you might begin by persuading the cook to send up some food," he said. "It's past noon-hour—yet I'm sure neither Mrs. Adams nor myself would care to leave. He might have some soup for Captain Welland."

"Yes, sir." Bates moved to the door.

"And take the key with you," Lord Randall added. "I want that door kept locked."

"Yes, m'lord." Bates slipped out and Lord Randall waited to hear the key turn. Then he went back to the bedroom.

Jennifer had recovered consciousness, and with consciousness, pain.

"Rufus—was that—was that Jonathan?" she whispered, and Lord Randall nodded.

"I—I thought so," Jennifer said. She swallowed and looked up at Rufus with desperate entreaty. "Rufus—what Jon—Jonathan said was right. I can't stay here. It's—it's not right—for—for you."

Silently cursing the absent Jonathan, Rufus said calmly, "You're going to stay exactly where you are, Jennifer. And I'm afraid, I'm very much afraid, I'm going to hurt you quite a lot. That shoulder of yours has to be bandaged."

"Rufus—" recollection came back to her eyes. "Rufus—did you—did you hit me?"

"Yes my dear, I did. And if it wasn't that I was afraid I'd crack your jaw, I'd do it again, because you're not going to enjoy this."

He was quite right—she did not. Neither, for that matter, did he, although his face showed nothing of his thoughts, as he firmly bound the shoulder and strapped her arm to her side so that she could not move it. In the course of strapping he had pressed on her ribs, and the cry of agony wrenched from her tight lips brought sickening realization that more than her leg was broken. He prodded as gently as possible, but even so she cried aloud when he touched the bruised area, where further examination revealed not one but two broken ribs.

There was nothing to do but set them and strap them tightly, and Rufus worked quickly and deftly, but Jennifer had fainted again before he was finished and he was not sorry that she had lost consciousness.

Bates tapped gently on the door. "I've brought up some food, sir."

Rufus glanced at Katie. "Go out and have something to eat," he said. "I'll stay here until you are finished."

She hesitated, but only for a moment, then she nodded and slipped out, and Rufus sat down beside the bed with his eyes on Jennifer's face and his fingers on her pulse. Katie had washed the mud and grime from the girl's cheeks, but there was a long graze where she had landed on the gravel, and her jaw was swollen angrily, starting to discolor where Rufus's blow had landed. He put up his hand, and, as his fingers brushed her cheek, she roused again with a deep shuddering moan and turned her head on the pillow.

"I guess I must have fainted," she mumbled.

"Yes, I think you did," Rufus said gently.

Her eyes darkened. "Rufus. What happened?"

"You had an unpleasant spill," he said briefly, and her eyes closed.

"I remember," she said. "Your horse. Oh—Rufus, you had to have him shot, didn't you? He gave me such a wonderful ride. Rufus, I'm so sorry." Easy tears ran down her cheeks and she caught her lip. "Rufus—the five hundred pounds— will you see that Captain Thurston gets it? He—he won the race, didn't he?"

"I'll see that Captain Thurston gets all that is coming to him," Lord Randall's voice was suddenly hard, but Jennifer did not notice—she was thinking of something else.

"Rufus—Rufus—Lady Bradbury. Rufus, you've got to see her. I said—I said I'd go back tomorrow."

"Yes, I'll see Lady Bradbury," Rufus said quietly. "Don't worry, Jennifer, I'll attend to everything."

"But Rufus—" her eyes were big with worry. "I told her that Jonathan was Jonathan—that his parents were my father and mother—that he was quite, quite respectable—

and I said I would—I would tell her more tomorrow, that I—I couldn't tell her the whole story then, because—because I couldn't. Rufus, I—I don't know—I don't know what you can do."

"Leave it to me," Rufus said quietly. "I'll attend to it, Jenny."

Her head moved restlessly on the pillow. "Rufus, Jonathan's right—I can't stay here. It—it's not right for you."

Lord Randall's jaw was set hard, a little nerve twitched in his cheek, but his voice was light, deliberately light, and Jennifer was too wretched to catch the undertone in it.

"Jenny—will you trust me completely? Will you marry me—now?"

Quick color flooded Jennifer's face. "Rufus, Rufus, you mustn't," she whispered.

"Will you trust me?" he said again. "Please, Jenny."

Her reddened eyes raised slowly to his face. "I always have, Rufus," she said simply, and Rufus, who had been holding her right hand, brought it up to his cheek and pressed it gently.

"It will be all right, Jenny," he said, "I give you my word."

She tried to smile at him, but the tears were very close and she closed her eyes and turned her head away.

Katie scratched at the door. "I brought some soup for m'lady," she said. "A spoonful or two will make her feel better. You go and have your meal, Lord Randall, I'll stay here now."

Lord Randall got up from the chair and seated her in it. "I've several things to attend to," he said, "but I won't be long." He left the room and quietly closed the door behind him.

He had indeed several things to attend to, and the first was to despatch Bates with a hastily written note to a certain house on the very edge of Halifax. His instructions to Jennifer's servant were concise but detailed, and included the hire of a closed carriage and the return to the hotel via the service entrance.

Bates left, and Lord Randall ate quickly, then wrote several notes, addressed them and fastened them with his own seal. These he put aside for Bates to deliver, then, pulling on his coat, he went in search of Jonathan.

He found him downstairs in the beverage room, as he had expected, and he was fortunately alone. Randall walked over and stood beside him and touched his shoulder, and Jonathan looked up morosely.

"What do you want?"

"Will you come upstairs?" Rufus asked quietly. "I'd like to talk with you."

Jonathan hesitated, but got to his feet and followed Lord Randall across the lobby and up the stairs.

"You threw me out before," he said sullenly, "and this time you say you want to talk to me—what's going on?"

Lord Randall closed and locked the door and motioned to a chair. "Sit down," he said, and Jonathan, after a would-be defiant glare, sat down. Rufus stood in front of him.

"Jonathan, there are occasions when I feel that your character would have been much improved had the rod been spared less, but for some odd reason your sister is fond of you, and I would do much to spare her grief. When you were in this room before, with a sudden excess of morality you declared it would not be proper if she were to stay here under my care, but that is a matter which will be rectified in the next hour. I'm going to marry your sister, Jonathan, and you're going to be here to witness the ceremony. That should satisfy your outraged sense of decency."

Jonathan opened his mouth to speak, but Rufus stopped him.

"I'm not finished. As soon as your sister is well enough to be moved, I shall take her to Boston to convalesce there until she is sufficiently recovered to undertake the return trip to England, which will possibly be in several months' time. Meanwhile, as long as we stay here in Halifax, you will remain at this hotel as Mr. Welland, behaving yourself with proper decorum and dignity, and courting Miss Markham, if she can tolerate the sight of you. I shall call upon Lady Bradbury tomorrow, and I shall confirm what your sister has already said to Lady Bradbury—that you are the son of Colonel Viscount Welland and his wife, Lady Mary Welland. Your sister, Lady Jennifer, is in Boston—remember that, Jonathan. This is not your sister here—your sister is in Boston. And Captain Welland is a cousin. Never mind what I shall say to Lady Bradbury—that is what you must say to everyone. Do you understand?"

He waited for Jonathan to nod, then he went on.

"Before we leave for Boston, I shall arrange that you will eventually take up your commission in the army. Then, as Lord Welland, you will be able to ask for Miss Markham's hand—if you so desire. Until that time you will be Mr. Welland. Is that clear?"

"But—but I don't want to go into the army." Jonathan protested, and Lord Randall's face hardened.

"I'm not particularly concerned whether you wish it or not," he said coldly. "If you wish to marry Miss Markham this is the only solution which can be considered at present. I cannot conceive that Sir Joseph, her father, would consider the suit of a gambling ne'er-do-well, such as you have represented yourself to be these past few weeks. You have to be a man, Jonathan, some time, you can't let your sister be your conscience and your strength always."

Jonathan had flushed a deep red. He attempted to justify himself, then his voice broke and he buried his face in his hands. "You don't think much of me, do you, Rufus?"

"I think you have always followed the easiest way," Lord Randall's voice had softened only slightly.

"Do you think I can ever make good?"

"Most people can, if they want to," Lord Randall answered. He hesitated, then he put his hand on the bowed shoulders. "Make no mistake, Jonathan, it's up to you now. Your sister is out of it completely—come what may. Lady Jennifer is in Boston—remember that. And the person who is ill here is your cousin. When your cousin leaves for Boston, you will be Captain Lord Welland. It is possible that you will have to leave, too, on that occasion, but we will face that later. Straighten up now, and come in and see your sister."

A tap sounded quietly on the door and Bates' voice followed, "Lord Randall?"

Lord Randall crossed the room and unlocked and opened the door. An elderly, kindly-faced gentleman in clerical attire was standing there with Bates, and he stepped into the room slowly.

"Lord Randall?" he said hesitantly. "I received your message."

"Thank you for coming, sir," Lord Randall said gravely, and nodded Bates in and closed the door. He introduced Jonathan. "This is Mr. Welland, Reverend Sanderson."

The reverend gentleman nodded courteously. "How do you do, sir." He turned back to Lord Randall. "Your message was somewhat obscure, my lord. I was not sure, but I came as I had promised you I would."

"Thank you, sir," Lord Randall said again. He gestured to a chair. "If you will sit down, sir, I will see that all is in readiness."

Bates took the Reverend Sanderson's hat and drew forward a chair, while Lord Randall went over to the closed bedroom door. He tapped gently, then entered.

Jennifer was still conscious, but her cheeks were flushed and Lord Randall, noting the signals of fever, hoped fervently that she would not collapse before the ceremony was over. He came up to the bed and he was smiling gently.

"Jennifer, Reverend Mr. Sanderson is here to marry us. Will you let him come in?"

"Whatever you say, Rufus," her voice was faint.

He hesitated but he could think of nothing to add, so he nodded and went out, returning shortly with the minister. Jonathan followed and looked anxiously at his sister.

Her gaze was fixed on Mr. Sanderson's face, and she did not look away from him as he spoke the solemn words that joined her to Rufus, Lord Randall. She gave her responses obediently, if faintly, but a quiver went through her when Rufus bent over and placed the wide gold ring on her left hand lying across her chest. Rufus, watching her face anxiously, saw her teeth close hard on her lip, and he held her right hand tightly as he repeated the final vows. Then, with deep solemnity, Mr. Sanderson pronounced them man and wife.

Rufus hesitated momentarily, but Mr. Sanderson was obviously waiting, so he bent over and pressed his lips to Jennifer's forehead before he straightened and turned to the old minister and ushered him from the room, rounding up Jonathan on his way.

Behind him, Jennifer, Lady Randall, lay with closed eyes, big tears running down her cheeks, the fingers of her right hand feeling the unfamiliar hardness of the gold ring on her third finger, left hand.

Chapter Twenty-four

The following afternoon, promptly at three o'clock, Lord Randall called at Government House and sent in his card to Lady Bradbury. As he had written her the previous day, she was expecting him and received him at once.

She gave him her hand as he came into the room and he bowed over it. "Thank you, Lady Bradbury, for permitting me the honor of calling upon you," he said formally.

Lady Bradbury inclined her head graciously and motioned him to a chair. "I understand that Lord Welland was removed to your rooms, Lord Randall," she said. "I do hope his injuries are not serious."

"Captain Welland is quite ill," Lord Randall said gravely. "He has a dislocated shoulder, two broken ribs and a fractured leg. However, the doctor assures me that the fracture is a clean one, which will heal without mishap, but meanwhile, there is a great deal of fever and, of course, pain."

"The poor boy!" Lady Bradbury was much distressed. "Is there anything more that can be done for him?"

Lord Randall assured her that he felt everything possible was being done, and went on to add that it was at the expressed request of Captain Welland that he had asked permission to call upon her this day. He believed that Captain Welland had been to see her the day before. Indeed, Welland had explained the entire interview to him and, with her permission, he would like to explain the remaining parts.

Lady Bradbury stiffened in her chair; her chin lifted slightly and she regarded him with a face from which all expression had been wiped. Then she nodded, slowly. "Pray continue, Lord Randall."

Lord Randall chose his words with care. He had thought much of what he was going to reveal, and he endeavored to say what was necessary in the fewest possible words.

His tone at its most dry, his face unreadable, he began by telling her who "Mr. Welland" actually was and, without attempting to either blacken or whitewash his character, gave her a succinct word-picture of Jonathan's aesthetic distaste for army life and all it entailed. He continued by outlining briefly how the person whom she, Lady Bradbury, knew as "Captain Welland" had offered to take his place, and how the masquerade had been entered into with the consent of both Jonathan and his sister, Lady Jennifer, who, all her life, had shielded and spoiled her brother.

Lady Bradbury might have been a china ornament, so still did she sit.

His expression unchanging, Lord Randall went on. His story was more difficult now; he was mixing fact and fantasy and the proportions had to be exactly right. Jonathan, he said, had decided to come to Halifax after all, to take over his commission, but in view of the esteem in which "Captain Welland" was held by his fellow officers, Lady Jennifer had refused to countenance an exposal of "Captain Welland," and accordingly Jonathan had introduced himself as "Mr. Welland" and, once his sister had left for Boston, to appear thus about Halifax.

He stopped there. It was time for Lady Bradbury to make

some sign either of distaste for such duplicity or at least of tacit acceptance.

The Governor's lady stirred. "You say that Mr. Welland—the gentleman whom we know here in Halifax as Mr. Welland—is in actuality Lord Welland?" she questioned, and Lord Randall nodded.

"Yes, Lady Bradbury, that is indeed the truth."

"And Captain Welland, then—you have not said who he is?"

Lord Randall hesitated. "A distant cousin," he said at last.

Lady Bradbury nodded. "Yes, I can see the family resemblance—it is very strong. But who is he, exactly?"

Lord Randall looked straightly at Lady Bradbury. It was a gamble, but he had wagered on fewer promising cards before. "*She* is my wife."

Lady Bradbury was pardonably agitated. "Your wife? Lord Randall, I fear you have mistaken me. I asked who was Captain Welland?"

Lord Randall nodded. "Yes, Lady Bradbury."

"But—" Lady Bradbury shut her mouth, and made a dazed gesture with her hand. "But—" she tried again, then she studied the man across from her narrowly. She saw the tight jaw, the steady eyes with their level gaze—she saw, too, a lot more than that. She said in a quieter tone, "I do not think that this is something that need be discussed further, Lord Randall. Captain Welland's honor and bravery are sufficiently well established in Halifax so that there would be no justifiable reason for besmirching his reputation. I would appreciate it, however, if you would trust me sufficiently to tell me the background of such an impersonation."

The muscle beside Lord Randall's mouth twitched, and Lady Bradbury saw that, too.

"Thank you, Lady Bradbury," he said, and with as few words as possible he complied with her request.

"I did not know I was in love with her until I returned to my estates and found that she had come over here," he ended at last. "I followed at once, but as you have observed, the reputation of Captain Welland was too admirable to darken by publicity proclaiming her to be who she really is. As soon as she is well enough to travel, I shall take her to Boston and she will convalesce there, and then we will return to England."

Lady Bradbury nodded. "A very intelligent decision, Lord Randall," she approved, "but the brother, Mr. Welland, what will you do about him?"

"I have considered two solutions, Lady Bradbury," Lord Randall said slowly. "One is that Lord Welland would sell out of the army, which would be a simple solution, but would have attendant difficulties for Jonathan. The second solution is that I should call upon Colonel Thompson shortly before my wife is well enough to travel, and explain much as I have explained to you now, up to a point, and suggest that Jonathan be allowed to take up the commission, but be transferred to another battalion. In that way the impersonation would soon be forgotten, and, should any of the present officers serving in this battalion meet with Lord Welland later—that is with Jonathan—they would perhaps not notice the difference in the two parties."

"I like your second solution best, Lord Randall," Lady Bradbury said after a pause. "I think I can help you with it. It will not be necessary for you to call upon Colonel Thompson. As Lieutenant-Governor and Commander-in-Chief of His Majesty's Forces in this part of Canada, my husband Lord Bradbury would be the final authority in any such transfer as you speak of. If you will leave all in my hands, I will see that a leave of absence is arranged for Captain Welland for three months, and then that a transfer to the 2nd Battalion shall be in order following his leave. No further explanations would then be necessary. I wouls suggest that Mr. Welland depart for Boston with you, and on rejoining the regiment in England in three months' time from that date, he would then, if he so desires, be able to call upon Sir Joseph—if he indeed wishes to marry his daughter. We have been very frank, Lord Randall, so I must add that I cannot feel that Jonathan is very good material for a husband. However, that judgment I will not be called upon to deliver."

"I think that Miss Markham would make an admirable wife for Jonathan," Lord Randall said carefully. "She is determined and strong, and has, I fancy, a fondness for the boy which she might not have for one of more definite character."

Lady Bradbury nodded in agreement. "You are possibly right, Lord Randall. Nevertheless, I confess I should not like to see one of my daughters marry a man to mature him. However, as I have said, that is not for me to decide." She arose and held out her hand. "Come to me when Lady Randall is well enough to travel, Lord Randall, and rest assured that I will see that everything is in order."

Lord Randall bent over her outstretched hand. "Lady Bradbury," he said quietly, "there are times when thank you is not enough, and yet there is nothing more I can say."

"There is nothing more you need to," Lady Bradbury said briskly, and added, "By the way, Lord Randall, you might perhaps be interested in knowing that Captain Thurston has resigned his commission and will be returning to England on the first transport."

Lord Randall's face hardened.

"Colonel Thompson considered that he had acted in a manner unbecoming to an officer and a gentleman, and suggested that he sell out without delay," Lady Bradbury explained. She walked to the door with him. "Thank you for coming, Lord Randall," and added, because the door was open, "Pray do not forget to let me know how Captain Welland goes on."

Lord Randall bowed to her again. "I shall not forget, Lady Bradbury," he promised, and turned and left her.

Six weeks later, "Captain Welland" was carried aboard the *Cambria* and carefully lowered onto the bunk in the largest cabin. A disconsolate Mr. Welland, who had taken a fond and somewhat tearful farewell of Miss Markham the night before, was in the party, which was further swelled by Mrs. Adams and Bates—who had a firm grip on George—while Lord Randall directed all operations. On shore to see them off were most of the officers of the garrison and many of the members of Halifax Society: Captain Lord Welland had been a respected officer of the Rifles, and the tale of his personal bravery coupled with the dastardliness of the two attacks by Captain Thurston had lost nothing in its telling. Too, it had also got about that Lord Welland had sent the five hundred pounds, which he had proposed as added stakes in the challenge race, to Captain Thurston, and this was regarded as further indication of the high qualities of the injured captain's honor. So the onlookers cheered the *Cambria* as she pulled out, and Jennifer begged Lord Randall to lift her so that she could see the last of Halifax as the shoreline slipped past the porthole.

"I suppose I shall never see Halifax again," she observed somewhat wistfully, as Rufus laid her down again gently.

"Never is a long time," he smiled, and went on deck to join Jonathan as the *Cambria* slipped past the Sambro lighthouse. He was being careful not to force himself in any way on Jennifer these days. After the long bout of fever and delirium had broken, during which it had sometimes taken Bates's strength as well as his own and Katie's to hold her still, he had watched every word and action in order to return to the safe ground of friendship until Jennifer was well enough and strong enough to know her own mind.

After a pleasant, uneventful three-day voyage, the *Cambria* sailed into Boston Harbor. Carriages were waiting for Lord Randall and his party on the wharf, and they were driven at once to a large, well furnished house which Lord Randall had engaged to rent for their stay.

The days and then the weeks passed pleasantly. Although Jennifer was tired from the trip, she was soon able to be carried downstairs to a comfortable drawing room, where some weeks later she took her first steps, with Rufus on one side and Jonathan on the other to steady her. Her shoulder had healed and her ribs had gone together well, while her leg, as the doctor had predicted, had been a clean break and had knitted evenly. She cried a little at the pins and needles, but she took six steps before she looked at Rufus pleadingly and gave in. He picked her up then, and carried her back to a long chair. However she was up the next day trying once more, and each day her leg strengthened and she was able to walk further.

At length she was walking unaided and Rufus suggested that perhaps they had better book passage back to England. The three months were almost up, and Captain Welland's orders to report would soon be due.

She twisted the heavy ring on her third finger and her eyes were on it. They were alone at the time. Jonathan was off shopping for a suitable gift for his Matilda, and Katie was in the kitchen.

She said in a small voice, "Rufus, do we have to go back to England yet?"

"It's almost time for orders for Captain Welland," he pointed out.

She nodded. "Yes, I know, but—but couldn't Jonathan go back alone? Besides that—if I went back, too, at the same time it would look, well—I think any person who saw us would know I was the one who had broken my leg and—well, it wouldn't—it would take more explanations, Rufus—and, well—"

"No, we don't have to go back," Rufus stopped her. "What would you like to do, Jennifer?"

Instead of answering him directly, she asked another question. "Rufus, you never told me why you went to Halifax?"

He looked across at her. She was sitting in a big chair by the window and the sun was glinting on her hair. He came and sat down beside her and took her two hands in his.

"Jenny, don't you know—truly?"

She shook her head but she did not meet his eyes. "No, Rufus, of course not." She tried to pull her hands away but he held on to them tightly.

"Jennifer, when I returned and called at Six Chimneys to find you were not there, read the letters which your guardian was so pleased at receiving, and realized where you were and what you were doing, I knew that I had been a fool for many years."

She was silent—she was waiting.

"In those few minutes, I suddenly realized that I loved you and had loved you for a long time, I knew, too, how *much* I loved you when I was furiously angry at the Duke for not seeing what was going on."

He was smiling. She looked up under her lashes.

"But—but weren't you angry at me, Rufus?" she said in a small voice.

"My dear, I could have turned you across my knee with the greatest of pleasure," Lord Randall said calmly, "and paddled you until you couldn't have sat down for a week—if I could have got my hands on you then."

219

"That doesn't sound much as if you loved me," she said childishly, and his eyes twinkled even as he said lightly,

"Some day I hope you'll learn as I did that your most violent feelings can be aroused by someone you love deeply."

She said, "But—but why didn't you tell me when you came to Halifax?"

"I didn't notice any sign of enthusiasm on your part to cast yourself on my tender mercies," he said dryly. "As I recall, you spent much time telling me to keep out of your way."

She colored. "Well, Rufus—I mean—it wasn't, it wasn't your troubles we were in."

Rufus' smile deepened, his grip tightened on her hands.

"I was content to wait, Jenny," he said. "You see, by that time I was very sure I loved you—to a degree which..." his voice trailed away. But there was that in his eyes which made Jennifer suddenly bite her lip.

"Rufus—" her voice was low, so low he could only just hear the words. "Rufus—I, I don't remember very much about it, but—well, it's, it's like a dream—only there's this ring. Rufus, you did marry me, didn't you?"

He nodded. "Yes, my darling, I did."

"Because you loved me, or just because it was the proper thing to do?"

He let go of her fingers and put his hands on her arms.

"Jenny, if it had been the proper thing to do, if I had been doing only what was right, I would have exposed you as soon as I arrived in Halifax. I married you because I loved you, as I would have married you the instant I came to Halifax had I been able. I'd have told you I loved you, too, before I did marry you, only that fool brother of yours had put his foot in it properly, and I could have boxed his ears—I very nearly did," he added grimly.

Jennifer laughed delightedly. "Rufus, do you really mean it?"

"I certainly do!" he returned. "You ask Jonathan." Then his face and voice were both very gentle. "Jenny, I love you."

She looked at him searching for a moment longer. Then she gave a little sob, raising herself to him, her arms closing about him. His hands went around her body quickly, lifting her, pressing her to him. Her mouth met his with an eagerness and passion which equalled his own, and his hold tightened on her as if he would never let her go.

CLASSIC BESTSELLERS
from FAWCETT BOOKS

THE GHOST WRITER   24322 $2.75
by Philip Roth

IBERIA   23804 $3.50
by James A. Michener

THE ICE AGE   04300 $2.25
by Margaret Drabble

ALL QUIET ON THE WESTERN FRONT   23808 $2.50
by Erich Maria Remarque

TO KILL A MOCKINGBIRD   08376 $2.50
by Harper Lee

SHOW BOAT   23191 $1.95
by Edna Ferber

THEM   23944 $2.50
by Joyce Carol Oates

THE SLAVE   24188 $2.50
by Isaac Bashevis Singer

THE FLOUNDER   24180 $2.95
by Gunter Grass

THE CHOSEN   24200 $2.25
by Chaim Potok

THE SOURCE   23859 $2.95
by James A. Michener

Buy them at your local bookstore or use this handy coupon for ordering.

COLUMBIA BOOK SERVICE (a CBS Publications Co.)
32275 Mally Road, P.O. Box FB, Madison Heights, MI 48071

Please send me the books I have checked above. Orders for less than 5 books must include 75¢ for the first book and 25¢ for each additional book to cover postage and handling. Orders for 5 books or more postage is FREE. Send check or money order only.

Cost $_____   Name _____

Sales tax*_____   Address _____

Postage_____   City _____

Total $_____   State _____ Zip _____

The government requires us to collect sales tax in all states except AK, DE, MT, NH and OR.

This offer expires 1 September 81   8105

GREAT ADVENTURES IN READING

THE MONA INTERCEPT   14374 $2.75
by Donald Hamilton
A story of the fight for power, life, and love on the treacherous seas.

JEMMA   14375 $2.75
by Beverly Byrne
A glittering Cinderella story set against the background of Lincoln's America, Victoria's England, and Napolean's France.

DEATH FIRES   14376 $1.95
by Ron Faust
The questions of art and life become a matter of life and death on a desolate stretch of the Mexican coast.

PAWN OF THE OMPHALOS   14377 $1.95
by E. C. Tubb
A lone man agrees to gamble his life to obtain the scientific data that might save a planet from destruction.

DADDY'S LITTLE HELPERS   14384 $1.50
by Bil Keane
More laughs with The Family Circus crew.

NEW FROM POPULAR LIBRARY